Shadow Stalking

Bloomington, IN　　Milton Keynes, UK

AuthorHouse™
1663 Liberty Drive, Suite 200
Bloomington, IN 47403
www.authorhouse.com
Phone: 1-800-839-8640

AuthorHouse™ UK Ltd.
500 Avebury Boulevard
Central Milton Keynes, MK9 2BE
www.authorhouse.co.uk
Phone: 08001974150

©2006 Linda J. Clark. All rights reserved.

No part of this book may be reproduced, stored in a retrieval system, or transmitted by any means without the written permission of the author.

First published by AuthorHouse 3/13/2006

ISBN: 1-4208-9168-5 (sc)

Printed in the United States of America
Bloomington, Indiana

This book is printed on acid-free paper.

WordShack Publishing proudly brings you the work of this new author. We began life as a web publisher in early 2002 and quickly gained critical worldwide acclaim for our award winning website and the literary quality of work displayed from primarily previously unpublished authors.

The work displayed on wordshack.com is now read and reviewed by thousands of readers and authors in 120 countries around the globe.

Our mission is exemplified in our corporate statement, "The author's first step to greatness." We search out the best new storytellers from around the globe and provide an opportunity for you to see their work in print.

This book represents our most recent foray into the world of traditional book publishing. After you have enjoyed Shadow Stalking, visit us at www.wordshack.com for information on our other high quality publications.

WordShack Publishing would like to thank Barbara and Ivan Shapero, Amy Starks and Sandra Smith for their unstinting support.

WordShack Publishing is a privately owned Trans-Atlantic corporation with offices in the United Kingdom and the United States of America. You may contact us at:

ukeditor@wordshack.com or useditor@wordshack.com

Acknowledgements

When it comes right down to it, publishing a novel involves so many more people than I thought it would. After all, no one else can write your thoughts or make your plot thicken without even knowing where the story is going! It is a solitary work. Or so I believed. But I've found there are others who move a book to its completed stage not as agents, editors or publishers, but as enthusiasts, cheerleaders, and encouragers.

I've been working on this novel for over ten years. Maybe I should be embarrassed about it taking so long, but I'm really not. I'm happy to have it finally ready to present and admittedly somewhat apprehensive.

That's were all those other people come into play. If it wasn't for my sisters, Elaine, Terri and Diana, and my mother, Joy, I might not have had the courage to submit my work to the publishers. They offered me ideas, insight and encouragement. They believed in my abilities and said I could do it. To them I say, "Thank you from the bottom of my heart."

To Lynda Blankenship of WordShack Publishing – Thank you for your words of wisdom and for allowing so many unknown authors the opportunity to be heard through your web site. Your thoughtful ways gently moved me forward and I truly value your opinions.

I have gained much of my inspiration from the students and faculty of GlenOak High School. Kids have such enthusiasm for reaching starry-eyed goals and they fill my days with adventure and excitement. Their energy is limitless and they give me the desire to live beyond the norm. Many thanks to all the students and friends whom I've had the pleasure of being with through the years in Plain Local Schools.

Most of all, I want to thank my husband, Dennis, for his support and my laptop computer. (It made writing so much easier!) Actually, watching my husband, my daughter, Jennifer and son, Jeremy, reach their own personal goals made this novel extremely important to me. They have accomplished so much and I just wanted to get on the bandwagon with them!

Kisses to my grandchildren, Allissa, Becca and Shane. It's so much fun getting hugs from them. (And by the way, life only gets better when you add a son-in-law and daughter-in-law to the mix. Thanks, Tim & Becky!)

Dedication

To my family, who have weathered the storms of loss and sadness these last few years, may we look forward to all the good times ahead.

In Loving Memory of:

Charles L. Clark, Max J Clark, Dorothy M. Clark
and 3 Tiny Angels now in heaven

Shadow Stalking

Chapter 1

1:48 AM- Jackie woke gasping for air. Flailing her arms at first, she finally found the pillow and tried to pull it off of her. She gasped again- sucking in oxygen. Her chest was heavy with the weight of a body pressing against hers. She fought back, but it didn't seem to make any difference at all. Jackie's mind began racing- *how do I get him off of me? Why is he doing this to me? Where are my children? Has he hurt my children?* She was frantic as she tossed her body from side to side praying for breath and freedom. He rolled with her from one side of the bed to the other. One moment he put her on her knees and the next he would roll her over and shove her into the mattress.

Again she twisted out of his grip until suddenly her body was careening off the bed and onto the floor. Quickly she began crawling away on her knees, but he was right behind her, grabbing her legs. A sharp kick to his face and shoulders forced him to lose his grip, which was all she needed to escape. She raced toward the balcony in her bedroom.

If she could just get away from him long enough to put a door between them, then maybe she would have a chance. But the french doors were locked. She shook them violently and shoved her foot against one door for leverage and began pulling at the knob of the other. It wouldn't budge. *Get it open, Jackie, get the door open!!*

She was screaming inside yet it was as if her body was in slow motion and no noise was coming out. Each movement was forced, every effort deliberate and calculated as if she was pushing her body to its limits without any results. Her mind wasn't working clearly. She couldn't find the handle to unlock the door. And then, the handle just appeared. *What was happening?* She turned the lock just as his arm came from behind and wrapped around her neck. She started choking. He lifted her up by the neck and she coughed and gagged from the pressure. She ripped the skin on his arms with her fingernails and yanked on his hair - anything to loosen his grip.

He shoved her body against the french doors shattering the glass with her shoulder. Jackie winced in pain, but continued to fight. With one swift kick against his shin, Jackie was free again. The french doors opened when Jackie fell against them and together they landed in a heap on the balcony floor. He was on top of her, but she wiggled out from underneath and began scrambling away. Her knees scraped against the wood planks, but it was the strong squeeze of his hands around her ankles that made her scream out in fear and pain. He was using her legs to crawl up her body. One arm over the other, he was making his way up to her waist. She kicked violently in an attempt to free herself once more.

She cried out for help, but there was no one there to rescue her. The woods below the balcony were deserted; her cries were silenced by the remote location of her home. The only ones who could hear her would be her children. *The children!* She panicked. She didn't dare scream anymore because the children might wake up and run to help her. Then their lives would be in danger.

Once again he was on top of her. There was no fight left in her. She knew it was over. He gathered her limp body in his arms and took three steps to the edge of the balcony. He held her over the railing for a moment - just so he could savor his victory - and then, without a word, he let go of her. She plummeted to the ground, fifteen feet below.

Jackie flung her body forward in bed as she woke gasping for breath. Had it only been a dream? It seemed so real. Her heart was racing. For a few minutes, she sat in disbelief clinging to Jonathan's pillow. The clock read 2:01 AM. *The children.* She had to check on the children. She dangled her shaking legs over the side of the bed and stumbled out into the corridor. Without turning on the lights, she made her way to Lizzy's room. She opened the door slowly, walked softly to her bedside and listened to her daughter's steady breathing. She was fine. Her little girl was fine. Jackie covered her with a blanket and Lizzy squirmed slightly before snuggling with her baby doll.

She reentered the hallway and tiptoed to Michael's room. Obviously he hadn't heard his mother's cries because he was sleeping soundly. How she longed to sleep peacefully like her children- just for awhile. Then maybe she could stand the pain of Jonathan's disappearance.

The kids were fine. Absolutely nothing was wrong. No one was waiting for her in the shadows. *Get a grip, Jackie!* Sitting on the first step of the back staircase, Jackie buried her face in her hands for a moment and then pushed her tangled, silky, black hair away from her face. She sat completely still and listened for any unusual noises. Nothing.

As she quietly descended the stairs, she cautiously made her way to her newly remodeled kitchen. The polished cherry cabinets glistened in the dark. For a moment she stroked the fine woodwork remembering how Jonathan had gone with her to the Kitchen and Bath Showroom to pick them out. They had playfully argued about the type of wood they wanted and what stain was the best. He liked a light oak, but she won when she pretended to whine. "Oh please Jonathan, you know it will be gorgeous, and besides, when was the last time you even made a cup of coffee?" For the first time since Jonathan's disappearance, a smile formed on her lips, but vanished almost as quickly as it appeared.

The light above the sink was still on. It started as a joke when they were first married over 12 years earlier. She'd flip it off; he'd turn it on. She was the conservative one and he was extravagant about everything. "Get real, Jackie," he would quip. "You really think a couple dollars is going to break us? If I want the lights on anywhere, I'll keep them on. And under no circumstances do I ever want the light above the sink off - day or night. If I'm hungry, I don't want to trip all over the kitchen in the dark just because you're too cheap to leave the light on."

Maybe it wasn't really a joke, but she had come to understand him so it didn't upset her. He was used to having his way, and he hadn't changed just because they got married. He was in control of everyone and everything and she liked it that way.

But now he was gone. And she was alone.

She turned on the faucet, cupped her hands under the cold water and splashed her face. Her eyes were swollen from crying and as she patted her face, her lips began to quiver again. She traced her cheeks with her fingers and then let them gently move down her chin and neck. She felt helpless as she walked to the kitchen table and sat down. How did this happen? *Where are you Jonathan?*

Chapter 2

After careful research, the house in the woods was put at the top of the list because it was secluded, but when real estate agent, Stephen Begg, began showing it, he apologized profusely for the disrepair. "The owners were very ill in their final years and they just couldn't manage it," he said.

The uncontrolled weeds winding through overgrown shrubs had long ago made the landscape unattractive. The tall grass was coarse and fighting to survive. Although the property was described as a wooded lot, the lack of sunlight through the thick branches and dense leaves made the place seem rather gloomy, even on a sunny day.

As they scoured the grounds the only thing the buyer could think was, *That's why the place needed upkeep. Upkeep wasn't quite the word for it. But that really didn't matter anyway, it would be sufficient.*

According to the potential owner, the consideration of this particular location was for a weekend retreat and hideaway from the city. The fact that there wasn't another house around for three miles in any direction was a bonus. There was little doubt that any other place could offer as much privacy as the '1950's cottage in the woods, fixer-upper' as described in the paper. The price was right too. It wouldn't take every penny in the bank.

As they walked around the outside, once again the agent reiterated how "just a little elbow grease would make the place a real gem again". *Well, it certainly had some things that would come in handy,* the client thought. There weren't too many places in the woods that could boast a detached garage, albeit a bit run down. As they opened the door, it was a bonus to find garden tools and a lawn mower.

"The husband died and the wife was forced into a nursing home a year later. It was just too difficult for her to maintain the property. She left everything pretty much as you see it and anything you see comes with the deal." He picked up an old runner sled, complete with rust, chuckled and then continued. "How lucky can you be? You got kids?"

The answer was quick, "No."

The real estate agent continued talking. "The hill will give you a good workout! The lake is down at the bottom." He pointed through the trees to the base of the hill. "The path is here somewhere. You want to go down?" He was praying for the words 'no' to come out, but instead, they were trudging down the so-called 'flag-stoned walkway to the private lake'. You could have fooled him. Oh wait, there was a piece of stone covered with overgrown grass and weeds. And then another. "Well, the ad was a bit overstated, but I guess you can…" Instead of finishing his sentence, the agent was tripping over a grapevine that had been sticking up out of the ground. He took a header down the hill and caught himself a few yards from the edge of the water.

The water was rippling slightly from the wind. As the agent lay at the edge of the bank, he could see how secluded the beach was. If there were any other houses around, they were buried deep in the woods as well. Duck Lake was very private, but large enough to accommodate twenty to thirty lake front homes.

As he cleaned himself off, he could see the client sauntering down the wooded landscape laughing. *Thanks for the help and the concern*, He thought to himself. After showing the dock and the uncovered, filthy motor boat, he turned to walk up to the house again.

"Does the boat work?"

"I'm not certain. Probably. Engines like that are a dime a dozen though and it wouldn't take much to make her run again. Just needs a little…"

"Elbow grease. I know." The client responded.

"Yes, hum, ah, well, shall we continue with a look at the house?" Stephen stammered, eager to get this showing over with. Something just didn't seem right, but he couldn't put his finger on the problem.

The cabin was built into the side of the hill, which allowed access to the basement through an old doorway. The small windows beside the door didn't let in much light. Anyone who loved the surroundings would certainly want to update the lower entrance with either a set of sliding doors or, better yet, french doors. As he approached the cracked door, he readied his keys, but the client beat him to the knob and turned it. It opened with just a twist.

"Guess there's not much need to lock up here anyway. Nobody comes around. This property is the only piece of land developed for miles. That's the beauty of it, private, secluded, quiet, peaceful- you name it, it's whatever you need."

"Yes, I believe it is." There was no need for much communication. The client just wanted to get on with the inspection.

Was that innuendo, or just another lame comment? The agent couldn't put his finger on this one. Agreeable, yes, but aloof and insensitive. Conversation was forced at best. Normally he didn't have any problem joking and talking with clients. Oh well, it didn't matter as long as he made the sale. It had been a rough couple of months for him.

The water heater, electrical box and furnace were in the cobwebbed corner along with boxes of unwanted magazines and papers. "I guess they weren't much on throwing anything out. We'd probably better at least move them away from the furnace. Fire hazard, you know." He began to pull them away as his client opened all the doors in the lower level.

The floors were wood planks with huge gaps between each piece. The dirt from years of poor housekeeping was imbedded in them. *Are those bugs crawling around in there?* It didn't seem to phase the potential owner of the run down cabin. A little sweat equity would restore it to its original state perhaps.

"Care to look upstairs now?"

"That would be fine. Thank you."

"There are only two bedrooms upstairs, but I think you can see the possibilities for a third, if you would need it. There's a lot of wasted space here." They walked up the creaky staircase with Stephen leading the way. "Now, the kitchen really needs a facelift." He paused and then continued, "As well as the bathrooms, but I don't have to tell you that. See for yourself. The good news is that there are two of them. You don't see that very often in an older house. There's one here in the hallway, and then there's one in the..." He coughed as he said the next words, "the master bedroom."

The master bedroom. That was a joke. It was a 12 x 12 room with a creaky iron bed frame taking up most of the space. How wonderful. They even left a bedspread on the musty mattress! Neither the agent nor the client wanted to sit on it, even though they were both still tired from the exhausting climb up the hill. The bathroom off the bedroom was definitely disgusting. It was cramped and uninviting to say the least.

They finished the tour with a look in the second bedroom down the hall. It couldn't have been more than a 9x10 room with two twin beds and a small dresser crammed in the space. Old wallpaper was peeling from the corner walls and water streaks darkened the pattern. It was time to move on.

"I need to get back into town. I appreciate your time showing me around. Is this the way out?" The client pointed to the front door in the dilapidated living room area. As they walked towards the front door they saw a tattered couch and one overstuffed, stained, dirty green chair positioned on either side of a small water damaged end table. The glance into the kitchen revealed painted wood cabinets that went to the 8 foot ceiling. One cupboard door had a crack through it and another couldn't shut properly. There were three drawers for utensils and an old coppertone stove and a white, one door refrigerator with a tiny freezer in it.

As they closed the door behind them and headed to the cars just up the hill by the road, the agent couldn't help but ask. "Are you interested? You could come by the office and write up a contract. I'm sure the sellers are highly motivated."

What came next was a shock since the client seemed uninterested. "I'll be there at 2:00 today. Is that doable?"

"Fine, um, that will be fine. See you at 2:00." He got in his car and watched as the probable new owner of the 'secluded getaway needing only a few minor repairs and updating' got in the other car. He smiled and waved goodbye to the not-too-bright client with a- he couldn't put his finger on it- yes, that was it- a sinister attitude. Not his problem. Money and a contract was all he wanted. He wasn't looking for some fabulous new friendship out of the deal.

The winding road led them both out of the woods after what seemed an eternity to the realtor. The client, on the other hand, switched on the radio and enjoyed the music- and the fact that of a storm cloud was about to let it rip. Perfect, just perfect!

Chapter 3

Had it only been one week since Jackie's family enjoyed the idea of a beach vacation? It seemed so long ago. They had arrived Saturday afternoon and by Monday felt settled in their new environment. Jackie could still hear the old man on the beach saying, "Where there are dolphins playing, you can be sure there are no sharks." And then he had thrown his baited hook into the ocean waves beating against the Atlantic shoreline. Summer by the sea, how wonderful!

The old man had obviously seen how anxious she was and was trying to calm her fears. She stared at the fins in the water desperately searching for a way to get Michael's attention as he swam. Michael was jumping the three-foot waves playing tag while the fish swam all around him. Crashing waves would swirl him around taking him under, but eventually he would pop back up. According to some, the dolphins never attacked swimmers. She hoped it was true. She needed to trust someone. This was her vacation. Peace, quiet, and rest - no schedule to keep, nothing special to do. It was her two weeks away from home and the chaos created by everyday living. Jonathan had whirled her away from the city so quickly that she hadn't even had time to pack anything. The new bathing suits, shorts, beach towels and anything else they needed - including toothbrushes and toothpaste - were picked up in the little merchant's store a few blocks from their cottage.

It was a beautiful setting. No crowded beach, no boardwalk, just miles of sand in both directions and an occasional cottage sitting back from the ocean guarded by a sand dune. The sandpipers swooped down to the ocean, snatched up their food and then blissfully carried their catch high above earth soaring away with their conquest.

Jackie continued to watch her children laughing and playing in the water as they ran from one wave to another. Thankfully, Michael listened to his father and paid close attention to Lizzy while they splashed in the ocean.

Jonathan had been very direct earlier that morning. "Michael, I'm leaving you in charge of the family while I'm not out here. Your mother and sister need you to look out for them. Can you handle that?"

"Yes sir!" He had replied. "I can take care of everything."

"I'll be back before your fingers turn to prunes from playing in the water too long!" Jonathan had a sheepish grin on his face. With that he tapped his son on the shoulder and kissed him on the head.

Jonathan was always cautious with the children's safety but recently he had become even more guarded. He would chastise Jackie if she let them play alone outside and insisted that they never leave her sight. But they were safe here. No one was around- except the old man, and he had vanished into his own cottage down the way a bit. The children were free to play in the sand and water while Jackie turned over on the blanket and let her back soak in the late afternoon sun. Michael and Lizzy built a castle using buckets of water to harden the sand on the top of their creation. Jackie was lulled into a light sleep from the gentle breeze and soft sound of the waves beating against the shore.

A sudden icy cold splash on the nape of Jackie's neck awakened her as two sand creatures attacked her. Lizzy was easily thrown off since her tiny frame and five-year-old features couldn't match her mother's 5' 2", 120 pounds. The other monster tried his best to wrestle his mother and pin her down, but he couldn't do it either. Soon they were heading towards the water screaming, "Run! Run!" desperately trying to reach the waves before she could get them. They knew they would be safe in the ocean because their mother was terrified of water and would never step foot in it. And they were right. Ankle deep in the waves they playfully egged their mother on yelling, "You can't get us! You can't get us!" She stood alone on the beach as they kicked the water at her.

As much as she wanted to play in the ocean with her children, she couldn't forget her past and what happened to Gina. She stood alone on the beach as they splashed her.

It didn't take very long though before Jackie found another way of enticing them out of the water. All she had to do was ask them if they wanted to have something to eat. It was, after all, 5:00 and definitely time for supper. They dried off haphazardly, dripping and running through the sand towards the cottage, leaving everything behind, including towels, buckets shovels and the blanket. Jackie loaded up her arms as she rolled her eyes. If she left everything where it was, the tide would sweep it away. She had no other choice. Digging her heels into the white sand, she made her way to the door, which thankfully they had left open.

Before she could stop either of them, Michael was offering Lizzy a sip of pop straight out of the two-liter bottle.

"Just one sip, Lizzy. Come on, that's enough. This is my bottle. Stop!"

Sharing wasn't something the Pennington kids did very well. *It's a wonder he even offered her a sip at all* Jackie thought to herself. Normally the children would be scolded for passing germs that way, but she decided not to say anything about the disgusting habit of drinking from a bottle and putting it back in the refrigerator, with the cap off, no less.

She dropped the towels and blankets into a pile in the middle of her bedroom floor and then went back to the kitchen to get an ice-cold glass of water. She pulled out a chair at the chrome table, sipped her drink and felt grateful for the comfort it brought to her parched throat. She closed her eyes for a moment enjoying the feeling, and then opened them again and looked around the living room. It was unusually messy. *Strange*, she thought. *I know I had this clean before we went back outside after lunch.* She looked at her watch. *Where is Jonathan anyway?*

On the table she found his scribbled message. Went for a jog. Won't be long. Love, Jonathan.

So disciplined. He won't even stop jogging on vacation. Well, I guess if I want him to look good, I've got to sacrifice the time it takes for him to stay in shape. After all, 35 is just around the corner for both of us. Jackie smiled. She loved putting her arms around his tanned, muscular shoulders and feeling his lean stomach next to her's. She imagined him beside her now. Jonathan kept long hours at the firm, so she was accustomed to dreaming about him.

Not long ago he had suggested they get a big dog to protect them when he was away. "Wouldn't you feel better having an animal trained to protect you in case a stranger got in the house?" Jonathan would repeatedly ask.

"More children are attacked by their own dogs than by some thief. No thanks. I couldn't live with myself if anything happened to my kids because I as afraid of being home alone. I'll just have to take up karate or something." Jackie would playfully reply.

Back to reality! "Michael, this place is a mess. Will you do me a huge favor and start cleaning it up while I give Lizzy her bath?" Without waiting for an answer, Jackie whisked Lizzy into the bathroom. She glanced around and nearly shuddered when she began filling the tub. No matter how she tried, she couldn't get over the fact that the plaster was cracked and the white porcelain around the tub was yellowing with age and rough to the touch. It definitely looked as if a do-it-yourselfer must have tried to patch the cracks in the walls and botched the job. Putting Lizzy in the tub was a bit disgusting.

Jackie still didn't understand why Jonathan was in such a big hurry to get to the beach. Accommodations are rarely good on short notice. Not that she was complaining. It just wasn't the way he usually liked to travel. Renting the cottage made her feel as if she was back in Indiana with her family. Although her childhood farm home was warm and cozy, it was constantly in need of repairs. Her mother and father lived day to day on their paychecks and watched how they spent their money. There was never much left over at the end of the week. When Jackie married Jonathan she found out what it meant to be able to buy what she wanted and afford nice things. She had grown accustomed to nice clothes, beautiful furniture and great food.

"Okay Lizzy, let's get this wet, sandy suit off and make your body feel good again."

At five years old, Lizzy was all legs and she wiggled them constantly.

"Stand still honey, I can't get this off with you moving so much." Jackie pleaded with her as she tugged at the bright purple flowered one-piece bathing suit.

"Mommy, I itch all over." Lizzy complained as she started scratching every part of her body.

"This will help." The suit landed on the floor and pieces of sand, gravel and even some tiny shells fell from the folds. "Looks like you brought the beach inside with you Lizzy!" Jackie began brushing the sand off as best she could with a towel and then wrapped it around Lizzy so she could give her a big bear hug. For a few seconds she just held her tightly and then she began kissing her sandy brow.

The cool bath water was just what Lizzy needed. The sun had scorched her shoulders and thighs. No matter how much sunscreen Jackie used on Lizzy, she seemed to draw the sun to her and burn any exposed flesh. It didn't seem right. No one else in the family burned that easily. Most of the day she had spent with a t-shirt over her bathing suit, and yet her shoulders were still red. Her hair, usually fine, had stiffened with the sand strewn in it and Jackie was sure it would take at least three washings to get the grit out.

Lizzy splashed in the water and played with the bubbles while Jackie washed her. So much energy! *Why couldn't I have some of that?* Jackie often felt tired and edgy but kept pushing herself because Lizzy never quit playing.

The only time she was still was when she finally collapsed into bed at the end of a long day of playing. Then it only took her two minutes to fall asleep.

While Jackie helped with Lizzy's bath, Michael flicked on the television as he cleaned. "How come I'm the only one who ever cleans up around here?" Michael mumbled to himself. It wasn't true, but he liked to think he was the only one who worked. After all, he was nearly ten and responsible for so much! He studied the TV while he gathered up the newspaper. Half-heartedly he managed to stack it on the old stand next to the couch. He picked up three pairs of shoes - all of them his father's. Jonathan's sandals, loafers and his jogging shoes were nestled around the furniture. "Dad can't even clean up his own things. I'd be dead meat if I left them sitting around. Probably wouldn't be allowed to play outside for at least a week!" He was really beginning to complain; especially after picking up orange peels on the floor- now that was just, just ... disgusting!

"Michael, the bathroom is all yours now," Jackie called out. "Try to hurry so you'll be ready for supper when your father gets home."

"Okay mom."

Lizzy was already dressed and snuggling up with her doll on the couch, a blanket twisted and laying near her feet. Cartoons kept her entertained as Jackie began supper. The table was set and the food was ready at 6:00, so all they had to do was wait for Jonathan.

Before long Michael reappeared dressed in a pair of shorts and t-shirt. His thick, black hair was neatly combed back and his face had a fresh touch of sun perfectly kissing his forehead and cheeks. He looked very handsome.

"What's for supper? I'm starving!" He lifted the lid so he could see what was cooking. "When can we eat?"

"I was hoping your father would be home by now, but I think we'd better start without him before you shrivel up and die from starvation." Jackie was just about to mess up his hair with her hand when Michael put a fast hand up and stopped her.

"Hey, don't touch the locks! I worked hard to look this good!" He said with a smile. She relaxed her hand and hugged him instead. Michael rolled his eyes. He didn't want his mother to know how much he loved her playful ways and her constant affection.

"What about Lizzy. Should I wake her?" Michael walked over to the couch and was just about to shake her when Jackie reacted.

"Let her sleep. She is exhausted!" she whispered.

Michael and Jackie sat at the table for nearly a half-hour before they began to clean up the table. "Go ahead, Michael. You can watch television now. I'll clean up in here."

"Thanks!"

Jackie was meticulous and deliberately slow cleaning up the plates and food, but was distracted. All she could think about was why Jonathan wasn't home yet. It was nearly 7:30. There didn't seem to be an explanation for him not being back by now. *He has a cell phone. Why isn't he using it?* Jackie's thoughts drifted...*Jonathan would have called because he knows how much I worry.*

Even though Jackie's breakdown was years ago, it was still a fresh memory for both of them. The doctor warned him about signing her out without his approval but they left anyway, with prescriptions to thwart off depression and anxiety. Jackie heard the doctor tell Jonathan that the drugs could be very dangerous. He was told to keep them locked up and give them only as prescribed. Another accidental overdose could leave her brain damaged or dead instead of just sick.

It had been a serious attempt, but the reasons were buried deep within her and therapy was long and tenuous. For months following the hospital stay, she saw her therapist three times a week, then two and then once a week until finally it was just once a month- so that the doctor could keep track of how she was doing. And she was doing much better. There were never any great revelations as to why she had been so self-destructive, but now, she no longer felt so hopeless. Now, more than ever, she had a reason to live, two reasons, in fact. Michael and Lizzy needed her. She vowed she would be there for them.

CRASH! There was a thunderous explosion of dishes breaking. The floor was spattered with tiny slivers of shining glass from two of them. Jackie bent over between the table and the sink and began picking up the pieces.

"Mom?"

"It's okay Michael. I just broke two of their finest pieces. Now they only have a set of three instead of five." *Careful Jackie. You sound a bit too cynical. It isn't necessary to make fun of other people's things.*

"Mom, where's Dad? I thought you said he'd be home soon."

"I thought he would be. I called his cell phone, but we must be out of range. As soon as I finish cleaning up I'm going to take the car out for a quick look around. You can keep an eye on Lizzy for me, can't you?" She wasn't listening for his answer. She swept the floors and continued. "Don't step over here in your bare feet. I'm not sure I got it all."

When she finished sweeping, she put the broom away and gave Michael directions. "Watch Lizzy and lock the door behind me. Don't let anyone in. I'll take the cell phone so you can reach me if you need to and I'll be back in a few minutes." She grabbed the keys and hurried to the door. Michael stood waiting for her to shut it. "Be…"

"I know, mom. Be careful. Don't let anyone in. Don't touch the matches. Don't let anyone know I'm home alone. I got it." Michael was teasing, but wanted her to know he was reliable and that he could be trusted.

Chapter 4

It had been early summer when the keys to the house in the woods were handed over to the new owner-five days after the initial run through and acceptance offer. As the client left, the real estate agent laughed and hummed down the hall on his way to the mortgage office with the check- payment in full! He was delighted to be rid of such an eyesore. It happened much easier than he thought too. For the life of him, he couldn't figure what draw that place had on someone obviously well enough off to have that much cash on hand. Maybe a place to rest after a hard week of work. Who knows? Who cared? He had his sale, his commission and another notch in his belt as he headed for salesman of the year. It worked for him!

The client reasoned that the house could use a professional cleaning, but that would have to wait. For now, the place would be stocked with food and supplies. Maybe renovations would follow at a later date. It wasn't that important to move forward without getting a feel of the surroundings. It was, after all, temporary. Timing had to be perfect. Opportunities were few and far between and it was important to be ready.

Chapter 5

Fifteen minutes later Jackie returned. There was no sign of Jonathan. Jackie was really getting worried now - really worried. This wasn't like him at all. Again she tried his cell phone with no luck.

Michael was sitting on the couch as she slipped past him without a word. He stared at her as she walked to her bedroom. He got off the couch and tried to follow her into her room, but she practically pushed the door shut in his face. She dialed 911.

"911. Is this an emergency?" The woman answered in a monotone voice.

"Yes, my husband is missing."

"Missing. Did you say missing?" She questioned, again mono toned but alert.

"Yes missing. He hasn't returned from his run and he is over three hours late."

"Mrs.?"

"Pennington. Mrs. Jonathan Pennington."

"Well Mrs. Pennington, missing person reports aren't validated until they've been gone over 24 hours if they are over 18." She seemed a bit flippant when she responded.

"This is different. He's not the type that would disappear on me." Jackie was defensive and angry that she had to argue with an operator.

"You can call the sheriff's office if you want. The number is 555-0895."

"Thank you." Jackie couldn't hide her frustration as she spoke. She dialed the number she was given, but fumbled the last digit and had to redial.

"Police? I want to report a missing person." She waited for the question and then replied, "My husband... three hours...twenty four hours? But you don't understand... No, we didn't fight... Please. He left a note saying he went jogging around 3:30 I think, and he never came back. I'm afraid he's been in some sort of accident or maybe he got sick... No I didn't call the hospitals...I don't know this area at all. I'm just here on vacation. I don't know anyone. I'm not familiar with anything and I don't know the names of the hospitals around here... Oh thank you! Yes I'll be here. Thank you. Oh, I'm sorry. Mrs. Pennington, Jackie...Just a minute." Jackie rummaged through some papers until she found the rental agreement. "Here it is, 2012 Seaside Drive, Cottage A. Thank you officer. Please hurry." She heard a knock on the bedroom door.

"Mom, can I come in please?"

Jackie wiped away the tears in her eyes and timidly approached the door. Michael had already opened it part way when she got there. "Michael, I think it's time you and Lizzy went to bed."

"What about dad?"

"He should be home soon. You need your rest so you can build that sandcastle again tomorrow like you promised. "

Michael knew better than to argue. He smacked the side of the doorway with the palm of his hand in defiance and trudged to the bathroom to brush his teeth. He swore he would listen for his father's return even if he had to stay awake all night!

Jackie went into the living room and found Lizzy beneath the blanket on the couch still fast asleep. It was easy for Jackie to pick her little girl up, snuggle her in her arms and carry her off to bed without waking her because she was so tiny. Gently she covered her up with a sheet knowing she would sleep through the night even without her supper. Just as she left, she made sure the bedroom door was open a little so light would shine in. Lizzy was afraid of the dark.

The overstuffed chair in the corner of the living room became a haven for Jackie. She collapsed into it and buried her head in tears. *Where are you Jonathan? Call me! Tell me you're okay.*

When the police knocked on the screen door, it was strong and startling. Jackie's pulse quickened as she raced to the door, hoping it was Jonathan. Instead a burly man with a rumpled shirt and one-size-too-small jacket peered through the screen door waiting patiently for it to be answered. Beside him stood a younger man, mid thirties, with a flick of golden hair falling on his forehead from the summer night ocean breeze. His features were flawless with a strong chin and piercing blue eyes. He smiled as he introduced himself and his partner. "Good evening, I'm Detective Ryder and this is my partner,

Detective Fortney. We're from the Beach City Police Department. We understand you are concerned about your husband. Is that correct?"

"Yes. Thank you for coming." She led them to the couch and offered them a seat as she continued. "I'm really worried about him. He left a note saying he was going jogging, but he never came back. I have the note right here." She handed them the scribbled message.

Detective Fortney reached for the note at the same time Detective Ryder did. After reading it, Detective Fortney began the questions. "When was the last time you saw your husband Mrs."

Jackie interrupted him to answer. "Jackie. Jacqueline Pennington. I came in around 1:00. He said he wanted to stay inside for a while and work on some briefs." She felt she needed to explain his work-aholic ethic. "He's a lawyer and he tends to take his work with him wherever he goes. When I got back inside around 5:00 to start supper I noticed the note. I didn't think too much of it since he can run for a couple of hours on a good day, but when he didn't show up by 6:00, I started to worry. It's nearly 10:30 now. I've been calling his cell phone and I went looking for him after supper, but I couldn't find him anywhere."

"Maybe a friend wanted him to stop for a beer or something. Or maybe there was an argument?" Detective Fortney was fishing for the truth - a fight of some sort.

"No, we don't have any friends here. We're on vacation and we weren't fighting at all. He just went for a jog." *Why don't they believe me?* That was all that Jackie could think. She insisted, "Look at the note!"

"Where did you find the note Mrs. Pennington?" Detective Ryder was examining it carefully.

"It was on the table in front of you. Right here." She was pointing to the corner of the coffee table.

"Is this your husband's handwriting?"

"Yes".

Detective Fortney read it aloud. "Went for a jog. Won't be long. Love, Jonathan."

Jackie buried her face for a moment and then sat down in the chair. It swallowed her tiny frame.

"Mrs. Pennington can you think of any reason why your husband is gone? Are any clothes missing?" Detective Ryder seemed much more compassionate than his partner.

"I never thought to check the closet. I'm sure nothing's gone. The bedroom looks the same as it did when I took the kids to the beach this afternoon. Nothing is out of place. The only room that looked different at all was this one." She was referring to the tiny living space surrounding them.

She continued, "Michael, that's my son, cleaned up in here." Jackie looked embarrassed as she noticed the way he had straightened up the room. There was a half-eaten, wrinkled-up orange on the end table. She picked it up and headed for the garbage pail with it.

"How tall is your husband?" Detective Fortney was busy with pen and paper taking notes.

"Six one."

"And weight?"

"Around 185 pounds."

"Hair color?"

"Dark brown and wavy."

"Any identifiable marks?" Detective Fortney noticed she seemed to question what he meant by that and continued. "Moles, warts, birthmarks, scars?"

"No, not really. Wait, he does have a scar on his left - no his right side. He was in a skiing accident a few years ago. It goes from here to here." Jackie was pointing to her own right side beginning at the breast and ending just above the hipbone. She began to cry softly. "I thought he was going to die. He was in ICU for three days."

Her mind wandered too much and Detective Ryder was concerned. "Mrs. Pennington, is there anyone you can call who could help you?" Jackie's reaction was slow. Too slow.

"Mrs. Pennington? Maybe you shouldn't be alone. Are there any family members you could call?"

Jackie wanted to scream out, "Yes, I have a sister. I have a sister!" But instead she stared straight ahead remembering how there was going to be one, but her mother miscarried Angela when she was eight months pregnant. There had been no explanation as to why the baby didn't make it. The cord wasn't wrapped around her neck, the placenta was intact and there were no abnormalities in the baby's development. She simply didn't survive. Angela was buried in a nearby cemetery. Since Jackie was barely three at the time of her death, she didn't remember her mother's tears or her father's sadness.

But when Jackie was thirteen, she found her mother's diary, quite by accident, after it had been left on the end table in the living room. There it was, plain as day…*I miss you every day, Angela Marie. I don't understand why God needed you more than me. It's been ten years and I've never gotten over the fact that you were taken from me before I even saw you take one breath. I held you in my arms and said goodbye without you ever knowing my voice, my kiss or my touch. Why God, why? No one should have to bury their children. It is too painful. I pray that you are resting happily in the arms of the Lord since I cannot be there to hold you myself. I still cry myself to sleep wishing you were with us and I've never stopped loving you.*

It was hard for Jackie to confess that she had read her mother's diary, but she wanted to know who Angela Marie was. Taken aback, Jackie's mother set her down on their aged couch and held on to Jackie's hands as she spoke. It all made sense as her mother told her about her little sister's death.

Jackie had remembered very few things from her early childhood, but she had always been haunted by a memory where her Daddy was walking away with her from a large, open area. Each time the vision returned, she could see him bury his head in her shoulder as they walked away. Was he weeping? The memory was so vivid, yet unexplainable. She remembered her father carrying her further away from her mother as her mother stood motionless, staring at the stones in the grass.

The memory became clear as her mother spoke of Angela's services. Her father and mother were the last ones at the gravesite. Her Daddy had walked away before her mother could leave the little casket with her baby lying inside. The memory had been recurring and had frightened Jackie for so long that when she heard about her little sister's death, she was relieved to finally get a real picture of what had happened all those years ago.

Jackie even began visiting the grave so that she could "talk" to her little sister. Often it was just to say mundane things like, "Dad and Mom just celebrated their anniversary and we had cake." Or "They talked about you again today." But Jackie needed to share so much more. She eventually told her about all the feelings she had that no one else could know. Sometimes she would sit by the head stone and start rambling on about her best friend, Gina, and how it was all her fault that she died. She'd dredge up the whole scene and plead for forgiveness that she wasn't able save her. Had Angela seen the whole thing from heaven? Did God take Gina because he needed her more than her own parents did? Why would he do that? Angela, why did he take you before I even had a chance to know you? I needed a sister to talk to. Angela, can you even hear me?

The one-sided conversations were never truly satisfying, but Jackie returned with every new piece of news- things she wouldn't share with anyone else and the things that didn't really matter. Years of guilt for surviving when Gina and Angela didn't took their toll on Jackie. She didn't feel she deserved to be happy when neither of them even got a chance to live.

She would lament over the decisions she was making and how it would affect her parents. If she got a bad grade on a test, she'd confess to Angela that she should have studied harder. If she knew a boy was interested in her, she'd tell Angela about him and then say she didn't dare go with him. He'd just leave her anyway. When she finally allowed herself to date as a senior in high school, she would visit Angela at the cemetery and tell her all about David and what they did. "We went for ice cream today. I bet you would have loved the ice cream. It was really good. Oh yea, he kissed me on the lips when he dropped me off at home. I don't think Daddy saw him do it, though."

On the day she left for college in Virginia, she spent an hour at Angela's grave talking about her decision to go. She was so afraid that her parents would feel like they had lost another child or feel abandoned. "I don't know if I should go. Angela, please give me some sort of sign about what to do. I don't want to hurt them. I'm not sure if Mom and Dad can take it. What do you think?" Of course, she never expected an answer. "I'll be back as soon as I can. I love you."

That was as close as she came to having a friend or confidant. When Gina died, she refused to get close to any other kids. She kept to herself and stayed at home to avoid them. If she felt the need for a friend, she'd just remind herself that she didn't want to be responsible for anyone else's safety and if she didn't spend time with them, then she wouldn't be. It was an isolated life, but Jackie felt safer tucked away in a cocoon. Her parents thought she was just a shy, little girl. They had no idea she was suffering from so much guilt.

"Mrs. Pennington?" The detective hadn't received a response to his question, so he asked again. "Any family or friends you can call?"

" Oh, I'm sorry, um no, not really. It's pretty much just Jonathan and the kids. Michael is nine and Lizzy, Elizabeth, is five. They're sleeping. I haven't told them anything yet. They just think he's late." She paused for a moment. "I don't know how to tell them he's missing."

"It's a little early to consider him missing. By morning all this worry may have been for nothing. You sure you don't want to call someone to stay with you tonight?"

"I'll be fine. But I need to call the hospitals now."

"We'll do that for you, Mrs. Pennington." Detective Fortney seemed eager to leave and was already at the door. "We'll check into this and call you when we know something. Let us know if you hear anything."

"Goodnight Mrs. Pennington. Try not to worry. I'm sure Mr. Pennington will be home soon. No man in his right mind would miss a night with you."

Detective Ryder's finger went to the front of his brow and he gave a gentle smile as he said good night.

Detective Fortney was chiding Detective Ryder as they left. "Putting the moves on the lady while her old man's away. Smooth man, smooth!"

"Just being friendly. She looked like she needed a smile, that's all."

From the window Jackie watched them check outside around the cottage. After a few minutes they returned to their car, started the engine and left. Jackie felt alone and frightened. Suddenly she was sick and before she could gain control, she was throwing up in the sink. *Wonderful. Look at me. Just like old times, isn't it, Jackie?* She was frustrated at her inability to handle the stress any better now than when she was 25. Getting sick in the sink wasn't going to bring Jonathan home. Neither was crying. But she just couldn't help it anymore. The tears began to flow and she found herself on the bed hugging his pillow, calling his name. "Jonathan. Where are you? "

She drifted in and out of sleep as she lay restlessly on the bed. Each hour passed slowly. It was 2:00 AM, silent, cold, windy... no longer the dream vacation she had hoped for, but a horrible nightmare.

Chapter 6

    Tuesday morning Lizzy rose with her usual spunk and made her way to her Mommy's bedroom and climbed into bed beside Jackie to snuggle. Jackie stirred and then abruptly sat straight up. When she reached for Jonathan she remembered instantly that he wasn't there. The pounding in her head upset her stomach- *a migraine. Where are my pills? Why haven't the police called? Where's Jonathan?* She stumbled out of bed and made her way into the living room hoping to find him asleep on the couch, but he wasn't there. She would have to tell the children pretty soon. But how? What would she say?

    "Mommy, why are you sleeping in your clothes? Where's Daddy? I'm hungry." Lizzy was constantly asking questions and rarely waited for an answer. Her tummy always came first.

    6:57 AM. Last night she thought morning would never come and now that it had, Jackie wondered why she cared. Without Jonathan nothing was worth it. She lifted her eyes toward the ceiling and mumbled, "Lord, give me strength."

    "What would you like for breakfast, sweetie? Cereal okay?"

    "Oatmeal, I want oatmeal!" Lizzy cried for her favorite breakfast. Of course she wanted oatmeal.

    "Oatmeal it is!" Jackie needed to keep her daughter happy and if all it took was a bowl of oatmeal, then so be it. Michael, on the other hand, would not be so easy. He would ask a million questions and then cry inconsolably.

    "Mommy, can we make a castle again today?" Lizzy began pushing a chair to the counter to watch her mother make the cereal.

    "I'm not sure. We'll have to wait and see." Jackie wasn't prepared to deal with the day. *Take a deep breath - 1, 2, 3, 4, 5. Again.* Too late. The tears were forming in her eyes. She turned around just in time to see Michael come stumbling out of his room rubbing his eyes. After a big yawn he came to life. "Hey, can I have some of that too?"

"Of course. Have a seat. It'll be ready in a minute."

"Dad still sleeping?" Michael was pulling up his chair to the table as he questioned her.

Jackie didn't think Michael would be so quick to ask. It was time. "Michael, Lizzy." Jackie took a deep breath. "Daddy didn't come home last night."

Michael's face went pale. His eyes filled with tears- not like Lizzy who sat silently watching Michael as he blurted out "What happened? Why didn't he come home?" Then he began to cry, so Lizzy cried too.

The smell of scorched oatmeal brought Jackie back to the stove. She shut off the flame and ran water in the pan to let it soak in the sink. Turning immediately back to her children, she swooped Lizzy into her arms and motioned for Michael to follow her. They plopped on the couch together.

"Until we hear from Daddy, we can't be away from the cottage. I'm sure we'll know soon where he is, so we'll try to do something fun another day. For now, we'll just have to wait. Okay Lizzy? Michael?" The look in Jackie's eyes and the inflection of her voice let the kids know she was worried.

Jackie turned on the television and watched the news. "And today's top story, Richmond police are looking into the identity of a body found last night... " Jackie jumped up and turned the television set up to listen more closely. "Authorities are only saying that it is a black female..." She hit the remote button so she didn't have to listen anymore.

"Mommy, can't I watch cartoons?" Lizzy whined, jumped up and turned on the set again, switching the channels until she found one that interested her. She sat down and stared at Big Bird.

They waited together for word from anyone- anywhere-while they sat on the couch.

Chapter 7

The hours passed slowly with no phone calls - nothing from Jonathan or the police. Jackie was restless as she sat beside her children. Both of them were cuddled up beside her trying to feel secure, all the while fidgeting or fighting with each other. Breakfast had burned, lunch was left untouched, and the games they had played on the dirty sand colored carpeting left them all feeling shallow and helpless. The television was on as a distraction. Lizzy would watch a few minutes and then pretend her doll could hear her and whisper in its ear. When the response from the doll didn't seem to be good enough for Lizzy, she hushed her with her tiny finger and then set her gently between her mother and her.

Jackie couldn't wait any longer. She left Lizzy with Michael and headed for the bedroom. The scratch pad with the policeman's number laid next to the phone and she dialed. "Is Detective Ryder in?"

"No, I'm sorry, he isn't. May I ask who's calling?" The dispatcher replied.

"Yes. This is Jackie Pennington. Detective Ryder was at my cottage last night and is looking for my husband. I haven't heard anything at all from him and I was just wondering if he called the hospitals or searched the area."

"I'm sorry Mrs. Pennington. Detective Ryder didn't mention the situation to me and hasn't come in yet this morning. His partner, Detective Fortney is here though. Would you like to speak to him?"

"Yes, please."

The inner office phone system was efficient and soon the voice on the other end of the line was speaking gruffly. "Fortney here."

"Detective Fortney? This is Jackie Pennington. You are investigating the disappearance of my husband and I was just calling to see if there had been any news." Jackie replied.

"Oh yea, Mrs. Pennington, the little dark-haired lady, right? Husband - uh let's see, Oh yea - Jonathan Pennington. Left the house to go for a run and was late getting back. Right?"

"He wasn't just 'late'. He never came home. You told me you'd check the hospitals and the area. Have you done that?" Jackie was totally unprepared for the detective's lack of concern.

"I'm sorry, Mrs. Pennington, no offense. It's just that so many of these cases come up solved the next morning when the husband cools off and wanders home begging to be forgiven for something he did or didn't do. I guess we just figured he was home by now. As soon as my partner gets in, we'll get right on it. I did call the hospitals though, and no one fitting your husband's description- in fact- no one at all was admitted through the emergency room since his-uh- disappearance. That's good news isn't it?"

"I guess so. But what if he's lying out there somewhere hurt and no one finds him in time? Please, this just isn't like him. I really need your help."

Jackie was not impressed with his attitude but didn't want to prolong the conversation. It seemed as if he wasn't working very hard to help her find Jonathan because he wasn't really "missing" yet. But provoking him wouldn't help either.

Detective Fortney felt guilty for not following through now, and he was apologetic. "Ma'am. We'll do whatever we can. Have you called anyone to come be with you yet? "

"No."

"Well, maybe you should."

"Thank you. I'll think about it."

He hung up with a simple goodbye and a promise to keep in touch.

Michael picked at the spaghetti in front of him while Lizzy swirled her milk with her straw. There was no conversation at all. No arguments, no encouragement from Jackie for her children to eat their dinner or drink their milk. Just silence.

They went through the motions of everyday living and at 9:00 PM - a full 24 hours from the first call to the police. Jackie put her children to bed. They didn't say a word. They brushed their teeth, went to the bathroom and got under the covers. Maybe they hoped if they pretended nothing was wrong, Daddy would come home. Or maybe they just wanted to hide beneath the blankets.

Jackie stared at the four unkempt corners of the cottage. Thoughts were swirling around in her head. *It's been 24 hours. Maybe now they'll start looking for him - if he's not dead. Stop it, Jackie! You'll drive yourself crazy again. We'll find him.*

Her mind was racing and she knew she needed to sleep or she would fall apart and she couldn't do that. Her children needed her. She opened the top dresser drawer and ruffled through her clothes. *There they are.* Her migraine pills - something she never left home without, but hadn't needed for a long time. *It won't hurt to take one. The children are asleep for the night and I need to get some rest*, she thought. She popped one in her mouth and made her way to the bathroom sink. The bed didn't look inviting, but Jonathan's pillow was. She picked it up and went back into the cottage's small living room, lay on the tattered couch and prayed for sleep to come quickly. Her tears slid down on the pillow.

Chapter 8

Wednesday morning a knock on the door woke Jackie. She checked her watch. 7:00 AM. She raced to the door, her heart pounding and her hands shaking. Her expression changed when she opened the door and saw Detective Ryder standing on the stoop.

"Mrs. Pennington, I know it's early, but may I come in? I assume you've heard nothing from your husband. Is that right?"

"No, nothing. Please, come in. "She led him to the overstuffed chair and began folding the blanket on the couch.

"I need to ask a few more questions if I may."

"Okay."

"Ma'am. Did you notice any changes in your husband in the last few weeks?"

She shook her head no and he continued. "Any mood swings? New friends? Unusual phone calls or unexplained absences?" Again she shook her head no.

"Anything suspicious at all?" He was pressing her for answers.

"No"

"Mrs. Pennington. Do you have any idea what your husband was wearing when he left the house?"

"Probably a pair of shorts and a t-shirt." She thought for a moment and continued. "And, of course, his running shoes." Jackie was grateful that he was finally taking her case seriously.

"Did you check to see if any of those clothes were missing? "

Before she could speak Michael walked in and was answering the question. "His shoes are in the closet, Mom. I put them there when you asked me to clean up."

Panic filled Jackie's face. She stood immediately to her feet and then ran into the bedroom to look for herself. There in the bottom of the closet were his running shoes. Just as Michael had said. *Why didn't she look for them before? How could she have been so stupid?* She picked them up and brought them over to the detective.

"He's right. Here they are." Jackie's throat was tight. "I don't know where he was going when he left. I thought he went jogging... the note said he went jogging...I don't understand... "Jackie could no longer speak and for the first time, she broke down in front of Michael and sobbed. Michael took her hand and pulled her to the battered couch. They sat down together and cried.

Michael pulled himself together. "Don't cry, Mom. I'll take care of you until Dad comes back. Honest. We'll find him. I know we will." Michael was scared, but he wanted to be brave for his mother.

Jackie lifted her head and kissed her son on the top of his tousled hair. "I know, honey, I know."

"Mrs. Pennington, perhaps you should call someone. I think you could use a friend right about now. What about your parents?" Detective Ryder's concern was genuine and he reached for her shoulder as he stood next to her. "I think you need them."

"It's just my mother now. Daddy had a heart attack and died before we got him to the hospital. Mother is too ill. She couldn't stand the trip." Jackie's response was more controlled, but she looked baffled.

"Isn't there anyone else you can think of?"

"Well, maybe Celeste would come. She's a close friend. Maybe I could call her."

"I think that would be wise. In the meantime, I'll keep checking out any leads. We've put an APB- All Points Bulletin - out on your husband and I'm sure we'll get some news soon. You said you lived in Richmond, Virginia, right? I'll contact the department there and they can get started looking too. In the meantime, sit tight. Hundreds of cases like this are reported every day, and most of them turn out all right. Hang on to that now, okay?" Detective Ryder was heading for the door as he spoke.

The case seemed more complicated than he originally suspected and now he was edgy too. "Michael is it?" Michael nodded. "Michael, make sure your mother calls her friend. And be a good boy now. She needs some TLC." Detective Ryder winked at the boy and left.

"Mom. What's TLC?" Michael asked as he shut the door.

"Tender, loving care. Just like you and Daddy give me all the time."

"Oh." He paused for a second then continued. "Don't forget to call Celeste."

"I won't."

Chapter 9

"Jackie. Jackie where are you? Come on Sweetie. I'm here now." Celeste always called everyone, Sweetie or Honey or Pumpkin- any endearing name that crossed her mind. She was just that way. Her inheritance had made it easy for her to learn the social graces of the elite, but her playful spirit could be misinterpreted. Her off-the-shoulder blouse revealed pampered bronze skin and her silky blonde hair rested at the edge of her shoulder blade. It was a sultry look, made to entice any gentleman she happened to encounter, and it worked like a charm. Money, good looks and attitude, Celeste had it all.

"Jackie, where are you?" Celeste found her sitting just off the dune watching the kids play in the sand. "Oh God, Jackie, you look terrible. Come on. Let's go inside and get you washed up and get some make-up on your face. You'll feel better. Then we'll talk."

Jackie couldn't get up. Celeste bent over and hugged her, then sat down beside her as Jackie began sobbing in her arms.

"Come on, it's okay. I'm here now. We'll find him." She held her close as she spoke. " Have you heard anything?"

"Nothing."

"It'll be okay. Honestly it will." Celeste struggled for the right words.

"C.C. Hey look Michael, C.C.'s here!" Lizzy squealed in excitement. Celeste was bombarded by the tiny frame approaching her in record speed. Lizzy's sandy arms covered Celeste's shirt, as she embraced her. Celeste squeezed her best buddy and held her tight. She loved these kids- more than anybody else. Anything Lizzy and Michael did was okay with Celeste.

"Hey there Beth, how ya doing?" Celeste refused to call Elizabeth "Lizzy". "A beautiful girl like you should have a beautiful name like Beth." Celeste was the only one allowed to call her that. "Michael, my man, how you hangin' in there? You being good for your mom?" With a shrug of his shoulders and a quick look at his mother for approval he nodded yes.

Jackie smiled and spoke quickly, "I don't know what I'd do without him!" Lizzy was pushing Michael out of the way as Celeste tried to receive the hugs Michael was so anxious to give.

Celeste stood to her feet, flung Lizzy across her waist, pulled Jackie from her sandy seat and then grabbed Michael's hand. "Come on everybody. I brought pizza. Let's eat." Suddenly everyone seemed to be able to eat again.

Lizzy went to bed early and while she slept, Jackie unleashed all of her fears about Jonathan's disappearance. Michael listened intently as they sat in the living room together. The evening sun went down without warning and soon Michael was ushered to bed as well. It seemed as if Celeste knew all the right things to do. As soon as Michael was asleep Celeste persuaded Jackie to take a long, hot shower while she cleaned up the cottage. Then she directed Jackie to her bed and handed her some medicine. Too tired to make any decisions on her own, she was grateful for Celeste's insistence. She swallowed the pills and drifted off to sleep. It was the third night without Jonathan and there was no sign of him at all.

It was Thursday morning already. Hard to believe they had been at the ocean since Saturday. Jonathan had disappeared Monday, which seemed so long ago. It felt appropriate that the rain was pouring down. Celeste spent most of her time playing with the children inside while Jackie made phone calls to everyone she could think of. The police had nothing. Everyone at the office had been alerted and no one knew where he was.

When Detective Ryder appeared at the door, rain pelting his umbrella, Celeste let him in and led him to Jackie. She offered him lemonade and sat next to Jackie as they talked.

After asking more pointed questions, Detective Ryder watched as Jackie twisted the wedding band on her left finger and played with the brilliant diamond. "Do you know how Jonathan proposed to me?" She asked. They waited for her to proceed. "He came into the University Library, bent down and whispered in my ear 'Come with me'. Then he reached for my hand, pulled me from my chair and started dragging me out." She chuckled and then went on. "I remember crying out 'my books, my books', but he just said, leave them there, we'll be back' and off we went. It was pouring outside. Kind of like today. We ran through the grass to the parking lot and my hair got soaked. He opened the driver's side of the car and pushed me in hoping I wouldn't get too wet."

Still chuckling, Jackie continued. "You should have seen it. There I was, crawling across the seat, my butt in the air and soaked from head to toe. We were laughing so hard I stopped moving, so he pushed on my rear again. I lost my balance and went flat on my face on the seat. Jonathan was trying to get in out of the rain too, so when he pushed me again, he fell on top of me. His legs were dangling out the door, his arms were all over me and I could barely breathe with him on top of me. "

"Eventually he got off me and we made it inside the car. He looked straight at me, said 'You are so beautiful' and then kissed me - wet head and all. Then he drove me to Virginia Beach and parked the car. The rain finally stopped so he stepped out, popped the trunk open and pulled out a picnic basket and blanket. We walked hand in hand to the beach, took off our shoes and dug our toes into the wet sand till we found the perfect place to sit."

Celeste didn't stop Jackie even though she'd heard the story before. She knew it was therapeutic.

"He pulled out two glasses, a bottle of wine and some bread and cheese. It was just like in the movies! I think we sat there sipping the wine for an hour. There was hardly anyone on the beach. It was so romantic. Just when I thought he was getting ready for us to leave, he reached into the basket again and pulled out a tiny package. I think it was the only time he couldn't find the right words. He was so flustered. I finally just said 'yes, yes!' even though he never got the question out. Then I kissed him!"

Jackie had played with her rings so long that Celeste finally touched her hand and spoke, "Hey, you'll wear your finger out if you don't stop it."

"Yea, I guess so." Jackie put her hands under her legs as she sat on the couch. "You know, when Mom and Dad said they wanted me to go away to college, I told them I didn't want to leave Indiana. But they said it would do me good and insisted, so I went. They were right. Jonathan was the best thing that ever happened to me and I never would have met him if I hadn't left home."

Jackie was drifting off in her own world. Celeste got up and ushered the detective to the door. "I'll take it from here."

"I think she should go home. See if you can get her to go. We'll let her know if anything turns up."

"Thank you. I'll try." Celeste touched his shoulder with the palm of her hand as she led him to the door.

Jackie finally agreed to go home, as long as the police would keep her informed and check on the cottage every few hours for his return. They began to pack.

"Let me help you with that." Celeste offered. "This is pretty tough on you, isn't it? I mean, not knowing where he is and all." She picked up Jonathan's new t-shirts from the pressed wood dresser drawer and placed them neatly in the new hunter green suitcase. She then placed two packages of unopened boxer shorts beside them. "Never even opened." Celeste noted to herself.

Reading Celeste's mind Jackie spoke. "Jonathan didn't give us time to pack anything. He said he wanted to get going." Jackie knelt down, staring at the bottom of the closet. "He said we'd buy it all when we got here- except for his shoes. He has really narrow feet and can't find too many places that carry the double AA width." Jackie picked up his running shoes and pulled them to her chest.

"Looks to me like he brought every pair he owned." Celeste observed as she bent over the sandals and dress shoes.

Suddenly feeling possessive, Jackie quipped back. "I'll take care of these." She scooped them up and then arranged them in the bottom of the suitcase next to her on the floor. "Would you mind getting the things out of the other drawers for me?"

Celeste stood to her feet. As she did, she brushed her hand across Jackie's shoulder and kept it on the crest of her slender form. Jackie reached up and touched Celeste's fingers, rubbing Celeste's forearm with her head. No words were needed and in a moment they both returned to their tasks.

Jackie could hear Lizzy in the other room. Michael offered to pack up the few things he and Lizzy had and was dutifully following through. Lizzy was sitting on the bed talking to her doll, Samantha. "We gotta go home, Samantha. Nothing we can do about it. See how Michael is packing?" She stopped talking to her doll so that she could instruct her brother on the proper way of getting things in the suitcase. "Michael, Mommy wants you to fold the clothes, not throw them!"

Michael starred at his little sister, but didn't argue. Under his breath he declared his *disgust for the stupid, lamebrain, ruin my life twirp that had his mother wrapped around her little finger.* It wasn't that he didn't like his sister. He just hated how much she got away with. *Look at her, sitting on the bed playing with her doll as if nothing was wrong. Dad was missing, for goodness sake. Can't she grow up? No. She just walked around carrying that stupid doll, talking to it as if it could hear her. Whatever!*

"Michael, don't forget my new bathing suits! Mommy left them in the bathroom." Lizzy demanded.

That was it, the final straw. He blurted out his next comments without control. "Don't forget my bathing suits." He mocked. "Don't forget my bathing suits!" He threw a pair of shorts at her as she sat on the bed.

Lizzy let out a shrill cry. "Mommy, Michael hit me. Michael hit me." With that, she began to wail.

Celeste was closer to the children's bedroom than Jackie by a few steps and she bounded in to see what was going on. Jackie followed her in and found Celeste wrapping her arms around Lizzy trying to console her as she glared at Michael.

Jackie led Michael into the hallway and knelt down directly in front of him. "Michael. Tell me what happened." She calmly waited for his explanation.

"Lizzy just gets so darned frustrating." Michael was almost in tears himself. "She won't lift her finger and then tells me how to pack the clothes up. I'm sorry, Mom. I just got mad and threw a pair of shorts at her. They barely touched her."

Jackie stopped him before he could say anything else. She leaned forward, pulled him close to her and put both arms around him. His arms hung at his side, ashamed of his behavior and certain he would break down and cry again if he reached out for his mother.

"It's okay, Michael. It's okay. I understand." Jackie waited for his response as she held him. He couldn't resist any longer and broke down and clung to his mother.

"I'm sorry, mom. I really am. I don't know why I did it."

"Michael, I know. It's okay, honey. I know you wouldn't purposely hurt your sister. I know how much you love her." She released her hold for a moment so she could look him straight in the face. "I know she can get aggravating, but she's just a little girl. She's not big like you are." She adjusted his shirt and wiped at his tears. "She doesn't understand what is going on with Daddy like you do. That's why I'm counting on you, Michael. I need you to be strong. I need you to help me be brave. Can you do that? Can you help us all be brave while we wait for Daddy?" Jackie wasn't sure if she was saying the right thing, but she continued. "You are always so good, Michael. Thank you for helping me with the packing, and for watching out for Lizzy too. It means so much to me."

Michael stood up tall and started to wipe his tears with his shoulder. Jackie walked into the bathroom and came out with a tissue. She handed it to Michael with a sheepish grin on her face. He took it, cocked his head and returned the smile. Then he blew his nose into it and threw it in a basket just inside the bathroom.

As Michael walked back into his bedroom his mother stopped him. "I love you. Michael. You know that, don't you?"

Why did Michael get embarrassed every time she said that? He lowered his eyes to avoid hers. "I love you too, Mom." He replied trying to slip past her.

"Hey, how about another hug? I could really use one!" Jackie didn't let him get by with any of that 'I'm too big to be hugged stuff'. She knew it was a phase. Kids just thought in order to be big they had to stop needing hugs from their mothers. Well, it wasn't true. Growing up didn't have to mean letting go. Jackie would make sure he always knew how much she loved him. She deliberately made the hug last longer until it was no longer awkward for him. He embraced her with all he had and didn't want to let go. He sniffed and then pretended to wipe his nose on his mother's shirt.

"Cute, really cute!" She backed him off and swatted his behind as he looked over his shoulder with a grin on his face.

"Gotcha!" He quipped as he re-entered his room to pack.

Celeste sat on the edge of the bed hugging Lizzy. "Beth is okay. Not even a mark, huh Beth? Michael, you should know…"

Jackie interrupted Celeste. "I've already spoken to Michael. Would you mind taking Lizzy outside for awhile? She could use some fresh air."

"No problem. Let's go, Beth! I've got a ball we can play with."

Michael packed in peace as Jackie took her time neatly folding the rest of Jonathan's clothes and personal items they had purchased together earlier in the week. When she got to his toothbrush and razor, she stopped and stared at them. *Tell me you will still need these, Jonathan. Tell me you're still alive.* She put the toothbrushes in a plastic bag along with the toothpaste and zipped it closed. She packed his shampoo, his hairbrush and picked up his prescription bottle. *His medicine! He doesn't have his medicine with him.*

Jonathan had been suffering for some time with acid reflux. The doctor had written a script for him that seemed to keep the episodes to a minimum, but he had to take it regularly in order to stave off the pain that would erupt when he went without them. Now Jackie stared at the bottle. It wouldn't kill him to be without them, but it could be tough on him. She found her purse and put the pills in it. She wanted them to be easy to reach when she finally saw Jonathan again.

"We're back!" Celeste and Lizzy came in from the beach looking wind blown and sandy. Jackie looked at Lizzy's little body and knew she should retrieve another outfit- panties and all. A bath was needed. Again.

"I'll get her cleaned up, Jackie. You about done here?" Celeste ushered the tiny five-year-old into the bathroom and drew a tub of water. "We'll be ready in just a few minutes if you are."

"That'll be fine. Thanks." Jackie walked into Michael's room, lifted the suitcase and took it to the door. "Come one, Michael. Let's check the rooms to see if we've left anything behind."

Together they checked under the beds and in the drawers and closets. The beds had been stripped; the pillows were now bare and uninviting. "Mom, is this dad's pillow?" Michael was holding up a pillow.

"Yes, thank you, Michael. We wouldn't want to leave that behind. Your father doesn't spend the night anywhere without it!" Then she thought of what she had just said. He had spent several nights already without it. *Where are you Jonathan?* She kissed Michael on the head and drew the pillow to her chest. "Let's check the rest of the place and then we'll go home and wait for your dad there. Okay?"

"Okay."

"We're ready, Mommy!" Lizzy looked great. Her hair was brushed with clips on either side so you could see her sparkling eyes and engaging smile.

"All cleaned up and looking fine!" Was Celeste talking about Lizzy or herself? Sometimes it was hard to tell with her.

"Could you give me a minute? Maybe get the kids in the car for me? I just want to check things out one more time."

"No problem. I've got you covered." Celeste picked up the suitcases and pillow and walked out the door.

A few minutes later they were loading the things into their cars, with Jackie fighting a blinding headache.

Chapter 10

The drive home was lonely. Lizzy rode with Celeste in her cherry red Honda Z3 and Michael rode with his mother. They pulled into the Pennington driveway less than three hours later. The long, winding, brick driveway was shielded on either side by mature oak trees. From the street the white plantation home looked grandiose. Once at the entrance, the massive front door and tall, white pillars brought an air of elegance and old money combined. The 1860's shutters were well maintained, weathered slightly, but with a fresh coat of black paint. The porch hosted four rocking chairs- two black, ladder back full size and two tiny black miniatures. Red impatiens flourished in their baskets next to the stairs inviting guests to enjoy the summer breezes. To Jackie it was just another reminder that Jonathan was missing. He was the one who planted the flowers.

Celeste let Lizzy slip out of her seat before Jackie got out of the car. Even though Celeste knew that it wouldn't be easy coming home to an empty house, she couldn't keep Lizzy from being under foot.

With little girl delight, Lizzy sprung open the door and bolted out of the car. Soon she was taking her mother's hand and pulling her towards the entrance. "Hurry Mommy, let's see if Daddy's home!"

For one brief moment Jackie too hoped that he would be waiting just inside the door - waiting to hold her and explain what had happened. Fantasy consumed her as she opened the door. But he wasn't there. She called out his name as they entered. "Jonathan! Jonathan, are you here?"

Their stately home was well decorated. To the right of the center hall was an exquisite sitting room with a baby grand piano that graced the front of the room with its beauty and splendid cherry finish. Dressing the side exterior wall was a handsome fireplace with a mahogany mantle and marble hearth.

On either side of the fireplace and on the front wall were four eight-foot long windows. Ivory drapes adorned each window with sheers underneath for privacy. Two love seats sat across from each other and offered a side view of the fire in the fireplace whenever it was lit. A small rocker took its place next to the marble hearth just close enough to be warm, but never too close to singe the child who would read by the lamp next to it. Beyond the sofa, to the back of the house, was a doorway leading to a den with mahogany pocket doors neatly tucked into the wall.

Flanking the doorway on both sides were mahogany bookcases rising to the ten-foot ceilings. A ladder lay against the shelves and was attached to railway so that anyone could reach the law books that filled up most of the shelving. Children's books were on the lowest shelves so they were easy to reach. The deep rose colored walls offered a rich glow as the lighting in the room came from several standing lamps with brass bases and ornate shades.

On top of the fireplace mantle was a Victorian collector's doll with long, blonde hair and eyes that seemed to follow whoever entered the room. Jonathan said he purchased her while on business a year earlier and had named her Camille because she seemed to have the ability to change expressions as easily as the mood changed in the household. Some days her eyes sparkled with the joy of laughter coming from the children, and other days they would reflect the loneliness Jackie felt while she waited for Jonathan to return from work. Today the doll's eyes looked very sad.

Jackie entered the room and went straight to Camille. She stroked her face as if wiping away a tear. *How do you do that? How do you always seem to sense the mood of our house? I swear you can make your eyes glisten and your mouth smile when we are all playing games together in here, and now, I know you sense the sadness.*

The children were upstairs with Celeste unpacking and settling in. Jackie went over to the cabinet, opened the door and stroked the tapes before pulling out one. Jackie turned on the television and pushed the button for the VCR before inserting the tape into the machine. Then she hit play. There they were, Mr. and Mrs. Jonathan Pennington on their wedding day. *Jonathan looks like a kid!* Jackie thought.

The ceremony had been fairy tale perfect even without a large wedding party. Jonathan didn't mind having just a best man. He would have been satisfied eloping, but Jackie was set on the white gown and flowers at the church, so he went along with it because it meant so much to her. Cindy was the only person Jackie could think of to be in her wedding, so she had asked her to be the maid of honor. She was a quiet, introverted classmate in college who spent most of her time studying, just like Jackie. The only reason they even got close was because they were both registered in the school of education and sat beside each other. On rare occasions they enjoyed eating out at Denny's restaurant together, but neither of them had the money to make that a habit, so mostly they just studied in the library. It had been over ten years since their wedding day, and Jackie had lost touch with Cindy.

As she watched the tape, Jackie noticed how often Jonathan kissed her on the dance floor. He held her so closely. She closed her eyes and imagined him pressing against her- just like he did when they were dancing that day. How she longed for his touch.

When she opened her eyes again, she saw herself gliding across the room with her father, her long flowing gown sweeping the floor. She brushed a tear from her cheek as she watched the film showing her embracing him while her mother looked on. Daddy, I need you!

In another moment, she was laughing with the tape as her new husband attempted to retrieve the garter from her leg, embarrassed that everyone was eyeing her as he slid his hands under her dress and felt her thigh. She was playfully trying to stop him, but he managed to secure it, slip it down over her foot and then twirl it above him in a victory dance.

Celeste walked in and sat beside Jackie in front of the television without saying a word. She just put her hand on top of Jackie's, silently studying the movie with her.

As the toast to the happy couple ended and champagne glasses saluted them, the camera angle deliberately moved to a large picture in a frame. Another salute was offered to the Pennington family. Jonathan's parents and twin sisters were gone, but not forgotten. He had made sure that the family portrait was put in a place of honor so they could be remembered. The accident had taken their lives, but they would live on in the memories of those who loved them.

Celeste gave Jackie a tissue and hugged her as she wiped her eyes. The movie suddenly turned fuzzy and both of them sat there waiting for the next big event-Michael's birth!

"Mom?" Michael didn't want to interrupt her, but he couldn't stand to see her so sad.

"Yes, honey?"

"Nothing. I just...never mind." Michael's eyes welled with tears. He was worried too.

"Come here Michael." Jackie drew him to her arms and ushered him to the sofa without speaking another word.

Celeste excused herself so they could be alone. "I'll get Beth settled in upstairs. I'll be back for the rest of the suitcases in a little while."

Lizzy carried her doll, Samantha, up the stairs. Dressed in hot pink and covered with a yellow and pink flowered blanket, Samantha almost looked real. Lizzy sat on the edge of her white canopy bed, gently re-wrapped her baby and then rocked her back and forth, sweetly humming her version of a lullaby.

After a few more moments together in the living room, Jackie lifted Michael's teary face from her shoulder and said, "Come on my little man. How about getting those suitcases in the house? We've got a lot of work to do. After we get something to eat we'll start doing some serious detective work. You'll help me, won't you?"

"You know I will, mom." Michael stood tall, taller than he had ever stood before. Now he was the man of the house and he wanted her to know that he could handle the job - at least until his dad returned. He headed for the door and brushed the tip of his nose with his sleeve. Remembering how his mother told him never to wipe his nose like that, he looked behind him out of the corner of his eye to see if she was looking. *Good, he thought, she didn't see that!* If he was going to be help, he had to start acting like he knew what he was doing all the time.

Finding something to eat wasn't going to be easy and Jackie knew it. When she was young and living with her parents, she helped prepare meals, but after she married Jonathan he convinced her that Mary should take care of the food. She didn't even know what was in the cabinets.

Jackie smiled as she recalled how sweetly Jonathan had coaxed her into having someone cook and clean for her. He said, "If we have help then you and I will be free to do other things together. " Then he gave her a sheepish grin, patted her on the behind and gave her a big squeeze. *He won, thankfully!*

She wished Mary were already with them. Mary did it all - cooked, cleaned and took care of the kids. *Well, Mary isn't here.* She would have to rely on her childhood experiences and whip up something easy. She could do it again.

Mary knew where everything in the kitchen was kept. She got permission to move it all around when she came years earlier, to make it easier to work. Mary had been injured in an auto accident and had suffered severe leg pain every day after that. She moved well enough, but climbing the stairs was tedious and she used a cane sometimes for balance. For convenience, Mary put everything she could on the lowest shelves so she didn't have to use a ladder.

Jackie's head was pounding as she checked the cherry cupboards for something edible. The pantry shelves had plenty of canned foods - all positioned so the labels faced out for easy reading. *Soup, vegetables - something good for the kids.* With her head splitting, the first thing she did was remove the cap from the Tylenol and take a glass from the cupboards, which slipped and shattered on the oak floor beneath her.

"Jackie, are you all right?" Celeste was running down the back stairs afraid of what she would find.

"Sorry. It just slipped out of my hand."

"Here, let me help you." Celeste reached for another glass. "Here's your water. I'll get the broom. It's in the closet, isn't it?" She opened the hallway door and found the broom and dustpan. "Jackie, why don't you go up to your room and take a whirlpool. It will relax you. I'll watch the kids. I'll even feed them!"

"Thanks. You're the best!" She climbed the center staircase and headed to the master suite to fill the tub.

Jackie could hear Lizzy shriek in excitement when she found out what Celeste was making for supper. "Pizza!"

Celeste began the order "One large mushroom and green pepper pizza- extra cheese." She looked at the children - both making horrible faces - and she changed her order. "Could you make that pepperoni and cheese? It seems the munchkins don't like mushrooms." A moment of silence and then she spoke again. "Delivery. Oh, just a second, I need the address, don't I?" She picked up an envelope addressed to Jonathan Pennington. It's 12246 South Coventry Boulevard - just west of Oxford Drive... forty minutes? That'll be fine. Thank you." Celeste returned the envelope to the desk where she found it. "Okay, kids, you have forty minutes to work up an appetite. How about a game of Chutes and Ladders?"

Michael went upstairs to get the game and met them in the living room. Lizzy was already sitting next to the fireplace as Celeste put pillows against the sofa to cushion her back. Suddenly sensing that someone was watching her, she looked up at the fireplace mantle. Just that stupid doll! Celeste's long, lean legs, tanned from sunning her body, were spread so that the game could fit between them. Michael began the task of opening the board game and putting the pieces out. Lizzy grabbed her "man" and placed the red figure in the start position. Celeste and Michael put their "men' on the board as Celeste shouted, "Let the games begin!"

While the children played with Celeste, Jackie tossed in her king-sized, four-poster bed trying to rest but juggling her thoughts and fears instead. *Why had Jonathan left a note saying he was going running and then not worn his jogging shoes? Why was the room such a mess when he disappeared? Was there a reason he was so quick to go on the vacation? Was someone after him?* The cell phone never left her side and she dialed his number again. No answer. She struggled with her thoughts - sometimes thinking he was dead and sometimes thinking she'd kill him when he came home for scaring her so much.

It had been four days and there was no sign of him and nothing to go on. *What was happening?* Jackie needed some rest, but the shadow dancing on the ceiling from the fan and the music she was playing only enhanced her anxiety. She turned off the C.D. player and reached for Jonathan's pillow so she could hug it. She lay down on the bed on her side and stared out the french doors at the tree limbs and waving leaves gently beckoning her to relax. But she couldn't.

The enormous bed now felt empty and cold instead of warm and comforting. The tailored balloon drapes cascading to the floor offered beauty, but not the love she longed for. The light was fading.

Celeste entered her bedroom quietly, hoping not to disturb her.

"It's okay, Celeste. You can come in. I haven't even been asleep yet. This headache is unbearable." Jackie wasn't usually a complainer, but she had been suffering with the same headache ever since Jonathan disappeared.

Celeste spoke softly as she came closer to the bed. "Jackie, I know you're not much on pill sharing, but if you want, I've got this medicine you can take. It really helps my headaches. I go right to sleep and when I wake up, they're gone." She continued cautiously. "It's no big deal. Just some sort of muscle relaxant. I even have some with me. Do you want one?"

"Oh, I don't know, Celeste. I don't think that's such a good idea. What happens if Michael or Lizzy wake up in the middle of the night, and I can't open my eyes to help them?"

"Don't be silly. The pills aren't that strong. Besides, the kids are already asleep. You need your rest. Here, take this. I brought up a sandwich and cola for you." Celeste was serious. She handed her two pills and a glass and watched Jackie as she took them. "You'll rest better now. You eat this sandwich and then cover up. You'll be sleeping before I even leave!" With a hug and kiss Celeste left the room.

As Jackie began feeling the effects of the pills, she could almost sense the separation of her body from her mind. Everything was beginning to float. The drugs seemed to be playing tricks on her as she heard voices whispering all around her. *"Daddy?" Get a hold of yourself, Jackie, your father's been dead for almost eight years now.* But the voices continued - not defined enough to understand, just mumbling.

Jackie remembered feeling the same way years earlier - like someone was talking about her, but she couldn't understand what was being said. She could hear the muffled accusations of how she caused Gina's death, and her father's death after her marriage-and all the other tragedies as well. She had fallen into a clinical depression which required hospitalization. Her recovery was a slow process, not yet completed.

Now she was hearing the voices again. 'You did this. You made Jonathan disappear. It's all your fault!' Those same fears she fought when she was younger were surfacing again. She never wanted to get close to anyone for fear they would die too, and now, Jonathan was missing. She should never have allowed herself to get close to another soul and now her husband and children were cursed. Maybe even Celeste!

As she lay in bed, she sensed the haunting shadows of her father's death and felt as if she were reliving Gina's accident. She began to toss and turn.

Gina was only seven when she died. Jackie had been her best friend and they did everything together in Indiana. They played with their dolls under the trees, had tea parties and slept over at each other's houses constantly. Living on a farm offered plenty of room for exploring as well, and Gina was always encouraging Jackie to join her in her adventures. Warnings about the dangers of being too far from home were ignored as they trudged through the brush and woods surrounding Gina's house day after day.

Rain had been pouring down almost every day for a week with no sunshine to dry up the ground. Jackie and Gina were clearly bored playing dolls and were ready to get out of the house and run around. When Gina's mother told them to stay away from the river and not get muddy, the laughter and gleam in their eyes set in motion a progression of play that could not be halted. Gina raced ahead, anxious to find yet another spot to mark as her playground. Jackie found it difficult to keep up as she slipped through the path Gina made. Whenever Jackie begged her to wait, Gina would just go faster and laugh. It was a game they played- who could get to the top faster without their heart bursting. This time it was Gina who won.

The hill was no challenge for her and when she reached the top, she started down the other side without waiting. Her momentum was strong and steady, but her pace changed when she stumbled under the slippery leaves beneath her feet. Suddenly she was tumbling over and over sometimes screaming in delight- other times screaming in terror.

Jackie was just reaching the crest of the hill as she heard Gina crying out. She could feel her heart beating hard, not so much from running as from the fear of danger that overwhelmed her. She didn't hesitate even a second to follow Gina down the hill, but slipped on the wet ground and fell backward onto a jagged, broken branch slightly buried underneath the muddy terrain. Quickly she rose to her feet, reached her hand around to wipe off her bottom and started down the hill again.

The screams were blood curdling and Jackie could see Gina struggling in the river below. The swollen water was pulling at Gina's body as her fragile arms tried to grab hold of the branches above her head. Jackie heard her cries for help and ran towards the edge of the river. Every attempt to grab hold of Gina was thwarted off by the angry swells of the river. Efforts to secure her footing on the murky riverbank left her more off balance.

Gina's eyes were bulging with fear and her hair was tangling in the weeds. She kept bobbing and fighting and began drinking in the dirty water gulping for breaths. One arm desperately clung to the twigs as the other reached for Jackie begging to be rescued. Jackie grabbed a branch near the edge and leaned in the water groping for Gina's hand.

"Grab hold, Gina" Jackie cried out in desperation.

"You're too far!" Gina was choking on the water.

Snap! One second more and Jackie would have had her, but instead, Gina's branch had torn away from the brittle tree. Now it was Jackie who was screaming.

"Gina!"

Gina's body was bobbing up and down in the water as she was carried further and further down river away from the shoreline. Jackie raced along the bank searching for anything that would extend far enough to reach her best friend and pull her to shore, but she couldn't find anything.

She stood frozen on the bank – staring helplessly into the river. There was no sign of Gina anymore. The only sounds around came from the water circling around buried rocks and swirling down the river. She turned pale and stood motionless. She didn't remember the man from up the road who approached the accident sight a few minutes after Gina disappeared.

She didn't remember the blanket being tenderly wrapped around her when the emergency team was called to the scene. Nor did she remember her parents' arms clinging to her as they wept openly when Gina's body was pulled from the river less than 400 yards from where she fell in. She only remembered the horror on Gina's face as she tried to reach her... to save her.

And that she failed and now her best friend in the whole world was gone and would never come back.

As a child, she proved to her parents that she could handle herself when her world was crumbling around her and she buried the horrible memories of watching Gina die as the dirt was shoveled onto her tiny casket.

That was the beginning of a tragic series of events for Jackie. Though she managed to survive the loss of her dearest friend, she really hadn't dealt with her feelings about it. Her life had been torn apart.

There were so many difficult times for her, first Gina, then later her father's death, Jonathan's family accident, her own breakdown, her mother's illness, and now Jonathan was missing. The shadows of her past surfaced to remind her that she was doomed to face one sorrowful moment after another.

She tried to go through every painful situation without showing her fears and her emotions to anyone. At her father's funeral, Jackie never cried and she never told her mother about the fight she and her father had just before his death.

The long distance phone call started off as it always did. "How's Michael?" Her father would ask.

Jackie's response was typical. "Growing like a weed, Daddy. How are you and mom doing?"

"We're fine, honey. Just a little lonely, you know?"

"I know, Dad, but it's just so hard to get away right now. Jonathan is putting in so many hours at the firm. His boss is considering him for a partnership already because he has brought in so many new clients. They really like him there."

"That's wonderful, Jackie. We're very happy for you both." She could tell by his tone that he was torn between the congratulatory comments and the sadness of being eliminated from their schedule for the sake of a career.

"Dad. I promise it won't be long until we get back home. I'll get Jonathan to take a long weekend off real soon."

"Yeah, I've heard that before."

"Dad!"

"I'm sorry, honey. It's just that your mother and I miss you both so much and I feel like Michael is growing up without knowing his grandparents!" Was that desperation in her father's voice?

"Dad. I'm doing the best I can. Don't make this any harder on me than it already is. You know I love you and Mom." Jackie protested as sweetly as she could.

"It's not so much me, Jackie. It's your mother. You know how she is. The minute you don't call, she thinks you're mad at her. She goes around the house all teary-eyed and says how you've changed and that you don't care about us anymore. It's pitiful."

Jackie thought to herself...*there it is again, the poor me complex. Might as well just pack my bags for the guilt trip I'm going on.* "Dad, you two need to stop it. I do the best I can and that's all I can do. Stop making me feel guilty for living away from home. You and mom were the ones who encouraged me to get away and the minute I did, you started to complain. You can't do this to me. I just can't take it."

"I'm sorry, honey. I don't mean to make things difficult for you. We just miss you. That's all."

"Dad, I've got to go. I'll talk to you later.

That was on Monday night. Jackie got the call from her mother on Thursday that her father was very ill. Her mother had asked her to come right away, but Jonathan was on a big case and it was really important that he finished. Jackie told her they'd drive back together with Michael on Friday night.

"Tell Daddy I love him, will you Mom? We'll be there on Saturday. I promise." Jackie never expected him to die so suddenly. She thought she had more time with him- years. He wasn't old enough to die.

She blamed herself when she got to the hospital and found her mother sitting by his bedside, holding his hand. He was still hooked up to the monitors, although now they were showing a flat line instead of a beating heart. Her mother just looked up at her from the other side of the bed, the tears long gone from days of crying. She said nothing.

"Mamma?" Jackie knew she spoke, but had no idea what she said. She was in shock. "Mamma, what happened?"

"His heart just couldn't take it. He started feeling bad on Monday night so I took him in to the doctor on Tuesday. They said stress. That's what they said, they said stress. I didn't think you could die from that." Her mother was wiping away a tear that fell down her cheek as her voice cracked. "They told me to take him home and let him rest. But he just kept getting weaker and weaker."

"They admitted him on Thursday night. That's when I called you. I told him..." she tried to regain her composure, "I told him you loved him and that you'd be here on Saturday, just like you asked me to. But by that time he was wearing an oxygen mask and couldn't speak. He just looked up at me, with those big, beautiful eyes," she faltered. "Your eyes- and I saw tears well up in them. I had a hold of his hand and he squeezed it so tightly I knew he heard me. He loved you so much, Jackie."

Jackie gently sat on the edge of the bed, looking at a man who had no breath left in him- her father. She leaned forward to give him one last kiss on the cheek and before she knew it, she was lying beside him, crying uncontrollably. "Why Daddy, why did you have to go? I told you I'd be here. I told you I was coming."

Her mother watched as her baby girl, now a mother herself, curled up next to her Daddy and sobbed. It wasn't until Jonathan came in carrying Michael that her mother stood to her feet and left her husband's side. She went to the foot of the hospital bed, touched his now cold feet as she passed them, and met her grandchild at the door of the hospital room.

Jonathan bent over to give his mother-in-law a hug. Michael was smiling as his grandma came next to him, but when he saw his own mother bawling he began to cry for her. Jonathan took his cue instinctively and withdrew from the room. He left Jackie alone to grieve.

How long had she been crying? How long had she clung to her Daddy's neck like that? Where did everybody go? Jackie sat up on the bed, brushing away her tears, looking around for her mother, or Jonathan, or someone. *Don't leave me here alone.*

The nurse walked in as Jackie straightened her clothes and smoothed her hair. Her kind words of condolences were appreciated, but as she began the 'body preparation' Jackie just stared at her father. *I did this to you. If I had just come home more often, or come right away when Mamma called, you'd still be alive, wouldn't you. I'm sorry Daddy. I'm so sorry.*

She watched the nurse clean him up, take the mask off his face and turn off all the machines. The only sound in the room was the sound of Jackie's weeping.

"They'll be coming with a gurney for him in a minute. Do you want to say your goodbyes before they get here, or will you be staying until they take him downstairs?"

"I'm staying. Daddy wouldn't want to be alone."

"That's fine. I'll let you know when they get here." She started to exit and then turned back as an after thought. "Your mother walked down the hall with a man and a little boy. She didn't say where she was going."

"Thanks." Jackie looked around the room. There were cards all over the board. In just two days her father had received get well wishes and flowers from so many of his friends. "I'm sorry Dad. I'm so sorry. You didn't even know how much I was thinking of you. I was too busy. I'm sorry. I'm so sorry."

The gurney was brought in by two men in white scrubs. Taken by surprise to find someone still in the room, one of them apologized for the intrusion and asked if she needed more time.

"No, it's fine. Do what you need to do. I just want to be here for him."

They brought out a black body bag and laid it close to her father, then rolled him over so they could move it under his cold midsection. His arm flopped and draped over the edge of the bed. Jackie stood immobile watching them as they rolled him back into the bag and began to zip it.

She couldn't breathe. *Don't do that. Don't zip the bag up. He won't be able to breathe. He won't be able to breathe.* She couldn't take it. Her knees buckled and she fell to the floor in the corner of the hospital room.

"Call the nurse." One of them said.

Jackie didn't see them roll her father out of the room. Jonathan was kneeling down beside her calling her name. "Jackie, Jackie, honey. It's Jonathan. Wake up, Jackie." Feeling he should excuse his wife's behavior he made sure they knew she hadn't eaten anything for quite some time.

They offered her some orange juice and a cookie, which she sipped and nibbled at out of politeness. Then, when she was stronger she stood to her feet, lifted her head and brushed off her clothing before she spoke. "Where's Mom?"

"She's right outside, with Michael." Jonathan helped her walk to the door of the room and kept a firm grasp on her arm as she turned to look at the empty hospital bed. "Come on Jackie." He supported her through the halls as her mother embraced Michael in her arms.

Jackie never cried in front of her mother again. She had failed her at the hospital, breaking down in the room, falling apart. It wouldn't happen at the funeral, at the internment site or back at the house. Her mother needed her to be strong.

So, she kept the secret of the argument that killed her father- the one that broke his heart and put him in the hospital; the one that brought her back to him too late because she didn't want to be manipulated by some hysterical false alarm.

She didn't mention to Jonathan or her mother how that conversation affected her the day she talked to her father. Or how awful she felt that she hadn't been home in so long. She didn't mention the fact that she didn't sleep on Monday night after they talked or about the terrible dream she had.

Or was it a dream? Her father was calling her name. She could hear him right outside her bedroom balcony. She had quietly slipped out the french doors as Jonathan slept. Haunted by her father's plea to visit, she thought she could hear him in the wind. As she let the breeze tousle her hair and flow through her long nightgown, she peered out into the woods. There, in the shadows of the moon, she thought she saw him coming towards her. *Dad?* She studied the gait of the shadowy figure that never seemed to get any closer until finally she realized no one was really out there.

She had to slow her racing heart and remind herself that she was always overly sensitive, reacting to emotions way too much. That was just a shadow stalking, not real life.

But this was real life and she couldn't hide her emotional scars. The hospital called it Post Traumatic Stress Syndrome. It was something she thought only soldiers returning from battle could get. Her war was fighting depression brought on by repression of painful memories. The first and most difficult memory was watching Gina die, and knowing that dirt would be shoveled over her tiny casket. That was the beginning of the shadows that would stalk and curse her. The doctor decided she should receive treatment- shock therapy and Prozac.

Sadly, she endured more pain and little else while under the hospital's care. After a month she was released and began outpatient therapy with Dr. Stanley. The results were slow and steady and she improved.

Now, she lay on her bed, drifting into sleep with the help of the pills Celeste had given her. But her dreams were vivid and disturbing. She even believed it was real when she dreamed that she was struggling to fight off an unknown assailant who was strangling her in her bed. The drop from the deck had made her heart race, even in her dreams.

After all her nightmares, she vowed her children would be allowed to weep openly and get help if they needed it. She didn't want them to feel the same way she had. Therapy from a good doctor was very important in recovering from severe trauma and if Jonathan didn't come back, they would definitely suffer loss. But they would not face the same destiny she had encountered from pretending to be fine. She would seek help for them.

Chapter 11

The sun hid behind the clouds as it rose on Friday. The trees in the woods behind the house whistled in the Virginia wind and tapped against the deck railing beyond the bay window in the dinette. Jackie had slept a few hours, a welcome relief, but by 7:00 AM, she couldn't lay in bed another moment. The narrow staircase, which led to the kitchen, was only a few feet from the master bedroom on the second floor. Slipping down the steps quietly so that she wouldn't wake the children, Jackie headed for the sink and a drink of water.

Celeste left the bottle of prescription pills on the window ledge above the sink. *Tempting,* Jackie thought, *but not a good idea. The kids need a mother who isn't drugged.* Instead, Jackie began cleaning up the pizza box and glasses. Celeste was great with the kids, but was a kid herself sometimes, forgetting that cleaning up was important too. It didn't matter. At least she had taken care of Michael and Lizzy for the evening and they were still sleeping because she had been there for them last night. Celeste made them feel secure. Jackie noticed a note on the refrigerator.

"Jackie, I called Mary last night and asked her to be here in the morning by 9:00 AM. She said okay. (She knows what happened. Hope you don't mind.) Love, C." The note was a welcome relief. Jackie really wasn't sure how to tell Mary about Jonathan and she needed someone to keep the place together while she fell apart inside. She looked at her watch. 7:15. She might have a little while before the kids woke up.

The kitchen was warm and comfortable, so Jackie made a cup of coffee and sat at the table. Suddenly she remembered the answering machine. *That's it. Maybe he left a message for me.* She raced to the desk in the kitchen. No messages. As she stroked the machine earnestly wishing it had produced some magical answer, she noticed an unopened, but formal, piece of mail addressed to Jonathan Pennington. The return address was listed as

>Clayton & Bromwell, Attorneys at Law
>1782 North Broadway
>Richmond, VA

She had heard of the firm before, but wasn't aware of any connections between Jonathan's firm and their offices. But then, she didn't know much about Jonathan's business. He was very private when it came to office talk. "Confidentiality" he'd say. She opened the letter hoping it was a lead.

"Mr. Jonathan Pennington,

You are hereby summoned to appear in court on Tuesday, September 21, 2004 to give witness to the following:

>5 counts grand theft
>1 count arson
>2 counts murder

The State of Virginia mandates your appearance beginning at 10:00 AM on the aforementioned date. Attached please find the information pertinent to this case and an accounting of the listed defendants.

Willful defiance of this summons will result in your arrest.

Frantically searching the rest of the paperwork, Jackie began to question what possible connection he would have with arson and murderers. It was time she started getting some answers. She felt certain her husband was in danger now. She reached in her purse to find the phone number for Detective Ryder.

"Detective Ryder, this is Mrs. Pennington. I found something at home that might help us locate my husband. It was an envelope addressed to Jonathan. What? Oh, the postmark is dated August 15th. That was two days before we left for the ocean.

Jackie was nervous as she continued. "The first page seems to be a summons for him to attend a trial for grand theft, arson and murder. I don't have any idea why he would be involved."

"Mrs. Pennington, I really don't have any jurisdiction in this investigation anymore, but I'd love to see what you've got there. Do you mind if I come over?"

"I was hoping you would."

"I've got your address from the files and I know the area pretty well, so I'll be there as soon as I can. Sit tight. Okay?"

Chapter 12

The phone rang a half dozen times between 9:00 and 11:00 AM. Even Jonathan's partner, Peter Anderson, phoned asking if there was any news. Not five minutes later, a call from one of Michael's friends.

Troy didn't know Michael's father was missing when he asked him to come over and play. "Hey, if my mom came to get you, could you come over and play? I got this neat trampoline yesterday. It's really cool. I can already do front and back flips on it!"

Troy's mother was in the background and heard her son talking on the phone. "Who are you talking to?"

"Michael. I just asked him to come over today." Troy was matter of fact as he answered his mother's question.

"Tell him you'll see him some other time and hang up."

"Mom!" Troy was not happy with his mother.

"I said, hang up the phone. NOW!" Her demand was obeyed immediately. Not even a goodbye to Michael.

Troy's mother had heard about Michael's father's disappearance on the morning news and didn't know what to do. Since the only way she knew Jackie was from her brief encounters when they made arrangements for their kids to be together, she wasn't sure it was appropriate to call, let alone visit. She took Troy aside and began with an apology. "I'm sorry I yelled at you to get off the phone. Come sit down with me for a minute." She patted the couch seat and Troy obeyed. "I heard this morning that Michael's father has been missing for several days. I know you didn't know it, but Michael probably is feeling pretty bad right now and I don't think we should ask him to come over. I'm not really sure what to do."

"Maybe we should go over there and see them." In his innocence, Troy had made perfect sense, at least to him he had. His mother wasn't so sure, but together they decided to prepare a basket of cookies and home made bread for the family.

The doorbell rang at the Pennington home and Mary limped from the kitchen to the foyer to answer it. Michael ran ahead of her and opened it wide to see a huge basket of fruit and a deliveryman poised on the front porch.

"Delivery for Mrs. Jonathan Pennington." The man said.

Michael took one look at the bananas on top and opened his arms for the deliveryman to place the basket in them. He was yelling for his mother as he turned to go. "Mom, mom, come look at this. Fruit!" He ran to the kitchen with the basket and then ripped open the plastic surrounding it. The apples began to fall out the basket and onto the table and Michael was awkwardly trying to catch them before they bruised.

Mary signed for the delivery and shut the door with a quick 'thank you' to the gentleman as he left. Shortly after he was gone, another deliveryman approached, this time with flowers. Mary opened the door again, signed the papers and walked back into the house muttering to herself, "This is crazy. Nobody died around here. Why would people send flowers? Course, it is a nice arrangement."

She looked at the card. It read, "Thinking of you as we wait for word, Your Family at the Firm." Mary muttered to herself again, " Family at the firm? They're family? I've never once seen or heard from anyone there. Not when Jackie was sick or when the kids were born. Family, my foot!" She limped into the living room and plopped them on the table behind the sofa.

She was on her way to the kitchen as the phone rang. "Pennington residence." She listened a moment and then answered. "May I ask who's calling?" Again she waited for a response and spoke, "Mrs. Pennington isn't available right now, but I'll tell her you called." She hung up without a goodbye.

Mary met Jackie in the foyer by the kitchen, "Who was that?" Jackie asked.

"Reporters."

"Oh." Jackie turned to walk away, then looked back. "Mary, thanks for being here. I don't know what I'd do without you. Do you mind taking the calls for me for the rest of the day? I just don't think I can handle it."

"I can take care of them, Mrs. Pennington. We've already had six or seven calls and two people stopped by to deliver things."

"I know. I guess the news has started to spread. I suppose we'll get a few more. I don't want to talk to any reporters, but if the detectives call, please let me know right away, will you?" Jackie wrapped her arms around Mary. "You're the best!"

They both jumped when they heard the doorbell ring.

"I'll get it." Mary was already heading to the door.

"Hi. Um, my name is Kathy and I work with Jon...Mr. Pennington. I was wondering if I could speak to Mrs. Pennington." Kathy's voice was strained.

"I'm sorry, Mrs. P..." Mary was interrupted by Jackie.

"That's okay, Mary. Let her in." Jackie escorted Kathy to the living room and motioned her to the couch.

"I hope it's okay that I came. I'm just so, I mean, we're all so worried about Jonathan." Kathy was stammering. "Have you heard anything? Has he called?"

"There's been no contact at all. I was hoping you'd heard something at work. In fact, I'm glad you came by. I have this summons for Jonathan. Let me get it so you can look it over." Jackie left the room to get the papers.

Kathy sat on the edge of the sofa in a dainty pose shifting from hip to hip. She noticed the doll on the mantle, stood up and without thinking, went to get a better look at it. She was stroking the dress as Jackie walked back into the room.

"I'm sorry. I didn't mean to be out of line. It's just that this is the only doll I've ever seen that seems to look right at you. Her eyes are so, so..." Kathy couldn't find the right words so she stopped mid-sentence.

Jackie walked next to Kathy and looked up at Camille. "I call her Camille. Jonathan brought her back from one of his trips."

"Atlanta." Kathy said.

"Pardon me?"

"Atlanta, Georgia. We got her in one of those little shops."

It was suddenly very cold in the room. "Oh." Jackie said.

Sensing the tension, Kathy tried to recover, "I had to travel with him on one of his cases. I just happened to be with him when he found it. He thought you'd love it."

"It's okay. I understand." Jackie handed the envelope to Kathy. "This is what I was talking about. Does it mean anything to you?"

Inspecting the contents carefully, Kathy tried to recall the names. "I really couldn't say. None of this sounds familiar at all. It may have been something very private. Jonathan, Mr. Pennington, was very careful about that. You know, confidentiality and all. Laptops make a huge difference. Sometimes he types his own stuff. I really don't know much about them. Do you want me to check into it? I could ask Mr. Anderson."

"Not yet. It's probably nothing. But thanks."

There was an unpleasant silence before Kathy spoke again. "Well, I should be going. I just want you to know how concerned we all are at the firm. If there's anything I can do, just call. I'll do anything, anything at all."

Jackie walked her to the door. "Thank you for coming. I appreciate it. If I think of anything, I'll call."

After the door closed, Jackie turned her back to the wall and rested against it. She thought, *that was harder than it should have been*, but she didn't have contact with the office staff. She'd never even met his partner. Jonathan made excuses for him at every gathering, either he was away for meetings, or on vacation, or busy in his office. It was almost as if he was avoiding the social aspect of the business altogether.

She checked her watch. *The detective should be here any minute.*

It was 11:00 AM when Detective Ryder was shown to the table. Mary asked the children to help make the beds so that Jackie could talk privately with him. He was already examining the summons closely. He shook his head as he tried to figure out what possible link this would have to Jonathan's disappearance. He began to question Jackie. "Mrs. Pennington."

"Jackie, please call me Jackie."

"All right, Jackie. Have you thought of anything that might help us since you found this letter? This isn't much to go on you know." His face showed more concern now than when Jonathan first disappeared.

"I wish I could come up with something, but I can't. I've been going over and over everything that happened before we left and all the things on his desk here in the kitchen and his office upstairs. Nothing seems unusual or out of place." Jackie spoke softly as she brushed the hair from her eyes. Even through all this she was beautiful and Detective Ryder noticed that. "Detective Ryder." Jackie continued.

"Call me Bob. If I'm on a first name basis with you, then you should return the favor." He was smiling as he spoke. "It's really Robert, but I never cared much for formality."

"I was hoping information would make me feel better, but I am more frightened than ever. I just can't imagine what this all means." The worry in her eyes was apparent.

"Listen. This may not mean anything, but there's only one way to find out. I'll start checking this out right away. That is, if you want me to. I think I can convince my boss to search here. If you don't mind."

"Mind? I don't know how to thank you." Jackie was putting her arms around his strong shoulders and squeezing his neck before she realized what she was doing. "Sorry, I guess I just got carried away. Really, thank you so much." She was embarrassed, but pleased that he had made such the suggestion.

Detective Ryder quickly rose to his feet and headed for the front door. He tipped his hat and promptly left. Jackie bolted the door behind him and headed for the kitchen to see if Mary needed anything.

Mary and Lizzy were busy at the kitchen sink, washing the last of the breakfast dishes when Jackie walked in. Lizzy was giggling while Mary attached tiny soap bubbles to her nose and then gently blew them off. It was a game they played all the time and Lizzy loved it. Jackie watched for a moment and then looked around the room for Michael. He wasn't there "Where's Michael? She asked.

"He said he was going out to the tree house for a while. I didn't figure you'd mind." Mary's statement was matter-of-fact as usual.

"No, that's fine. I just need to talk to him for a minute." Jackie opened the french doors next to the kitchen and hurried outside. She didn't want to appear frantic, but ever since Jonathan disappeared, she was frightened for her children. She heard noises in the house she never remembered hearing before; sounds of footsteps- or was it wind- creaking through the hallway, or down the basement steps, or breaking the silence of the moment with a crack. But she continually reminded herself that it was because she was so tense. *Every sound is deafening when you're scared of your own shadow.* Something else she seemed to sense lately- a presence in the house-like a thief- stealing her peace of mind. *She had to find Michael - now.*

Up in the tree house, Michael was tapping on the floor rhythmically. Tap, tap, tap tap. "Michael, is that you?" Jackie thought of the foolishness of the question, but continued. "Can I come up? I need to talk to you."

"Suit yourself, mom." Every day Jonathan was missing she could see the despair growing in her son's eyes. Before, he was always running around the yard with a toy laser gun, or building a fort out of anything he could find lying around the house, or practically swinging from the tree limbs surrounding the Pennington house. Now, he was almost reclusive, if he could get away with it.

"How you doin' Michael." Jackie put her arm around her son.

Michael shrugged his shoulders and stared down at the stick he had been using to tap the floor of the tree house. Desperately he tried to fight back his tears, but one escaped and trickled down the side of his cheek. He quickly wiped it with his shirtsleeve hoping his mother wouldn't see him crying. After all, his father left him in charge at the ocean - just before he disappeared. His answer was not convincing. "I'm fine."

"Fine, huh? You don't look so fine". Michael didn't answer so Jackie continued. "Listen, I think you're having as much trouble with this as I am, and I'm tired of waiting on the police to find your Daddy, so..." Jackie took a deep breath." I'm going into your dad's office to see if I can find anything that could tell us where he is."

Michael's face lit up. "Can I come too?" He watched the expression on his mother's face and could tell that she was not going to say yes.

"Sorry, Michael. I'm not even sure they'll let me in his office. And besides, I really need for you to stay here with Mary and keep Lizzy company."

Michael knew better than to think his mother would change her mind, so he just hung his head and began tapping the twig again. Jackie leaned into his cheek and kissed him. "Will you be okay?"

"Yea."

Chapter 13

Troy and his mother, Tracie, arranged the gift basket neatly, a lace napkin covering the bottom. The cookies were individually wrapped in colored cellophane at Troy's insistence and the freshly baked bread, done to perfection, was placed gently on end extending out of the basket. It, too, had been wrapped in cellophane, although Troy wanted it to be a different color. Each cookie was tied with a piece of twine to stay fresh. It had taken them several hours to bake and prepare the basket, but they were finally ready to head to the Pennington's.

Four minutes later, as they were pulling into the long Pennington driveway, they were nearly hit by Jackie's car. Both vehicles came to a screeching halt, the drivers unable to move as they recovered from narrowly missing each other.

Jackie got out first. "I am so sorry, I wasn't expecting anyone to be driving in. Are you okay?"

"I'm fine. How about you, are you hurt?" Tracie was walking up to Jackie as she talked. "I'm really sorry. I was just on my way in to see you. Troy insisted that we bring you some food, so we made a basket up for you. I hope you don't mind."

"That was so thoughtful of you both. Is Troy with you?' Jackie was scanning their car trying to see in her tinted windows.

"He's there, in the back." Tracie motioned to Troy to get out of the car. "Troy, get the basket for Mrs. Pennington, will you?"

Troy proudly held the basket up to Mrs. Pennington. "Here you go. I'm sorry your husband is missing."

"Troy!" Tracie was embarrassed by Troy blurting out such a comment.

"It's okay, Tracie." She bent down to Troy as she spoke, "Troy, Michael could use a friend right now. Any chance you're free for a while to play with him? I know he's kind of lonely." She looked for approval from Tracie.

"That would be fine with me, that is, if you want to, Troy." Troy said, "yeah" before she could retrieve the basket. He shoved it into Jackie's hands and raced up the driveway.

"I'm so sorry for the way Troy behaved." Tracie said.

"Don't apologize. It was nice of you to think of us. It's really very kind of you. Honestly. I don't know how to thank you." Jackie understood children and related better to them than adults. With Troy gone, there was a lull in the conversation.

"Well, um, I just feel so bad about your husband. I, um, I don't know what to say. I'm just so sorry." Sputtering her condolences, Tracie struggled to relay how horrible she would feel if her own husband disappeared.

"Thank you so much for stopping by. It means a lot to me. The basket is such a thoughtful gesture. The kids will love it." Jackie hugged Tracie and then offered more information. "I haven't had much success with the police. They don't think of him as being kidnapped, so they aren't looking very hard, so I'm on my way now to the office to see if I can get some answers."

"Oh, yes, of course. I should let you go." Tracie was already heading to her car. "Should I pick Troy up in an hour, do you think?"

"That'd be great. And thank you again." Jackie waved and waited for Tracie to leave before she gently placed the basket in her back seat on the floor. She wanted to get to the office and taking it back to the house would just delay her. She fastened her seat belt, checked in her rear view mirror, and drove away.

The twenty-minute drive to Jonathan's office was tense for Jackie because she hated the horrible traffic. Richmond was a beautiful city, and Jackie loved to go uptown for the plays and nightlife, as long as Jonathan drove. Tourists traveled chaotically, missing exits and stopping suddenly to take in the sights. Taxi cab drivers weaved between the cars erratically picking up their fares and speeding through the intersections. As one passed her on the right, she wished she were sitting in it - letting someone else drive through the mess.

Richmond locals didn't mind the traffic or tourists. They loved the city, but for Jackie it was the opposite. She enjoyed growing up in a small town where going the speed limit meant you risked getting your car caught in a pothole the size of a tractor tire. In fact, home made signs placed on the side of the road used to say things like "watch for falling road ahead" or "travel at your own risk". Jackie smiled as she remembered the sign she and her cousin,

Joe, had made for one such crater. "Whoops, too late! For tire repair, see Joe's auto shop two miles north." Joe didn't have a shop at all, but it made the quiet days and peaceful nights more enjoyable for them adding a little bit of humor. Jackie wished Joe were around so that she could lean on him.

Startled by the honk of a horn, Jackie kept pace once again with the traffic. Before she knew it, Jonathan's building was in view. She turned into the parking deck and found a spot open on level three. Her dark green Lexus fit perfectly in the space. Jackie sat frozen in her seat for a few moments. Then, gently, she began stroking the fine leather seats as if they had suddenly become human. She let her head fall against the backrest and closed her eyes. Stepping into her husband's office without him guiding her every move was harder than she imagined. Her delicate, manicured hand flowed from the seat to the steering wheel and her fingers wrapped tightly around it. Tears once again were threatening her composure as the radio softly played "Anything for you, though you're not here. Since you've been away, it seems like years..." She shut off the engine, and the song.

With a deep breath and a quick release again, she buried her head in the wheel. *Come on, Jackie, get a grip!* She opened the car door and unexpectedly tapped the white Lincoln beside her. *Great, that's all I need now!* She examined the car carefully to inspect the damages, but noted none. *Thank you God!* She thought as she locked her doors with a press of a button and then slammed the door shut. The heels of her shoes on the concrete were screaming "I'm here" as she walked towards the elevator. She felt as if everyone could hear her clipping along and studied the deck looking for anyone who might be disturbed by her clomping but no one was around.

She entered the elevator and pushed the button for the fifth floor. As she felt the elevator move, her face immediately flushed and her heart began racing. She knew it was an over-reaction to her phobias and she tried not to think about it. But she couldn't help it. Every time she stepped into an elevator, she remembered how frightened she had been as a child when she was trapped between two floors, terrified that no one could help her. And she just couldn't stop the flashbacks.

It had been a first for five-year old Jackie and her family- an exciting vacation in Chicago. Her mother and father had taken her to the windy city to see the skyscrapers and museums hoping she would love the sites as much as they knew they would. The Grande Hotel, in the heart of it all, was the fanciest place Jackie's parents had ever stayed and it cost them a lot more money than they had planned

to spend. Though it worried her mother, Jackie's father told her to stop fretting so much and start enjoying her vacation. He wanted to splurge just once.

While her parents registered for a room, little Jackie slipped away unnoticed to explore her surroundings with her doll, Sandy. Sandy's limp, left arm was dragging behind the five-year-old as she entered the elevator.

As the doors automatically closed, Jackie's eyes widened in fear as she noticed her dolly's arm hanging across the opening. She yanked on it, but the sleeve caught on the threshold and she couldn't free it. Tangled by the barrier, Jackie tugged at Sandy's arm trying to release it. The doors smashed the cloth doll's arm as Jackie began frantically pulling at it. Suddenly, the arm ripped at the shoulder and Jackie fell backwards against the wall. Sandy's severed arm landed on the floor of the elevator as the rest of it flew to the back. Stuffing sprinkled out all over Jackie.

Weeping, Jackie crawled along the floor trying to pick up what was left of her doll as the elevator came to an abrupt halt. It was stuck and Jackie was alone. Jackie was only whimpering as she clutched her mangled baby but as the hours slipped by, she went from crying, to screaming, to pounding her head against the wall and then into a fitful, exhausted sleep.

After three hours of being caught in a broken elevator, a sudden shift scared her once more. A rope appeared as the ceiling opened above the tiles. Within minutes, two men were hovering over her with a blood pressure cuff wrapped around her tiny arm and a heart monitor listening to her breathing. She was unhurt, but scarred for life.

From that moment on, Jackie couldn't bear to be separated from her family in unfamiliar surroundings. She became a frightened, emotionally dependent child.

※

Jackie stepped off the elevator on the fifth floor relieved, once again, to have escaped its confinement and her fear. The entrance to Jonathan's office complex was inviting in soft, plush, muted tones with a large sign reading, Anderson, and Pennington Law Office.

"Mrs. Pennington, how are you? I didn't think I'd see you again so soon." Kathy said.

"I'm fine. I'd like to take a look at his office and see if I can find anything that might be helpful. Would you be willing to help me hunt? I could use someone who knows what is really going on here." Jackie's voice was controlled in an attempt to maintain some semblance of confidence.

"Of course I will. I have all of his messages and mail in order on his desk."

"Thanks." Jackie entered Jonathan's office with Kathy leading the way. *That was hard.* Jackie wondered many times if Jonathan and Kathy were having an affair. She had even gone so far as to ask her husband if he was seeing another woman - to which he defiantly responded no. The issue was dropped, but the questions in her mind continued. Kathy was still too close to him and now she knew they had been in Atlanta together.

But today she faced Jonathan's disappearance, her traffic and elevator fears, and the reminder of her suspicions of Kathy's involvement with her husband all for the sake of finding any clues to why Jonathan was gone. *Dr. Stanley would be very proud of me,* she thought.

Together they entered the inner door. Emerald green carpet bordered by a cream accent strip cushioned the mahogany desk. The multi-lined phone was placed to the right of his seat- to the left, a notebook. Mini blinds were opened at an upward angle on his large window for indirect lighting. Jackie had seen him relax in his burgundy leather, high-backed, overstuffed executive chair, sipping a glass of Jack Daniels. His well-equipped bathroom to the side of the office allowed for showers and shaves and a suit and clean shirts hung in his closet for emergencies.

The light from the wall-to-wall window brought security to Jackie. As Kathy proceeded to the desk, Jackie stood motionless scanning the room for indicators of anything unusual. Nothing.

"Ouch" Kathy was wincing in pain after hitting her side on the open right hand desk drawer. "Now who would've been in here and left his drawer open?"

Spoken more for her own ears than for anyone else's, she was almost surprised by Jackie's response. "What?"

"Oh, I'm sorry. It's just that I don't remember opening his drawer- let alone leaving it ajar. I'm kind of klutzy and I tend to keep things closed so I don't run into them. You know what I mean?" Kathy's words were clumsy and Jackie could tell she was a bit uneasy around her.

Jackie began circling the desk looking for other things out of place. The mail was mislaid; messages rummaged through and in general his large desk looked cluttered. Not at all as Jonathan would have it. He was meticulous, right down to where his pencil was positioned. Jackie was certain Jonathan wasn't the one going through the mail. "Who else has access to this room?"

"No one, really. Just me. Of course, the cleaning lady comes after hours, but she never touches the desks. She just cleans the bathrooms and floors mostly. Let me check with Cindy. Maybe she knows if Mr. Anderson has been in here trying to get a handle on Mr. Pennington's work load."

"Thanks." With that said, Kathy left Jackie alone to explore the room. She eyed the desk again and began picking up the mail. Nothing seemed out of the ordinary until she found another notice from the same firm that sent Jonathan the summons. She picked it up and stuffed it into her purse. That was definitely something she wanted to review in private.

She began to search the desk drawers, including the one that had been left open that contained his personal items. Jackie wasn't very careful as she rummaged through it. She was definitely surprised at what she found. *"Dixie Chicks" What in the world? Jonathan hates listening to country music and it isn't even a C.D.* How odd. There was no explanation for it. She made a mental note of it, left the tape in the drawer and closed it.

Turning her attention to the filing cabinet near the closet, she opened each drawer and randomly began searching. *Organized and color-coded. That's more like it.* Green for financial affairs, blue for divorce settlements, black for criminal charges and an unidentified red label. Odd, a single file was behind it and when she picked it up, it appeared to be empty. *Why would you put an empty folder in a file drawer, Jonathan?* Behind each coded topic there were single folders with client's names on them. Jackie found a double folded note, which had fallen between two manila file folders, apparently misfiled. "James Mason" was printed neatly on the topside of the page. It was Jonathan's handwriting. On the other side was an address - 2122 West 32nd Street. That was all. Jackie decided to keep the paper with her. *Maybe it means something, maybe not.*

Once she had finished looking in the file cabinet, she searched his closet. There were two white shirts and a pressed suit dangling from their hangers on the brink of falling. *That's weird. Jonathan never hung his clothes haphazardly.* His emergency dress attire was extremely important to him and even his shoes were stored neatly underneath his suit with a pair of black socks draped carefully over the tongue of the shoe. But not this time. The socks had been flung to the back and his left shoe was overturned. Nothing else was in the closet.

Jonathan's bathroom appeared to be untouched, except for a rumpled towel and his electric razor precariously close to the side of the sink. Just as Jackie was picking it up to put it back, Kathy reentered.

"I'm sorry Mrs. Pennington, no one seems to know who might have been in here. They did say a temp has been cleaning lately. Maybe that's why she's temporary- because she won't keep her hands off of other people's things. We'll check into this, I can assure you of that."

"Thanks, Kathy. I appreciate that. I really haven't been able to come up with anything, so I think I'll go home. If you hear anything, please let me know, will you? And if it turns out that the temp has been going through his things, I hope someone will consider firing her."

"I'm sure they will, Mrs. Pennington. Have a safe ride home."

Jackie left the office and headed for the stairs to get to the parking deck. Once was enough for her in the elevator. She was a bit surprised to hear footsteps above her as she descended the steps and her heart began to pound when she reached her car. She fumbled for her keys- looking over her shoulder as she unlocked her door. *Now you think people are following you.* She revved the engine and backed out of her parking space. The white Lincoln was already gone.

Traffic was even heavier as rush hour began, and Jackie's uneasiness continued to rise. She glanced in the rear view mirror and felt certain someone was keeping pace with her. *Yes, there it is again, the same car.* Every turn she made, it made. Jackie began to speed up. The other driver kept enough distance between them so that she couldn't make out the license or recognize the driver.

With a sudden, unexpected right turn, Jackie beat the red light and fooled the driver behind her. Speeding up, Jackie continued her trip home- the long way, continually watching in her rear view mirror to see if anyone was still following her.

It seemed to take forever to get home and as she drove in the driveway, she saw Michael peering through the curtains in the living room, waiting.

Michael raced to the door and opened it wide. His face brightened and he hugged his mother- and wouldn't let go. "It was getting kind of late. I thought maybe you weren't coming home either."

"Oh, honey, I'm so sorry. The time just got away from me."

Mary and Lizzy were on the floor by the fireplace playing Chutes and Ladders together. There were three markers on the board, but two of them were almost at the top and one was barely off the first path. It was obvious to Jackie that Michael had given up on the game much earlier and had been watching for her to come home for quite a while.

"Mommy, Mommy, Mary waited supper for you, and I'm starving. Can we eat now?" Lizzy was already pulling Jackie's arm towards the kitchen as Michael followed behind. Mary struggled to get off the floor and under her breath was cursing her bad leg for making her so clumsy.

Shadow Stalking

Once in the kitchen, Jackie was happy to see the table set and the food ready. Waiting, hoping and worrying about Jonathan was so all consuming that Jackie was grateful for Mary's support. Michael and Lizzy sat across from each other and Jackie stared at the empty chair opposite hers. *Jonathan's.* The conversation between them seemed almost distorted as they ate.

"Mom, did you hear me?" Michael was insistent in his questioning.

"What? Oh, I'm sorry Michael. I guess I wasn't listening. What did you say?"

"I said did you find out anything at dad's work today?"

"Not much, but I'm not giving up. And neither should you!" She could see the disappointment in his eyes as she answered him. "Please Michael, I'm sure everything will be all right." Changing the subject she continued. "Now maybe you and Lizzy had better finish eating. I bet Mary could use your help cleaning up around here."

They ate quietly and Jackie noticed a tear rolling down Michael's cheek. He was picking at his chicken and mashed potatoes and had barely eaten anything. Mary noticed how quiet the children had become and she turned on the radio and began humming as she took away the dinner dishes. "Come on, you two. Don't be lazy. Help me out and bring your plates to the sink. Okay?"

Jackie took her dishes to the sink too and then went into the living room again. She felt spent as she let her tiny frame fall into the wing back chair. Next to the chair was a highly polished, mahogany table, which held a picture of the family; Jonathan, Jackie, Michael and Lizzy sitting next to the Cape Hatteras Lighthouse. Their sweaters were all in coordinating colors and their hair was gently tousled by the breeze. Of course Lizzy was squinting, but that just made the picture even more enjoyable to look at. Jackie picked up the frame and stared at Jonathan. The tears came again. This time she reached for the phone and dialed.

"Hi! I'm not home right now, but you know what to do don't you? So, just leave your own special message and I'll definitely get back to you as soon as I can- maybe!"

"Celeste, this is Jackie. Are you there? I really need to talk to you. Come on pick up the phone. Okay, maybe you're not there. Call me right away. Okay?" *Funny, Celeste said she'd be home all evening. I wonder where she went.* Jackie pulled the blanket from the back of the chair and wrapped up. The comfort was momentary as she shifted from side to side. She was too fidgety to sit down so she got up and paced the room. As she headed for the foyer she remembered her purse.

The number for Detective Ryder was buried in the back of her wallet. She thought he should know that she'd been followed, or at least she thought that she had been. Just as she walked through the darkened hallway, she saw a flash of light at the window. Her heart began to pound as she ducked into the living room to avoid being seen. She crept to the window and peeked out. No one was there. *Maybe I imagined it*, she thought.

She was letting go of the drape, when out of the corner of her eye she caught a glimpse of something- or someone- running across the grass towards the woods at the side the house. Again her heart raced as she went to the side window beside the fireplace. She strained her eyes in the blackness of the night hoping to see who was lurking around her house, but she couldn't see anything. She dropped the curtain and frantically went looking for the children.

"Michael, Lizzy? Where are you?" She didn't want the panic in her voice to give her away, so she smiled as she entered the kitchen. Mary was still humming softly as she washed the counter and stove off while Lizzy was busy playing in the soapy water. Michael was staring aimlessly out the french doors. Quickly Jackie went to the door, checked the lock and then gently touched Michael's chin and kissed his forehead.

Careful Jackie...don't scare the children. "Michael, why don't you and Lizzy come upstairs with me for awhile? I could use the company. Mary, leave the rest of the clean up for later, will you? I want you to come too."

From the unusual invitation to join them, Mary knew something was wrong. She put her washcloth down, picked Lizzy up off the chair she'd been standing on to reach the sink and began drying her hands- and arms and elbows. Just as she was wiping off the soapy beard Lizzy had on her face, Jackie's eyes met Mary's.

Without another word, Mary stopped wiping and began walking towards the back staircase with Lizzy on her hip. Michael followed close behind as Jackie lightly pushed on his shoulder to move him a little faster. They reached the master bedroom and Mary instinctively knew her next move. She led Michael and Lizzy to the love seat in the corner of the room and took the book from the table beside it. Then she began reading it to the children.

Jackie locked the door behind her and Michael noticed. "What's wrong, mom? Why are you locking the door?"

"I just feel safer when the door is locked, that's all. Jackie was checking the windows again as Mary came to her side.

"Keep them busy will you? I'm going to call the police. Someone is outside. Make sure you keep them away from the windows. Okay?" Jackie was whispering her plea to Mary.

There was no time to wait for a reply as Jackie reached for the phone by the bed. Mary's limp was more noticeable as she headed back towards the kids. It always seemed worse when she was under stress.

"Police?" Jackie was whispering in fear of being heard. "There is someone outside our house. No, I don't think so. All of the doors are locked. What? Oh, my children and our housekeeper. In the master bedroom, second story. No, no one else is here. Please hurry. All right. Thank you."

Jackie hung up and tiptoed to the window as if the prowler could hear her. *Anyone could be out there. The three and a half acres surrounding the house were covered in darkness.* The seclusion was frightening now and it seemed like forever until the police arrived. Jackie's skin tingled and she jumped when the doorbell rang.

"Stay here." Jackie demanded. "I'll get the door." She looked at Mary. "And lock this after me. You understand?" Her eyes showed her desperate attempt to keep her family safe.

Mary nodded as she closed the door behind Jackie. They waited in silence as Jackie nervously made her way to the front door. She peered through the window and was relieved to see a uniformed officer standing on her porch. She opened the door and allowed him to enter.

"Good evening, ma'am. Did you report a prowler? I've already checked around the house, but didn't see anyone." The officer was polite as he questioned her. Just then the phone rang.

"Jackie, it's me, Celeste. What's up? You sounded upset on the machine."

Staring at the police officer, Jackie answered her. "The police are here. Someone was outside. I saw a light of some sort at the front door."

"I'll be right there. Sit tight and don't worry. And do everything the police tell you to do!" Celeste was adamant.

Jackie put the phone back on the cradle and when she turned back around the policeman was gone. She found him in the kitchen searching her broom closet. He motioned for her to step away and her heart began pounding, fearing he had found someone hiding there. She stepped back into the hallway and peered into the room waiting for his response. He shut the door and walked to Jackie shaking his head.

He spoke quietly. "I haven't seen anything unusual yet. Dispatch said there were others in the house?"

"My children and our housekeeper are upstairs in my room." Jackie's response was timid.

"Let's check upstairs."

Together they went to the second floor and reached the master bedroom. He jiggled the door handle before Jackie could say anything. The children began screaming and she could hear Mary hushing them. Jackie was trying to calm them down through the door. "It's just me. Let me in Mary. The policeman is with me. Everything is fine."

The door opened a crack and then widened to let them both in. The kids ran to their mother and held on to her. Lizzy looked up and cried "I was so scared, Mommy."

"It's okay, I'm here now. "

"Are you all right in here? " With his hand on his gun, the policeman circled the room. He was checking the door to the master bathroom as he addressed them. "Has anyone been in here?"

Mary shook her head no and he continued to check under the bed and in the closet for any sign of an intruder. No one was there.

"I'm going to check the other rooms on this floor before I search the rest of the house again. You stay here and lock the door behind you."

Michael paced the floor- first going to the french doors to look out and then back to the love seat where Jackie sat with Lizzy on her lap. "Michael, stay away from the windows."

"Where'd the cop go?" Michael was angry with him for leaving them alone.

Correcting him, Jackie replied. "Policeman, Michael, and he went downstairs to check out the rest of the house. Now come over here and sit with me for a while, okay?"

Mary sat in the chair near the armoire and the waiting continued for sometime. They were motionless and quiet- afraid to move for fear someone would hear them and find out where they were.

Jackie wasn't comfortable waiting for the officers to check the house without her near by. She wanted to make sure they weren't missing anything. So, she left the children with Mary and headed back downstairs.

The officer was already on the first floor heading back to the kitchen to check once more in all of the closets and small spaces where someone could hide. He opened the door to the basement and once again had his hand on his gun as he descended the steps. His approach was cautious as he searched for the light switch.

The 150-year-old house definitely was not well equipped with basement lighting and the officer continued with just his flashlight. At the bottom of the stairs there was a string hanging from the ceiling. He pulled on it and the bulb lit up. Boxes were completely covering the wall to the left of him and were stacked about three feet tall and on a plank, probably a water problem, he thought. The stone walls were deteriorating and crumbling granules lay at the base of the wall.

He inspected the tiny window determining entrance from it was impossible. Even a small dog would have a problem negotiating that space. The floors seemed dry, but it smelled a little musty and the patrolman silently chuckled at the thought of such an expensive home having its musty, old basement problems just like regular folk. Shadows filled the basement and moved about as the hanging light bulb was blocked by his moves. A spider had built a huge, dangling web near a cellar door. He walked toward the web and brushed it out of the way.

An old wooden door was near the back of the basement. He reached for the rusty door handle and opened it slowly- one hand on his pistol, the other pushing slowly against the door as it creaked. It gave him the creeps to be in such a dark space looking for an intruder. As he opened the door he recognized the area right away. It was a cold storage pantry.

He began feeling the walls for a light switch when he brushed up against a handful of hair. He screamed in alarm and heard a loud crash at his feet. Pressure and stabbing pain pierced his legs and he felt an oozing of blood trickle down to his foot. Sweat dripped from his forehead as he grabbed his gun and cocked it. At the same time he flung the door wide open to let in more light. He held his breath, looked around the room and then collapsed to the floor. He could now see what had been attacking him and was glad that no one else had seen the expression of fright on his face. What he thought was human hair was simply a very old coconut with strands of "hair" growing out of it.

The cut on his leg came from broken glass that had toppled off the shelf when he jerked his hand in fright after brushing against the coconut- the one he thought was a head of hair. His breathing returned to normal and he rolled his eyes and spoke under his breath "Well aren't you an idiot! Scared of a coconut head. If anyone finds out, you'll be laughed out of the force."

Jackie heard the commotion and was quickly at the top of the steps. "Are you okay?

"Yes ma'am, I'm fine. But I'm afraid I broke a jar down here. I'm really sorry. I was just checking out this pantry and it fell." He wasn't about to tell her how close he came to almost shooting a coconut to death.

"Don't worry about that. There's nothing important down there anyway." Jackie's olive complexion was ashen as she spoke. Her jeans hung limp and her wedding band slipped around her finger. She had lost weight since Jonathan's disappearance, and now this intruder was threatening her home. She was jumpy and frightened.

"Well, I'm just about finished checking things out down here. Are there any exits?" He was anxious to get out of there and his voice was edgy.

"Yes, but it hasn't been opened in years. It was locked by accident and we lost the key. Since we never used it, we didn't replace the key. It's on the side of the house. Do you want me to show you?" Jackie prayed that he'd say no.

"No thanks. I'll take care of it. You stay up there. I'll be right up." The officer headed for the boxes but stopped abruptly when he heard Jackie screaming in the kitchen. He raced to the top of the steps. Jackie was standing in front of the french doors with her hands clenching her face. As the officer approached she collapsed in his arms. He carried her limp body to a chair and gently placed her in it. She was shaking and cold, but not in immediate danger, so he looked back towards the door she had been staring at. There on the window was a note scribbled, but legible- "You're next!"

The officer immediately opened the door and carefully stepped onto the patio, gun positioned and ready. He checked the area surrounding the patio and then called for back up on his radio. The darkness of the evening and the wind rustling the trees made his search for the intruder nearly impossible alone- especially if he wanted to make sure the residents were safe. He returned to the house, closed and bolted the doors, then helped Jackie to the second floor master bedroom where he checked on the others.

The doorbell startled the officer as they approached the bedroom, and he rushed her into the room and drew his gun while approaching the door. The bell stopped and the pounding started.

"Jackie, Jackie are you in there? Jackie, it's me, Celeste. Come on, open the door. Let me in Jackie!" She was emphatic.

The officer hurried to the door as Jackie stood at the top of the stairs. "It's all right, it's my friend Celeste. You can let her in."

Instantly Celeste pushed past the officer and headed for the stairs. "Where is she? Where's Jackie. Is she okay? Where are the kids?" She saw Jackie at the top of the stairs and cried. "Honey, are you okay? What's going on?"

The officer closed and bolted the front door and then followed her up the steps. The children were sitting on the bed with Mary in the middle cuddling them. Michael was fearful, but tearless and Lizzy clung to Mary's neck whimpering. They saw Celeste come in behind their mother, but they were immobile for a moment. Then Lizzy spoke. "C.C., somebody's outside. Mommy saw him."

Celeste picked Lizzy up and Lizzy wrapped her arms around Celeste's neck. There was no letting go as they clung to each other. "It's okay sweetie, I'm here now; I'll take care of you."

Michael sprang into action. "I'm gonna get whoever's out there and blast them away." He ran to the closet and began to reach for the box on the shelf above his father's shirts.

"Michael, get away from there. What are you doing?" Jackie had no idea that Michael knew Jonathan owned a gun, let alone where it was. Frantic now, she continued, "Michael don't touch that!"

Police were using their sirens as they approached the house and Celeste reached for Jackie's hand while still hugging Lizzy. The officer excused himself and took the steps two at a time to meet the other policemen who were now waiting at the door for someone to let them in. The waiting seemed endless. One policeman stayed with Jackie and the rest of the family while the others checked the estate again.

"I'm sorry, Mrs. Pennington. We couldn't find anyone anywhere. We'll write a report and keep an eye on the place." What else was he supposed to say? The note taped to the door was the only piece of evidence indicating someone had been prowling around the house, and that wasn't much to go on.

"Fine." Jackie was too upset to say any more.

"Ma'am, do you have anywhere else you could go for the evening? I think it might be better if you didn't stay here tonight."

Celeste spoke up quickly. "They can stay at my place." Looking for Jackie's approval she continued, "Honey, you know it's for the best. At least for tonight. Come on. I'll help you get packed." Turning back to the officer Celeste continued, "You'll stay until we get a few things together, won't you officer. By the way, what did you say your name was?"

"Officer Richard Henry, ma'am. And yes, I will be happy to stay."

"Thanks Mr. Two Firsts. We appreciate your help!"

Jackie looked at Celeste and then at Officer Henry. It was obvious that Celeste was flirting with him and he loved the attention.

"Two Firsts? " His face distorted when he questioned her.

"That's you handsome! I always give the men in my life my own pet names. I wouldn't want you to feel left out now, would I? After all, you saved our lives! You have two first names, so I figured your nickname should be Two-firsts. Okay with you?" Celeste batted her long black lashes and winked her eye at him.

Jackie finished her packing for the night and they all headed for the door. Officer Henry followed them down the stairs and out to Celeste's car and then leaned into the driver's side window to talk to Celeste.

Lizzy screamed, "Wait, wait. I forgot Samantha." She hopped out of the car and raced up the steps to her bedroom and retrieved her doll, Samantha. Celeste didn't mind waiting as long as a man was paying attention to her and Officer Henry was happy to oblige. Jackie could see that he was preoccupied and ran back inside to make sure Lizzy was safe. When Lizzy returned, Jackie buckled her in Celeste's car and got in her own car with Michael.

With a flirtatious wave and a smile, Celeste led the way out of the driveway. The house was secured and everyone was safe, for now.

Chapter 14

The beat of the music was pulsating in Jackie's head as she woke in Celeste's apartment. She opened her eyes slowly and peered through her slits trying to focus. Her head ached, her eyes watering. *Too much tension.* Beside her bed on the table was a new prescription of medicine that Celeste had gotten for her. Two tablets and a glass of water were waiting for her on the nightstand. She took them without a second thought. This nightmare was too much for her. First Jonathan disappears- then someone stalks her and puts her children in danger. *But who? Why? What do they want?* With the pain throbbing, she closed her eyes again and put a pillow over them to block out the morning light. *Make it all go away.*

But it wasn't going away. It was getting worse. Much worse. And no one had any answers for her. It was Saturday already. It had been six days since Jonathan had disappeared and still no clues. Now someone was threatening her children and her. But for a moment they were all safe in Celeste's apartment. It was a tight fit since it was so much smaller than their home. Two bedrooms and a bath and a half is sufficient for a single woman, but when two small children and another adult take refuge there as well, it becomes confusing. The children were safe, sleeping in the spare room- Michael on the floor and Lizzy on the day bed, her doll safely tucked in her arms. Celeste had slept on the couch so that Jackie could sleep in her bedroom.

The noise from the music was piercing. Jackie couldn't sleep, and she needed a cup of coffee, so she rolled out of bed, slipped into a robe and shuffled into the kitchen. Celeste was startled at the sight of her friend. Her hair was a tangled mess, dark circles under her eyes and a pained expression on her brow.

Celeste began the conversation with an apology. "Oh God, Jackie, I'm so sorry. I didn't even think that the music might wake you. How are you doing today sweetie? Feeling any better? " She was stroking Jackie's hair, pulling it back off her face and trying to show her genuine concern and comfort. "You look awful. You want some coffee? It'll be ready in a minute."

"Coffee sounds great. My head is splitting. Are the kids up yet?"

"Not yet, they were really tired! Poor kids. They just plopped down in bed and fell fast asleep. Not a peep out of them all night!"

"Listen, do you think you could watch them while I go down to the station? The police want me to come in and talk about last night."

"Are you sure you don't want me to come with you? Mary would probably watch them if you wanted her to."

"No thanks. I'd really appreciate it if you were with them when they woke up. You know what I mean?" Jackie was sipping her coffee and leaning on a stool by the counter top.

"Celeste poured a little more coffee in her cup before speaking. "No problem, if that's what you really want. I don't have anywhere I need to be today anyway. How soon are you planning to go?"

"As soon as I get a shower. I want to get this over with so I can start looking for Jonathan again. Will you get some breakfast for the kids when they wake up?"

"Sure." Celeste turned back to the refrigerator, examining the contents for breakfast. Not much there, but she could make do. Popcorn?

Chapter 15

The trip to the police station offered Jackie nothing. There was no new information from them or her regarding the person who was stalking the house and leaving threatening notes. Jonathan's disappearance had no new leads and the grilling of the events from the night before only tired her as they pressed her for a better description of the person who was outside her house.

Jackie had trouble communicating. Her headache was still sending jabbing pains through her skull, and the medication made her feel as if she was living on the outer edge of her body, ready to fall away any second. They continued to ask her for the details. *No, I couldn't see his face. No, I'm not sure if he was carrying anything else besides a flashlight. He was wearing dark pants- tight fitting, like joggers wear, I think and a bulky over shirt- maybe a sweatshirt- black. His hair? Dark, I think. It was covered with a cap. Around 9:30 PM. Mary and I took the children upstairs to my bedroom and locked ourselves in until the police came. The officer arrived shortly and Celeste a little later. That's all I know.* Over, and over, and over again.

Jackie returned to the apartment two hours later frazzled and worn. Celeste was lounging on the sofa with Michael and Lizzy and they were watching television together. "Hey girl, how'd it go? Did you find out anything?" Celeste seemed almost too bright. *Sometimes she just doesn't get it.*

Jackie replied "Nothing new" with a heavy sigh and flopped down on the sofa as Celeste pulled her knees to her chest to make room for her. She rested her head on the pillow attached to the sofa and rubbed her forehead with her fingertips.

Celeste hopped up and went into her bedroom. When she reappeared, she held two more pills cupped in her manicured left hand and a glass of water in the other. She reached the sofa and stretched out her arm for Jackie to take the pills. Long ago Jackie would have refused, but it seemed easier each time she was offered them now. She popped them in her mouth, took the glass Celeste offered and began to swallow. Tipping her head back quickly to help the flow of the water, she then lifted her deep brown eyes thankfully up at Celeste. She was being such a great friend. Jackie laid her head back on the couch again and closed her eyes. *Just a little rest - for a minute.*

A minute turned into hours. When she woke, she was groggy and disoriented, but fought off the urge to close her eyes again. Lizzy and Michael were still sitting in front of the television. Looking at her children staring at a screen made her feel uncomfortable, so Jackie forced herself to sit up and brushed back her locks of hair.

It has to be safe enough for us to go home. Mary could continue to help them work on spelling and math and that would keep their minds off of their father's disappearance. Staying with Celeste would just be giving in to her fears and she didn't want to do that anymore. She stood up, caught herself against the couch arm as she began to sway and then straightened up again.

"Lizzy. Michael. You ready to go home? I have some things to do and I bet you guys could really help!" Jackie felt woozy and thought she was slurring her speech a bit, but she fought off the feeling.

Both children sprang to their feet. They missed their rooms, their beds, their toys, Mary and their father. Lizzy grabbed her dolly and ran to watch her mother begin packing up the few belongings they brought along when they left the house the night before.

Celeste protested helplessly as they busied themselves getting ready to go. "Jackie, I don't think it's such a good idea for you to leave. The policemen thought you'd be safer here at least for a few days, and it hasn't even been twenty-four hours. Please don't go. I don't want to be worrying about you."

Over protest Jackie responded quietly. "Honestly Celeste, we'll be fine. I promise to bolt the doors and make sure the windows are locked tightly.

Chapter 16

Jackie felt desperate as she walked into her home again. Bolting the door behind her as promised, she dragged the bags toward the center hall stairs. Mary had offered to return for the evening, but Jackie didn't want to inconvenience her, so the house was empty and still. Step by step, with the children by her side, they went through each room inspecting the contents for disturbances. Nothing seemed touched and the doors were just as she had left them the night before.

"Mom, what are you looking for?" Michael was inquisitive and confused as he asked.

Lizzy held her doll, Samantha, close to her chest and wrapped both arms tightly around her. Jackie was kneeling beside Michael's bed, lifting the skirt to see what was underneath. "Mommy?" She choked on her cry.

Michael and Lizzy were standing in the doorway watching their mother sneak up to a door and swing it wide open and then creep into the room. One hand was cautioning the children to stay where they were- away from the danger that might be around the corner. Lizzy was wiping the tears from her eyes. Michael's mouth hung open and his eyes widened more at each new room. Jackie wasn't aware of the sound that made Michael jump. "Mom," he whispered. "I heard something."

Startled by his whisper, Jackie was at their side in seconds. She tightened her shoulder hold on both of them and moved them into the bedroom. "Stay here" she commanded as she put her finger to her lips "Shhh". Before she got to the staircase, her children were grasping at her hands. Neither of them wanted to be left alone. Not knowing where the sound had come from or if there had even been one, she did not go any further. Instead she motioned for the children to sit on the top step with her and wait for the next sound.

Why did she come home? If only she had asked Detective Ryder to meet her here and go through the house. But she didn't want him to see her unraveling, or frightened.

They sat quietly waiting for the next sound to come. Nothing. "What did you hear, Michael?" Jackie's voice cracked as she asked, hoping he would say the floor creaked.

Shrugging his shoulders, Michael replied, "Noise. I heard a noise."

"What kind of noise?"

"Just a noise. I don't know." Michael was flustered as he spoke.

For a few more minutes they were fixed in their spots. No one made a sound- except when Lizzy sniffled. *Was she getting a cold?* Jackie ushered them quietly down the steps. Tiptoeing through the hall, they reached the kitchen together just in time to see a bird flying into the french doors. As it floundered against the window Michael recognized the sound. "That's it! That's what I heard!"

The look of relief covered Jackie's face. "Okay, now that we've got that puzzle solved, who is hungry?" *Could the children tell how close she was to losing it?*

Rummaging through the cupboards, she chose tomato soup and decided to toast some cheese sandwiches for them. Michael crunched the blackened edges and then spit it into his napkin without his mother noticing. Jackie was stealing glances at the window with every bite wondering who was out there and if they were watching her now? Lizzy pushed her crackers around the bowl of soup.

Michael paid close attention to his mother as she stared out the window. "Mom, do you think dad is coming home?" The words were out of his mouth before Jackie could stop him. *Too late. Now Lizzy would start up again.* But Lizzy wasn't listening. She was talking to her doll, Samantha, pretending to feed her.

"Michael, everything will be fine. Just remember that. After supper I'd really like to rest for awhile. Will you and Lizzy play quietly in my room if I turn my TV on? We'll skip the bath tonight and get one first thing in the morning."

As if saluting, Michael's body stiffened. Being the man of the house was important to him and he didn't want to disappoint his mother.

The sun had set, and the ten o'clock news smattered bits and pieces of the headlines across the screen. Michael and Lizzy were sprawled across the carpeted floor sound asleep. "Concern is growing in the disappearance of Jonathan Pennington, last seen while on vacation with his wife Jacqueline..." *I can't listen to this* was all Jackie could think. Picking up the remote, she turned off the television and picked Lizzy up. Although she wanted them to sleep with her, keeping them on the same routine - in their own rooms - seemed to be the best thing for them.

"Mommy, will you tell me a story?" Lizzy's sweet little pleading eyes were irresistible to Jackie.

"It's late, Lizzy. And I'm really tired tonight. Can we do this tomorrow."

"Please, Mommy, just one story. I promise after that I'll go right to sleep."

"Right to sleep? You mean it?" Lizzy nodded enthusiastically as Jackie rose to get a book from her shelf. "Okay then, what story do you want to hear tonight?" She picked the smallest book up and carried to the bed.

"Not that one Mommy. Tell me a story."

"Oh, honey, can't we just read a book tonight? I don't feel very creative right now."

"Please Mommy. Tell me a story about you and Daddy."

Jackie loved to talk about how she and Jonathan first met, but it was painful now that he was missing. What if he never came back? How would she face life without him?

"Not tonight. I'll read you a book, if you want."

"I don't want a book. Tell me a story, please!"

"Okay, but just one." Jackie couldn't resist Lizzy. She was such a sweetheart and she gave the best hugs and kisses- something Jackie needed right then. Lizzy squeezed her mother's neck so tightly that Jackie had to help release the hold. "Don't choke me. I won't be able to tell the story if I can't breathe!" They embraced for a moment longer and then Lizzy settled in beside her mother on the bed, pillows propped against Lizzy's headboard. The story began.

"Well, let's see. How about I tell you how your Daddy and I met? It was the spring of…" Jackie was interrupted.

"No, tell it like a real story." Jackie had a puzzled expression on her face so Lizzy began her explanation. "You know, once upon a time…"

"Oh." Jackie was smiling and softly chuckling. "Okay, you ready now? No more interruptions, okay?"

"Okay."

"Okay, then. Once upon a time, long, long ago, there was a handsome prince named…"

Lizzy interrupted her. "Daddy."

Correcting her, Jackie spoke softly into her ear. "Jonathan. He wasn't a Daddy yet!"

"Oh yeah."

"Jonathan was so handsome that all the girls in the kingdom wanted to be at his side. Prince Jonathan was very smart. His father, King Robert, saw to it that his Prince had everything needed to rule the kingdom one day. He made sure that his son got the finest schooling in the land of Uni." Lizzy looked up at her mother with questioning eyes. "That's short for University." Jackie explained.

Lizzy was satisfied with the land of Uni, so Jackie continued.

"Anyway. All day long Prince Jonathan followed the king's command. 'Study hard, my son, so that you will be worthy of such a kingdom!' Jackie spoke in a deep voice mimicking a man's. "And he listened to his father. He attended all that was required, read all the books he could and tried to ignore the things that would take his mind off his goal of one day being the king."

"You mean, like girls?"

"You know this story too well, don't you? Yes, like the Ladies in Waiting. Those Ladies wanted to marry the Prince and live happily ever after in the castle he would soon own."

"But not you, Mommy. You didn't want to marry Daddy, did you?"

"It's not that I didn't want to marry Daddy, I didn't even know him. Now, may I continue?" Jackie took her finger and playfully poked at her daughter's stomach and Lizzy giggled.

"Prince Jonathan had spent seven years in the land of Uni before poor, little Jacqueline took her head out of the sand and noticed this wonderful, attractive, charming man. Many a year had passed. Alas, she knew this prince could never love such a lowly peasant girl. After all, so many Ladies in Waiting doted on him everywhere he went."

"What does 'doted' mean, Mommy?"

"Doting means, um," She wanted to say it meant all the girls were hanging all over him, hands touching him and their breasts falling out of their clothes. But instead she stumbled for a tamer description. "They tried to meet the Prince's every need at his command."

"Oh."

"Now, where was I? Oh yes, the lowly, hand maiden, Jacqueline, watched from a distance certain that the Prince could never love someone so meek and pitiful."

"What does pitiful mean?"

"It means Mommy didn't think she was good enough for Daddy." Michael interjected as he walked into Lizzy's room and sat at the foot of the bed. He wanted to hear the story too.

"Is that right, Mommy?" Lizzy was hugging her mother's middle as they sat together.

"I guess so. It's just that your Daddy came from money and was so well educated and I lived on a farm in Indiana. I didn't think he could love someone so…"

"Mommy, the story. Finish the story." Lizzy put Jackie back on track.

"Okay, anyway, where was I? Oh yes. Jacqueline didn't believe she was worthy of the Prince's attention. Besides, she had someone back in her own kingdom waiting for her to return. But that didn't stop her from staring at Prince Jonathan every chance she could.

One day, while she was walking to her class in that same land of Uni, she slipped on a bit of black ice and down she went! Her books flew out of her hands, her head hit the sidewalk and she fell asleep right there by the steps of the library. All the people swarmed around her like bees buzzing about." Jackie pretended her hand was a bee and "buzzed" her way to Michael. He swatted at her hand and tried not to smile. After all, he was almost ten and he'd heard the story before.

"Mom!" He protested.

"Prince Jonathan was coming out of the library, saw maiden Jacqueline lying on the cold, hard ground and ran to her rescue. He pushed the crowd away, knelt at her side and brushed the hair from her face. He commanded his followers to fetch the nearest doctor and took off his own cloak to lie across her to keep her warm until she awoke.

Prince Jonathan bent even further over her to see if she was breathing. She was, but her eyes did not open. He wanted to call out her name, but didn't know it. In fact, he had never seen her in his kingdom before. He looked at those around him and asked if anyone knew this beautiful maiden, now lying so still on the ground.

No one knew of her, and as the good men of the emergency squad came to her aid, Prince Jonathan held her hand and whispered in her ear. 'You'll be fine, my princess, you'll be fine. But, pray tell, what is your name," he whispered.

Maiden Jacqueline opened her eyes, briefly, to see the most wonderful, handsome Prince touching her shoulder, asking for her name. But all Jacqueline could say was 'Jackie' before they whisked her away.

"Wait, wait, Prince Jonathan begged. Let me go with her. But the men denied his request, put her in a carriage and slapped the reins against the horse. Off they galloped, leaving Prince Jonathan bewildered and alone. How would ever find out who she was?"

"I know, Mommy. I know. He looked in your books cause your name was in them."

"Hey, Lizzy who's telling this story, you or me?" Jackie snuggled with Lizzy and winked at Michael.

"Sorry!"

"Prince Jonathan asked again if anyone knew who the fair maiden was that had fallen so gravely ill at his side. But alas, no one knew her name. He was crushed. He had fallen madly in love with a mysterious maiden whom he did not know. But wait! Her books. They had fallen from her hands as she slipped. Surely they would have her name in them. He ran to the stairs and retrieved them. He opened one and, behold, there was her name. Jacqueline Tanner. The woman who would one day be his bride, Princess of his kingdom- that is, if she lived. He vowed he would find her, court her, and win her heart.

He had no idea that she had already given hers away. The end."

"That's not the end." Lizzy put her hands on her hips and looked miffed at her mother.

"It is for tonight. Maybe tomorrow I'll tell you more. It's way past your bedtime now. Kisses?" Michael crawled up the bed to his mother, hugged her and got up off the covers waiting for his mother to say goodnight to Lizzy.

Lizzy held on tight to Jackie and cried. "I miss my Daddy."

"I do too, Lizzy. I do too." They hugged one more time, then Jackie asked Lizzy to say her prayers.

"Dear Jesus, please bring my Daddy home so Mommy and me won't cry anymore." Lizzy kissed her Mommy and then her doll.

Jackie tucked her into bed, shut off the light and wished her sweet dreams. She motioned for Michael to leave with her and then gently closed the door, but did not latch it.

When Michael was in his own bed, he could barely whisper his prayer. "You know what I need; can you do it for us?" Not long ago his prayers were emphatic, "Dear God, I miss my dad and I want him to come home. Please keep him safe and help him come home now. Amen. Oh yea, help mom feel better."

There was no way to understand why Jonathan hadn't called. No matter how many times she tried his cell phone, it was always the same thing –

his voice mail. Sometimes she called it just to hear his voice. "Jonathan Pennington speaking. I'm not available, please leave a detailed message and I'll get back to you." *You said you'd get back to me. Why aren't you???*

Now Jackie was saying her prayers - praying that Jonathan would be found- alive. Praying that the medication she was taking would keep her calm enough to cope with his disappearance and still take care of her children. Praying for sleep that wasn't filled with nightmares and tossing and turning- sleep that would drown out the noises that echoed through the empty halls of her lonely house.

Since Jonathan's disappearance she heard noises everywhere, creaking floors, soft, distant muffled cries of the wind-even an occasional cracking of the air conditioning unit when it kicked on. If it weren't for those eerie sounds, perhaps sleep could be more restful. Each time she drifted off, noises would startle her and her heart would pound harder and faster. Strange that the noises never bothered her before.

Time to sleep now, Jackie. She couldn't stand the crying of the wind as she stared at the clock- just watching the minutes tick away. 12:15, 12:16, 12:17... like counting sheep. She hugged Jonathan's pillow and yawned. And then she heard it again. It was a muffled, nearly undetectable sound, barely audible, and never describable. She couldn't ignore it anymore. She slipped her robe on quietly and reached for the gun now placed in the drawer of her nightstand. Her footsteps were light- lighter by the day as she lost weight. She opened the door slowly and stepped into the hallway.

The open staircase allowed visibility to the front door below and she focused on the lock. It appeared secure. She scanned the first floor and stood perfectly still listening for the sound that had lured her out of the safety of her room. Why did it always seem as if someone was walking the floor below her? The creaking was frightening. Now there was nothing - no noise at all.

Jackie lowered her gun and moved toward Lizzy's room. *Not a sound- be quiet!* Panic filled her heart as she checked out the surroundings. She raced to the bed as her stomach turned upside down. *Where's Lizzy? Where's Lizzy?* As she was about to fling the covers back, she noticed the tiny frame sleeping peacefully in the corner. She bent down and checked Lizzy's breathing. Everything was fine- slow and steady. Samantha was tucked neatly under her arm nestled in the soft blankets that hid them from a mother's view. Lizzy and her dolly were inseparable. Lizzy had a blankey, and so did Samantha. Whenever Lizzy felt insecure she would grab her blanket and rub the silk edge against her cheek, sometimes sucking her finger. Eventually the silky was tattered and thread bare, but Lizzy wouldn't give it up. *Another noise! What about Michael?*

Michael lay across his bed with the covers going every direction. His legs were over the edge. Below his head on the floor was his pillow. Locks of black hair swirled around his forehead. He was fine.

It was important to check all the rooms, again, so Jackie made her way down the back staircase and into the kitchen. She was glad the light was on above the sink. Jonathan was right- as usual. Keeping the light on was smart. Rounding the corner to the main hall and into the rooms felt eerie and she peeked out the drapes to see if anyone was outside. She didn't want to call the police again so soon. They'd think she was crazy.

The gun was getting heavier by the moment. Suddenly she felt foolish carrying it with her while she checked out the noises an old house makes. *Stupid, really stupid.*

After another look around the house, Jackie climbed the stairs to her bedroom, returned the gun to its drawer and slipped out of her robe and under her covers. Sleep - please.

Jackie wasn't dreaming when she heard a loud bang from downstairs. The sun was up and the birds were chirping at her balcony. She once again slipped on her robe and went to the door to listen. *Humming? Mary!* Mary let herself in at 7:00 AM and was busy preparing breakfast. Jackie just shook her head in amazement at how jumpy she was.

The forecast was for sunny Sunday and 85 degrees. She knew Mary would want to take the children outside, but it didn't seem safe. With them underfoot, it would be difficult to think. She needed to concentrate on all thoughts running through her mind - Jonathan's disappearance, the prowler and note, the person who followed her from Jonathan's office, even the noises in the house. Nothing added up. Then she remembered the subpoena left on the desk in the kitchen. Maybe she should check into that more closely. And what about Jonathan's address book? Someone had to know details that could lead her to him.

"Mary, I'm going into Jonathan's office again today." Jackie was rummaging through the kitchen drawers as she spoke, switching to a hushed voice, "Don't let the kids play alone outside today. Don't even let them out of your sight." She stopped abruptly and turned to Mary. "No don't even let them go outside at all. They can play indoors." *Have you seen my keys? I can't remember what I did with them - again!*" Jackie seemed agitated and hurried.

"Slow down a minute. If you just relax and give yourself time to think, I'm sure you'll remember where you put them." Mary was merely stating a fact considering Jackie often misplaced her keys and had to spend time retracing her steps.

"Ah, here they are. Right where you left them!" Jackie said teasingly as she picked them up.

"I never touched…"

"I know that, I was just teasing you. It's been a while since I've smiled and I just wanted to see the expression on your face!" Jackie was chuckling.

"Funny, really funny!"

"Mary, have you seen that envelope that was on the desk? I can't find it." Jackie was throwing the unopened letters and bills around the desk searching for the official summons she had seen when she returned from the ocean.

"I put it on his desk so it wouldn't get lost. It looks like that was a good idea considering the way you're shuffling the mail around." Mary was already heading to the library to retrieve the letter. Back in a moment, she replied, "Here it is. It was right where I left it."

"Thank you." Holding it up and shaking it like it was her finger she continued. "This could be very important. I can't lose it now." She shoved it into her oversized purse, picked up her keys again and headed for the door.

"I'll try not to be too long. See you soon."

Chapter 17

Before she knew it, she was in the parking deck at the office. She looked over her shoulder before opening the car door, just to make sure that the car that followed her the last time wasn't anywhere around. It looked safe, so she opened the door, then shut it again before she got out.

Sunday. No one will be in. Wait, maybe that's better. After all, what would she say to his secretary? "Hi Kathy. Just thought I'd snoop around the office looking for more clues." *If there was something there that would shed some light on Jonathan's disappearance, she hadn't found it before. What made her think she'd find it now?* She started to open the car door again and stopped. *But there was something. What was it? Think, think.*

Suddenly her sharp, brown eyes widened and she remembered. She had seen the top drawer open, things in disarray and a tape of the Dixie Chicks. *That's not Jonathan! Dixie Chicks- never. That's got to mean something.* She now stepped out of the car and confidently headed for the elevator. *The elevator! Must I?* She drew a deep breath and entered.

Even though she was pretty sure no one would be in on Sunday, she was cautious. It was important that she avoid the staff as much as possible. She didn't like the way she felt around them anymore. When the elevator door opened at the law offices of Anderson and Pennington, Jackie peeked out first before stepping onto the rich, blue carpet. *No one around. Good.* She slipped past the receptionist's desk and picked out the key to Jonathan's office on his key chain. It went in smoothly and turned without a sound. She was in his office without anyone seeing her. *Thank you God!*

The desk drawer that had been ajar the first time Jackie searched the office was closed and everything else seemed to be in the same place as it was before. Getting to that drawer was so important that she didn't notice the noises in the hallway until she was at Jonathan's desk. Now she could hear the sounds from the hall. Someone was turning the knob on his office door. Jackie ducked behind his desk and began to panic. *Did I re-lock it?* The knob was being jolted and the door shook. And then nothing. She waited, her small frame fitting easily between the drawers on either side of the desk top. Her breathing was erratic and labored as she waited to see if anyone entered. Nothing.

She crept out from underneath the desk, still on her knees, and slid the drawer open searching for the tape. *There it is!* She read the title again. *Dixie Chicks.* After a little more rummaging, Jackie determined that the tape was the only thing she needed from the desk. She shut the drawer as quietly as she had opened it. Then standing to her feet, she made her way to the bathroom. Just as she stepped into it, she heard the door open and someone enter the office. She was sure that he didn't know she was in the bathroom, because he lumbered around the room without trying to hide his presence there.

Jackie peeked through the frame of the bathroom door and watched as the shadow opened and closed file drawers and looked through the papers on Jonathan's desk. He turned his large frame around to see if anyone was coming. Piece by piece, he examined everything and put it back where he found it.

Jackie couldn't see his face so she couldn't tell who it was. As he came closer to the bathroom, she put her back to the wall, drew in a breath and held it. Even the sound of her breathing could give her away. Then as if he wouldn't see her if she couldn't see him, she shut her eyes. He brushed by the bathroom door, pushed it open a little further to look inside and she tightened up more. *Don't come in! Don't come in!*

He took a step toward the sink, but quickly shifted his glance to the sound coming from outside the office door. He turned on his heels to put his ear against it. Certain there was someone in the halls, he listened carefully for several minutes, then left Jonathan's office when he felt it was safe.

Jackie slipped to the bathroom floor right where she was. Whoever he was, he was there looking for something too. And she didn't think it was someone who had any business looking through her husband's office. Her head was suddenly thumping as much as her heart. Collecting her thoughts she remained stone still, straining to hear activity in the outer offices. *I need to get out of here!*

The office door had been latched when the man left. Twisting the knob, she pulled the door open slightly and peeked out. It was hard to see through such a small opening, but she didn't want anyone to spot her. When it seemed safe, she stepped into the hall, checking her pocket to make sure she still had the tape. She hugged the wall as she walked down the hall hoping no one would see her.

Just as she got to the receptionist area she heard the shuffling of paper and the copier running. She stopped short and once again peeked around the corner into the copy room. A secretary had her back to the door and was busy sorting paperwork. Jackie picked up her pace and headed for the stairwell. It would be safer to descend the stairs rather than be caught in the elevator with someone she knew. At this point, she didn't feel she could trust anyone in the office.

She was fairly certain no one had noticed her in the building, but the man who had just been searching Jonathan's office knew he was not alone by the perfume she was wearing. He hid behind an office door to wait for her to come out. Not sure at first who she was, he followed her to the exit, quietly opened the door to the stairwell so he could watch her descend the steps. He silently moved to the stairs, leaned over the edge and saw her sleek form scurrying down.

He recognized her trim figure and beautiful hair from one of the few encounters he ever had with her years ago.

It was one of those ridiculous office parties- the first one Jonathan and Jackie attended shortly after he was hired. Everyone was gulping down their favorite drinks and inhaling the appetizers. Peter watched his staff suck up his profits with a stupid party designed to raise morale. Why did he have to foot the bill for a gathering he didn't even want?

His secretary, Terri, told him everyone at the firm was feeling the pressure from being overworked and underpaid. She said that a party would boost their spirits. All he could think was 'welcome to the real world' but Terri assured him that morale affected the productivity of the firm. They were feeling unappreciated and threatening to quit. If experienced staff members left, the partnership would suffer. And after all, experience built profit margins. Would he really want to start over training new, inexperienced graduates instead of contributing a little money to a party that could make the employees feel more appreciated? Though he really didn't care if anyone left, the ramifications of losing trained help didn't appeal to him either. What else could he to do? They would have an employee appreciation party.

She then suggested a gala event at La Shae's, the trendy new downtown club. Peter nearly choked on the suggestion. "What in the world do I want to take them there for? Do you know how much it costs to buy a drink at that place?"

Terri saw his face flush and backed off the idea right away. "Well, it doesn't have to be there. If you want, we could organize a party here in the office. I could arrange the catering and get it all together for you. That shouldn't be too expensive and it would make everyone feel more important."

So, it boiled down to either losing staff or having a Christmas Gala Event. Peter remembered thinking "Whatever!"

Terri had taken care of all the details. He just had to show up. Oh yes, and everyone was supposed to bring their "significant other". That meant his wife, Amanda, would want to be there. Again, whatever!

Peter stayed in his office for most of the party trying to ignore the blaring music and ruckus from the crowd. Why was it that normally intelligent people turned into idiots whenever they were drinking? Alcohol never enticed him and he found it vulgar that people would lose their dignity and standards when they were drunk. Women who seemed controlled during work hours somehow came unglued, flirting with married men in front of spouses and falling down drunk.

Even conservative Kathy was putting the moves on her boss, the newcomer. Peter's reaction to her play for Jonathan was immediate. His face reddened, his palms got sweaty and his blood pressure rose. He wanted to strangle her. He controlled his emotions for the sake of his wife. If he reacted to his disgust and attacked Kathy, Amanda would have known it was because he wished he was the one that Kathy was hanging all over.

Instead, he watched as Kathy put her hands on Jonathan's muscular chest and played itsy, bitsy spider up his white shirt until she reached his face. She drew her body closer to his and pressed it against him. Jonathan was sitting on the edge of the desk in the reception area, but immediately stood to his feet to escape her.

Jackie stood in the corner of the room, hugging the wall, sipping a coke. She was a beautiful woman. Her black, knee length dress was perfectly molded to her model thin, sexy body. There was no doubt that Jackie was furious with Jonathan for being involved with Kathy. Peter could see her quietly seething in the corner of the room, keeping her distance, not willing to make a scene in front of the staff.

He smiled as he thought about how much trouble Jonathan would be in once they were home and Jackie could scream at him. Too bad, he thought. Jonathan should've been more careful with his secretary-at least while the wife was around.

But then Jonathan, as politely as he could, attempted to smother her advances by grabbing her wrists and pulling her arms off of his neck. His eyes met Jackie's with a plea of forgiveness, but Jackie lowered hers the minute they made a connection.

Peter had overheard a conversation between Jonathan and Jackie as he passed the office one day while Jonathan was on the phone with her. He was obviously upset and nervously trying to explain his behavior regarding Kathy. Peter heard him explain that Jackie's fears were totally unfounded and that he didn't love Kathy, he loved her. Now, seeing the way Kathy wrapped herself around Jonathan at the party, Jackie's suspicions were confirmed. Peter could see that as well as Jackie. Kathy was interested, even if Jonathan wasn't.

Peter watched the entire scenario play out- Kathy making a move on Jonathan, Jackie seeing the action from the sidelines and Jonathan embarrassed about the whole thing.

At that moment Peter realized a few things, the first being that the Christmas Gala Event was the last firm party he would attend. He would make excuses for any invitations he received and if the firm got together, he'd make sure he wasn't around for it. He wouldn't subject himself to such distasteful actions ever again. As far as he was concerned, women were all tramps.

He also now understood that people didn't necessarily perceive him the way he saw himself, an attractive, albeit, older man. He wore designer suits, kept in shape and, though his hair was thinning, he thought he looked pretty good. So, why did Kathy choose Jonathan over him?

Kathy had put him in his place one day, shortly before Jonathan came to the firm. She had refused Peter's advances and even threatened a sexual harassment lawsuit if he ever touched her again. When he saw her throwing herself at Jonathan during the party, he was humiliated. It was all too apparent that she preferred Jonathan to him. That was infuriating and just one more reason to skip any office festivities. He wouldn't be embarrassed again by some lame secretary, even if no one else knew how he felt about her.

Every day at the office was hard for Peter. He had to watch Jonathan and Kathy work side by side, laughing and talking together. Why couldn't that have been him? Even now, years later, he had those same feelings- wanting Kathy and yet distrusting her.

Yes, he knew who was hurrying down the stairwell. It was the same woman who watched as a tramp put the moves on her husband at the office party. The same woman who looked gorgeous in her tiny black dress and high heels. He knew who had been in Jonathan's office while he was searching it.

It was Jacqueline Pennington. *She could spoil everything if she knows what's going on,* Peter thought.

What was she doing in Jonathan's office anyway? His secretary had warned him that Jackie was snooping around his desk, but he didn't think she'd come back so soon. He hoped he'd have more time to find the evidence that Jonathan was threatening him with, but so far he had come up empty handed.

How did Jonathan find out about NewStart Clinic anyway? Peter lamented to himself. It really bugged him that Jonathan was always asking questions about the firm's finances, but there wasn't anything he could do about it. Peter was the one who invited him to be his partner a few years back, and that gave him access to all the files and account information. Ultimately he had only himself to blame for his problems.

In the beginning of Peter's career, he had established himself as a powerful attorney. He built his firm by dabbling in many venues until he decided business law was his forte and began concentrating on that specialty. He did very well and soon living comfortably with his wife, Amanda.

If it wasn't for Amanda, he could have managed the firm without needing another attorney to bring in more revenue. Long ago they discovered he was infertile, so it seemed a child was out of the question unless they poured money into experiments and invetro fertilization. They did, but all their attempts failed and nothing happened. They exhausted their finances, looked into adoption but eventually Amanda dropped the idea altogether. Amanda adapted quickly to the idea of being a rich wife with rich friends. To keep up with them, she furnished her new, executive home under the supervision of an interior decorator. It really didn't matter to her if Peter liked the style. It was, after all, expensive and exactly what her decorator had suggested. When he asked her to cut back on spending, Amanda just shopped more. She wanted more things for the house, more vacations, more designer clothes. That was the real reason he'd invested in the NewStart Clinic.

"Just think," his best friend Dr. A.J. Ferguson said. "We can make a fortune on this project- and with the government's blessing to boot!"

He had continued melodramatically using his hands to gesture. "I can see it now. We'll be the good guys, shelling out medicine to all those poor souls addicted to drugs and then we'll bill Medicaid. We won't have to wait for private pay to come through and government paperwork won't be a problem. We'll hire someone off the street at $5.50 an hour to sit in the office and work. We'll be giving someone a job, there'll be fewer druggies on the streets, and fewer trips to the hospital emergency rooms 'cause they'll go to the clinic instead. Everyone will be happy. Piece of cake. In fact, we'll be applauded for being community leaders!"

Now Peter Anderson was kicking himself for listening to his good buddy, A.J. Ferguson. All the front money came from his pocket, which wasn't that deep to begin with. Dr. Ferguson was in charge of the day-to-day needs of the clinic. He had managed to find another doctor who was willing to help with the caseload, but their capital outlay was only a quarter of what Peter had invested.

He was in way over his head, his life savings tied up in worthless real estate nobody wanted and a pitiful group of no-good, crybabies begging for prescription drugs every day.

Thankfully their newest venture was turning a profit and he was recovering some of his losses. It didn't matter that it was both illegal and dangerous as long as he made a few bucks.

If it hadn't been for Jonathan snooping around, the scheme would have made him very wealthy. But no, he had to stick his nose in where it didn't belong. That's why he had to search Jonathan's office. All those comments Jonathan was making about financial discrepancies were making him nervous. He had to see for himself if there was any concrete evidence that could be used against him.

If only he knew exactly what Jonathan had on him. Jonathan never said what it was. It sounded as if it was all conjecture, but Peter couldn't be certain. And he couldn't take the risk of Jonathan going to the police. There was too much at stake.

Peter returned to the office after watching Jacqueline disappear at the bottom of the stairwell. He was nearly run over by Kathy as she walked towards her office. The bundle of copied papers scattered on the floor. Frantically she bent down and began drawing them to her as fast as she could. Her hands shook as she arranged the copies and drew them to her chest.

"Mr. Anderson," she said, her voice quivering. "I didn't know you were here."

"Ms. Alton, what are you doing here on the weekend?" Peter was eyeing the papers, trying to see exactly what she had been duplicating at the machine. He spoke again. "Helping out with Jonathan's work load while he is missing?"

"I, uh, I", she was obviously struggling to find the words. "I found a few files that needed to be moved into position for transfer to someone else's case load. I thought maybe I should get them ready for Monday's staff meeting. I hope that was alright."

"Really? You took it upon yourself to do this, did you? How very resourceful of you." His long, drawn out 'really' threatened Kathy's security even more. "Perhaps I should take a look at them." He said.

She squirmed and backed her way to her own office. "Yes, well, it might be better for me to, uh, reorganize these before presenting them to anyone. They got a little, uh, they're just a bit uh," she searched for words, "They are so messy right now. I should just get them together first if you don't mind." She unlatched her door and slipped inside, quickly closing it behind her.

For a moment Peter just stared at the door wondering what just happened. He put his hand on the knob to turn it and then thought better of it. If he approached her now, demanding to see what she was doing, it might arouse suspicion. Or she might make up a story about sexual harassment like she did before. Playing it low key would be advantageous for him. He walked back to his own office.

Kathy sat at her desk shaking. She had been holding her breath for so long she felt dizzy. When she was certain that he wasn't going to follow her into her office, she let her head fall and inhaled. *Whew*!

After she regrouped, she began sorting the papers she had copied. All the while she talked to herself. "You are really an idiot. What made you think the office would be empty today? I hope you're happy now, because I doubt that Mr. Anderson believed you. This could mean your job, you know. And where exactly do you think you'll find another one? Do you realize how lucky you are that Jonathan kept you on? What other man would have been willing to work things out after what happened?"

She never forgot how embarrassed they both were when she put the moves on him at the firm one day. They were dangerously close to the point of no return and Jonathan didn't like that at all. He had lost control and was infuriated that he had betrayed his wife by giving into Kathy's advances. He recommended that she look for another job, but she had begged him to forgive her and keep her on. He reluctantly agreed- on the condition that their relationship be strictly professional.

Strictly professional was really tough. She loved everything about Jonathan.

She stopped shuffling the papers, went to the door and locked it, then walked to the window. Just as she stepped closer to view the ground below, a bird soared past it, nearly hitting the pane. She jumped back, letting out a breathy gasp. *Just a bird.* As she reapproached the window, she noticed a man exiting the building. It was Mr. Anderson. Good, she thought, he's gone. She watched him walk down the street.

He walked down the street. *That's strange*, she thought. He always drove to work. *So where was he going?* Kathy stared down at him as he looked over his shoulder and picked up his pace. It didn't make any sense to her at all. She'd been working for the firm for ten years and had never once seen him take a walk. He rounded the corner a half a block away.

She realized she was staring and blinked. Where was Mr. Anderson going? Did he know what happened to Jonathan? Did he even care? She knew that there was a problem between the two of them recently. She could tell by the way they interacted with each other. Before the relationship was strained they used the intercom, bantering back and forth with random questions, jokes and comments. Now, most of the time communication was only by email.

They even stopped going to lunch together. Jonathan said it was just a time commitment problem, but Kathy really didn't think so. It wasn't her fault that she could hear everything from Jonathan's office. The door between them just wasn't very thick. Besides, she often left it slightly cracked so there was no strain when he called for her to take a memo.

Sometimes she left it open so she could listen to his phone conversations. She couldn't help it. It drove her crazy when she had to transfer a call to him without knowing who it was. Some people, mostly women, were secretive and refused to give their names. Who'd they think she was, some clerk at a convenience store? She was supposed to screen his calls, even if he accepted them anyway. She'd pretend to file at the cabinet near his door and listen to his one-sided conversations. His voice was so low sometimes it was barely audible at all. *Why did he do that? What was so private that even his own secretary was kept in the dark*, Kathy wondered.

On some occasions while he was taking those calls, Kathy would walk into the office with a file and plop it down on his desk. She'd wait until he acknowledged her with his 'thank you' nod and then slowly leave the room. More than once he had turned his head away from her as he spoke, almost burying his chin in his chest as he whispered. She was pretty sure it was the same woman on the phone every time he was so quiet. That frustrated her so much.

Returning to the work at hand, Kathy went back to her desk; picked up the files she had been copying and walked straight into Jonathan's office. It was important that each folder was returned to the exact location it was found. She didn't want anybody to notice anything out of place. After all, she was lucky she kept her composure when Jackie saw the open desk drawer during her first search of Jonathan's office. Kathy didn't want a reoccurrence of the same mistake. No one needed to know she was rummaging around in there. It was none of their business what she was looking for.

When she returned to her desk, she put the copies of the papers she had dropped in front of Mr. Anderson into a brief case, neatly banded this time to prevent another scattering. After checking to make certain that her office was tidy, she opened the door to the hall and stepped out. Her skirt had risen up her thigh, so she smoothed it out before strolling nonchalantly to the elevator hoping that she wouldn't arouse suspicion if she ran into anyone else. In minutes she was in the parking deck slipping into her two-door Mazda, her slender body fitting neatly behind the wheel.

Chapter 18

Bounding down the stairs, Jackie reached the parking deck in record speed. After glancing around, she slipped into her car and headed for home. Thankfully, no one had seen her upstairs. Or had they?

Only when she was certain no one was following did she think to listen to the tape she took from her husband's desk. Not certain what to expect, she hoped there was more than music on the tape. Jackie slipped the copy of "Dixie Chicks" into the car stereo and began listening to fiddles, recorders and banjos strumming. Then the lead singer started singing about being ready to run when someone said she'd look good in white- *whatever that meant*!

Fifteen minutes into the songs, she started fast-forwarding through the tape looking for something besides music. Chastising herself for being so foolish, Jackie heaved a heart-wrenching sigh and reached to push eject. Just as her fingers touched the button she heard an abrupt end in the middle of the song and a familiar voice came on. Jonathan! Straining to hear him speak, she turned up the volume on the stereo. "Update- overheard conversation between Peter Anderson and Dr. A.J. Ferguson regarding NewStart Clinic. The center has been under investigation for illegal drug dispensing since early last month. Peter has been very evasive lately and I've noticed an edge to his personality. I am almost certain he is in over his head with this Center- perhaps even dealing. His cash flow appears to have greatly increased. Must keep a low profile at this time until I can discover what's up." Jonathan's taped voice was low- as if he was whispering into the microphone.

I knew it. The office staff couldn't be trusted with this so he was hiding his notes. Jonathan. What is happening, Jackie thought.

She pulled into the driveway at home and cut the engine. Automatically she ejected the tape, stuck it in her pocket and practically ran to the front door.

"Mary, Michael, Lizzy, I'm home! Where are you?" It was later than she thought. There was no answer from them. "Mary? Where are you?" She walked from room to room searching for them until suddenly she heard a scream from upstairs. Racing to the bottom of the staircase, she heard it again. Dashing to the top toward the sounds of Lizzy cries, she nearly cried when she saw her son tickling his little sister as she rolled on her carpeted floor screaming and laughing. Jackie leaned on the bedroom door fame and then touching her forehead with two fingers - rubbing and pressing against her skin. *I've got to get rid of this headache!* Just then the phone rang.

"Jackie? It's Detective Ryder. I was just wondering how things are going. Have you heard anything from Jonathan?" His voice was warm and welcoming.

"Nothing at all. But I found something today that I want to check out first thing tomorrow." She couldn't hide the excitement in her voice.

"What are you talking about?"

"Jonathan found out his partner was involved with NewStart Clinic downtown and it has something to do with illegal drugs."

"Let me do some investigating first and then we can scope it out."

"That would be wonderful. I felt pretty vulnerable today at Jonathan's office when I found the tape."

Detective Ryder was suddenly and momentarily very quiet. "What tape?"

"That's how I found out about NewStart Clinic. It was on a tape in Jonathan's desk." She was almost giddy and very proud of her find.

"Does anyone else know you have that tape?" Though he wanted to sound calm, his voice was edged.

"I'm pretty sure no one saw me, but, I saw someone. He was rummaging through Jonathan's office looking for something and I hid in the bathroom behind the door scared to breathe for fear he'd find me there."

"Who was it?"

"I couldn't tell. I only saw his frame, never his face. I don't think it was one of his partners. No one else should even be in there, let alone snooping through his files. I don't think he found what he was looking for either. He slithered out the door when he heard noises outside the office. I was so scared I couldn't move for a long time and when I finally did, I left the building as fast as I could. No one saw me. I'm pretty sure of that."

"I don't know, Jackie. I think you're in over your head! Have you told the police?"

"I'm telling you!" She was adamant as she spoke.

"Yes, but it isn't really my case. I'm just helping you out as a favor."

"Well you're the only one who seems to be working it. I think the police believe he took off on his own. They don't seem to be working on it very hard if you ask me."

"Maybe you should be contacting them more often." Right after he spoke he chuckled to himself. *Yeah, right. They'd like that*, he thought.

"They already think I'm crazy. I can tell by the way they talk to me. It's so condescending. I figure if I check some things out on my own maybe they'll look into it when I have something to really go on."

"Okay, I'll be there tomorrow about 10:00 AM. Don't do anything until I get there. You got that?" She could tell the detective was serious.

"Yes sir!" She quipped. "See you tomorrow morning." Just before she hung up she added " And detective, thank you so much."

"Bob, remember?"

"Bob." The sound of her hopeful tone made the detective smile as he hung up.

Chapter 19

Jackie began looking for her children and found Lizzy sitting on the floor in the corner of the living room, looking at the scrapbooks. She couldn't resist sitting down beside her little girl as she studied the pictures. Stroking the protective cover on each page of her life, Jackie thought about how important the 'memory books' really were to her now. Without Jonathan there, the only thing she had were her memories of him. And now his entire family was gone. NO! *Jonathan was not gone. Missing, yes. Gone, no!* She couldn't think that. He would be home soon. She couldn't bear it if he didn't come home.

"Mommy. Who's this again?" Lizzy was pointing to one of the girls in a family photo. It was a picture of three children surrounded by a mother and father. The formal portrait was the last one taken before Jonathan started law school.

"That was your Aunt Jennifer. And this one was your Aunt Jessica." Jackie was pointing to the identical twins. It had been difficult for her to tell them apart when they first met each other. Finally, after Jonathan repeatedly told her which one was which, she got it straight. Jennifer, the older twin by two minutes, had a tiny beauty mark next to her right eye. Jessica was the one who was always smiling. Both the girls loved to joke around and only behaved when they had to. The rest of the time they were mischievous and ornery. But they were good girls.

Lizzy poured over the pictures, checking them out as if she'd never seen them before. "Look at this Mommy. That's Daddy, isn't it?"

"Yes, that's your daddy. See the funny hat on his head?" She pointed to the graduation cap he was wearing. "And see that white thing in his hand? That's his diploma. It's something they give you when you go to their school and finish their classes. And that's your Grandma and Grandpa Pennington on either side of your Daddy. They were very proud of your father. See how your grandma is hugging your father? She was like that. She loved to hug everybody, especially her kids." Jackie hugged Lizzy and then continued. "She was a very special lady."

Jackie always wished her children had known their grandparents and aunts, but that wasn't the way life worked out. Instead, she tried to keep their memories alive by talking about them.

"Grandma Pennington loved to have company. She liked it when the girls brought their friends over. When your father brought me home to meet her, she walked right up to me, gave me a big hug. She would sit right here in this living room and sip her lemonade and talk about anything you wanted. And she and your grandpa loved each other very much. You could tell that by the way they held hands in the picture. See?" They took a closer look at the picture.

"You love Daddy like that too, don't you Mommy?"

"Of course I do. I love your father very much." Jackie could feel the tears well up in her eyes. She wasn't going to be able to finish looking at the pictures this time, so she got up and started walking away.

"Stay here, Mommy. Look at the pictures with me."

"I can't right now, honey. Maybe later." She walked away from the conversation, wiping away her tears, but Lizzy followed her and pulled her into a seat.

"Anybody home?" Celeste let herself in the front door.

"In here." Jackie replied.

"Mommy, can I go outside and play?" Lizzy was squirming as she sat on her mother's lap.

"I don't think it's a good idea right now, honey." Jackie was desperate to keep her children safe, but afraid her conservative approach would make them even more paranoid if she kept them cornered in their own home.

"Why not?" Lizzy was insistent and Jackie struggled to come up with an answer.

"I can't be out there with you right now and I don't want you to play alone."

Michael walked in the room just then and stood next to his mother listening to her explanation.

"Michael will take me, won't you Michael." Lizzy looked up at her brother with pleading eyes.

"Yea, I'll take her, Mom. We'll be fine. I promise I won't leave the yard." Michael had already grabbed hold of Lizzy's hand and was pulling at her.

"I don't think so, Michael. I think you should stay inside and play a game." Jackie clung to Lizzy as she was hopping off the chair.

"Mom, Please!" Now Michael was pleading too.

Celeste had been in the kitchen helping herself to an apple and sauntered back in the living room chomping on it. "I'll take 'em outside for you if you want. They'll be safe with me."

"I don't know, Celeste." Jackie put her arm around Lizzy and drew her closer.

Celeste directed her next comment to the children. "Hey kids, why don't you go get an apple? I'll be with you in a minute. Okay?"

Michael took Lizzy into the kitchen where she quickly convinced him that he should cut up the apple.

While the children rummaged through the cupboards looking for other treats, Celeste approached Jackie in the living room. "Are you planning to hold them prisoners in their own home?" She paused for a moment, then continued. "You can't do that, Jackie. They'll be fine with me. I can watch out for them. I'll bring them back inside every half hour if you want me to. Just let them play outside for awhile."

Jackie rose from her chair, drew back the curtains at the window and looked outside. "What if he's still out there Celeste?"

"The police didn't find anyone out there Jackie."

Jackie was indignant, turned, glared at Celeste and retorted. "I'm not imagining any of this, Celeste. Jonathan is missing. There was someone who followed me home from his office the other day and someone was out there stalking the house! I don't know who, and I don't know why, but someone is out there. Do you really think I can send my children out to play knowing they may be in danger?"

Celeste's response was defensive. "If I thought they were in danger, I would never suggest taking them outside. I am sure I can keep them safe for a half hour." She stopped for a moment and relaxed before speaking again. "Jackie, they need some semblance of normality, Jackie. I'll take care of them. Honestly, I will. Besides, you could use a few minutes of peace and quiet. Why don't you take your medicine and get some rest. I can handle the munchkins."

Jackie turned away from the window and looked Celeste in the eye. "You promise not to let them out of your sight?"

Celeste nodded.

"Only for a half hour, and don't take them into the woods. Make sure they stay in the backyard by the kitchen doors. I want to be able to see them all the time. Deal?"

"Deal." Celeste was already running to the kitchen yelling for the kids to get their shoes on and join her out back.

Jackie swallowed two pills, sat down at the kitchen table and watched Celeste and the children play kick ball together for ten minutes. Then she let her guard down and relaxed, believing they were safer than she originally thought. She sipped a cup of tea, trying to settle her stomach. Her headache made it difficult to concentrate so she put her head on the table and closed her eyes for a minute. Just a minute.

Lizzy was the first to stray from the back yard. The ball had gotten away from her and she chased after it into the woods. Soon Michael was following her with Celeste yards behind. "Wait up, you two. Don't get so far ahead of me!"

The kids weren't afraid to play in the woods. They knew every inch of the estate. Their father took them for walks to hunt for wild flowers whenever he could. Of course, they had been warned to always have an adult with them, but they weren't disobeying orders. Celeste was right behind them. She just couldn't keep up, that's all.

"Look!" Lizzy squealed. "Look what I found!" Lizzy had stopped dead in her tracks to pick up a black scarf.

Michael was just about to take it from her when Celeste joined them. "Let me see that." She insisted. Without hesitation she grabbed it out of Lizzy's hands to inspect it. "Well, what do you know! It's my scarf. It blew off my neck one day over a month ago. I figured I'd never see it again! Wow, Lizzy, you are really an explorer! Let's see what other gems you can find out here."

Celeste shoved the scarf into her jeans pocket and pointed to a toad stool. "Is that a mushroom? I'm getting a little hungry and mushrooms are yummy when you fry them up in a pan!"

Both Michael and Lizzy laughed.

"What? What's so funny?" Celeste looked at them for an explanation.

"That's not a mushroom, that's a toad stool." Michael picked it and pushed it into her nose. "Dad says if we eat these we'll get sick. Didn't you ever learn how to tell the difference between mushrooms and toad stools?"

"You don't know that either, Michael." Lizzy defended Celeste's ignorance and grabbed hold of her hand to lead her out of the woods and back to the yard. Michael followed, stick in hand, batting at the trees as he went.

"Michael, stop that. You'll damage the trees!" Celeste demanded as she extended her hand for the switch. "I'll take that, if you don't mind."

"Whatever!" Michael gave it up willingly and ran on ahead towards the house.

Inside Jackie awoke feeling groggy. She had an indentation on her face where her head had rested on her hand and her back ached from sitting at the kitchen table, sleeping. As she stretched, she suddenly remembered her children had been outside playing with Celeste and she looked at her watch. She'd been asleep for over and hour. Why weren't they back? Celeste promised to come in every half hour.

Panic set in as Jackie pushed her chair back and tripped over its leg racing to the door. *Where are my children, Celeste?*

Just as she opened it, Michael ran in. "Hi, Mom!"

She didn't want to appear overly protective so she simply replied "Hey buddy."

As she watched Lizzy and Celeste enter, she eyed Celeste with a questioning look and then motioned to the clock on the wall.

Celeste shrugged her shoulders before replying. "Lost track of time. Sorry. You kids better go wash up now."

Jackie was relieved that they were okay. She knew Celeste could be a bit over zealous with her children and often lost track of time, but that was probably a good thing since she was painfully aware that as a mother she could sometimes be too tough. What a balancing act!

"Hey, Jackie." Celeste was calling from the front door. "See you around. I gotta run some errands."

Jackie's response was reserved. "See you."

Mary shuffled into the kitchen and opened the refrigerator door. "Almost time for supper, " she said. "It should be ready soon."

"What would I do without you, Mary?"

೩✈

With supper over, Mary said goodnight shortly after 7:00. She was putting in twelve-hour shifts caring for the children while Jackie was searching for Jonathan, but she didn't really mind. She loved Michael and Elizabeth.

"Michael, get Lizzy and come sit with me before bed. I have one of your favorite books!" Jackie did her best to keep things upbeat for the sake of the children.

Lizzy scampered in and jumped on her mother's lap as Michael slipped behind the sofa and leaned over his mother's shoulder. He suddenly felt too old to be read to and didn't want to appear eager to be coddled.

"Aren't you going to sit bedside me, Michael?" Jackie knew what was going on in his head, but she decided to coax him to her side anyway. Michael shrugged his shoulders, then came back to the front of the sofa and sat down next to her. It felt good to be hugged as she put her arm around his neck and gently kissed the top of his head. They read for an hour and then Jackie said.

"Bedtime!"

Chapter 20

Monday morning. "Scattered showers will dampen the area surrounding Richmond today and…" Jackie listened to the weather report with little enthusiasm. It really didn't make any difference to her what the weather was like. Rain or shine, without Jonathan, life was just a necessary evil so she could take care of the kids. It wasn't worth anything to her alone. So many things were happening that Jackie couldn't figure out. Nothing was making any sense.

※

In the city, at Jonathan's office, the Monday morning routine was about to begin.

"Good morning Mr. Anderson." Terri was professional, as always. "Did you have a good weekend, sir?"

"Good enough." Peter walked by her desk without acknowledging anyone else at all. The receptionist looked at Terri, then turned her attention back to the paperwork at her desk.

"Everyone ready?" He was referring to the meeting in the conference room.

"Everyone is here except Kathy. She didn't mention that she would be late today, so I called her house, but no one answered. I'm not sure where she is." Terri replied with concern. "It's not like her to miss work without calling."

"Yes, well, we'll begin without her. I'm sure she'll be along shortly." As an after thought he added. "Make sure you dock her pay. I won't tolerate tardiness in my staff."

"Yes sir."

The usual chatter around the conference room ended the minute Mr. Anderson walked in the room. All eyes were on him. He stood at the head of the table and cleared his throat. "As you know, there's still no word about Mr. Pennington. At first we hoped it was just a personal situation and he needed time away from the office, but now we are afraid foul play may be suspected. Although we here at the firm are very concerned, there isn't much we can do but pick up his caseload and move forward for the sake of our clients." The staff sat quietly as he spoke.

"To that end, I've interviewed some candidates looking for someone who can step up to the plate- until Jonathan returns, of course. Within the week we will hire an intern to help us. In the meantime, we need to keep working. I'm sure Jonathan would want that." Mr. Anderson was cool and collected as he sat down and began discussing the agenda for the week.

Terri was astounded. She always knew that Peter was aloof, but she had no idea he was that cold-hearted. However, it really was all about the money with him. She knew that. But what about Kathy? It wasn't like her to miss a day without a phone call or explanation. Was she hurt? Terri wasn't so sure she liked the atmosphere in the office anymore. There were just too many secrets and lies.

What Terri didn't know was that the police found Kathy's car abandoned on Saturday night. The right front tire was completely flat, leaving the Mazda disabled. A cell phone was flipped open, lying just underneath the front seat, as if it had fallen during a sudden stop. There was no sign of Kathy.

Since it appeared to the patrolman on duty that someone had abandoned the car to find help, he radioed for a tow truck to haul it away. The standard destination for vehicles left unattended was a fenced in lot where it would sit until it was claimed and a hefty fee had been paid.

Chapter 21

Back at the Pennington home, the phone rang. It was Celeste. "Hey Jackie, I thought you were going to call me and let me know what's going on. What's up?" She had an accusatory tone in her voice that wasn't well hidden.

"I'm sorry. It's been a little hectic around here and after the kids were asleep I took one of the pills you gave me. Man, those things really knock me out. I'm really not sure I should be taking them."

Celeste jumped on the comment, interrupting her, "Jackie, you know you need them. They help you get some sleep. And all those headaches you've been having. You are still getting the headaches, aren't you?"

"I don't think I ever got rid of them. It's been one long headache ever since Jonathan disappeared but I think I've got a lead..."Jackie was interrupted again.

"A lead? What do you mean a lead? You think you know what happened to him?" Celeste seemed startled as she spoke into the phone.

"Not sure yet, but Detective Ryder and I are going to NewStart Clinic together later on."

"NewStart Clinic? What's that?"

"I think it's like a free health care facility, but I'm not really sure. All I know is that he was very worried about it."

"How do you know?" Celeste's curiosity had peeked.

"I can't get into that now. I've got to get ready to go. Detective Ryder is picking me up soon." Jackie held the cordless phone to her ear as she was dressing. "Coming over today?" She asked with hopeful intonation.

"You know me, I can't stay away too long or I have Beth withdrawal!"

"Thanks. She loves seeing you too and Mary seems to be getting awfully tired. I think I'm overworking her!"

"Don't worry, I've got your back!" Celeste was so bubbly and a little too happy sounding for Jackie.

"Thanks." Was all Jackie could say. Just then the doorbell rang. "The doorbell is ringing. I've got to go. That's probably the detective at the door." Jackie hung up without saying goodbye.

Detective Ryder was greeted by a stunningly beautiful woman. Jackie looked fabulous in her casual black pants and a white button down blouse. Her flawless olive complexion, deep brown eyes, and long, smooth, black hair made her look drop dead gorgeous. He was almost speechless as he tipped his cap, "Mrs. Pennington. Nice to see you." *Oh brother*, he thought, *how stupid did that sound? Nice to see you. Couldn't you come up with anything more original than that?*

"It's Jackie, Detective. Remember?"

"Ready to go, Jackie?" He held the door open for her as she stepped outside.

Jackie turned her head back and called out, "Mary, I'm leaving now. Thanks for watching the kids. I'll see you later!" She felt nervous about going, but she knew she had to.

The ride into Richmond was quiet. Jackie couldn't think of anything to say and Detective Ryder was thinking of all the wrong things to talk about. So, they didn't speak at all- until they reached the city.

"Jackie, let me do all the talking. Don't do anything unless I tell you to. Okay?" He had reached his hand over to touch hers as he spoke.

"Okay." Jackie didn't know what else to say. She was feeling a little nauseous.

"I don't expect to uncover much today, so don't get too excited. This is just a preliminary investigation, you know, checking out the building and who services it. We haven't got anything to really go on yet. Don't forget that."

"I know. I understand."

"Hope you don't mind, but I brought you an old pair of jeans and this flannel shirt." He pulled a paper bag off the floor as he drove, nearly side-swiping the car in the lane beside him. "Whoops". He recovered and straightened out his driving and then rummaged through the bag until he got a grip on a pair of faded jeans with holes and a frayed pant legs. "I know these aren't what you normally wear, but if someone sees you, you need to fit the part.

Jackie examined the clothing and rubbed the flannel.

"I know, it's not your style. Sorry about that!" Bob watched her expression as she stroked the material.

"Actually back home this is pretty much all I wore- including the holey jeans, just not this size!" Her expression lightened as she spoke.

"You can crawl to the back seat and scoot down to put them on. I won't peek. I promise." He winked at her and chuckled.

She obeyed him immediately. Within moments her look was transformed and she climbed back over the seat to the front again.

Bob reached his hand out to her head and let his fingers gently run through her hair and then without warning ruffled it with intensity. "Got to mess up these locks a bit. There probably aren't many clients going to that clinic looking as good as you. In fact, maybe you'd better try to get your lipstick off too."

"I'm not wearing any lipstick."

"A natural beauty. Wow!" Now he was embarrassed. He'd gone too far. "Sorry, that just slipped out."

"It's okay." It may have been okay, but it made her blush to hear him say anything about her looks. It was suddenly silent in the car again.

Detective Ryder broke the silence. "There it is." He read the sign: "NewStart Clinic-We're Here To Help. What kind of help do you suppose they offer? Uppers? Downers? Or maybe just good old pain killers. Yes sir, the doctor is in and can give you whatever you need. Just make sure there is enough money in your pocket cause he won't do it for nothing!"

"Do I detect a little cynicism detective?" Jackie cocked her head and looked at him as if to say shame on you.

"Stay here Jackie." He parked the car and was opening his door as he cautioned her.

"Oh no you don't. I didn't put on this gorgeous outfit to be left out in the car. I'm coming too."

He wanted to say no way, but instead he replied. "Can't stop you, can I? Okay then but remember…"

Jackie interrupted him, "I know, do what you say and nothing more. Got it!"

They parked the car around the corner from the clinic to avoid suspicion. As they opened the front door a buzzer announced their arrival and a girl in her early twenties came from behind the counter in the center of the room. "Can I help you?"

"Yea, we wanna see the doctor. I got a really bad cold." Bob sneezed and let the spray fly straight at the girl, then wiped his nose with his sleeve as he sniffled before continuing. "I can't seem to shake it and I need some pills."

Totally disgusted, the girl took two steps back before she asked her next question. "And you, miss?"

Before Jackie could speak, Bob chimed in. "Oh, she just needs birth control pills, don't ya sweetie pie?" He pinched her on the rear and then embraced her, pulling her extra close.

Jackie looked up at him as he planted a big, wet, stubbly chinned kiss on her cheek. She played into his hands to keep up the charade.

"Well, I'm really sorry, but the doctor left about ten minutes ago and I don't expect him back until tomorrow." She turned to leave.

"Wait just a minute." He raised his voice for affect. "I need to see a doctor now. What am I supposed to do? Make an appointment?" He took a few steps toward her as she spoke.

"It's generally walk-ins, but we close at 11:30 so the doctors can go to their offices. The girl was repulsed by his attitude and offered little compassion as she answered his questions. "Dr. Tender comes in on Mondays and Fridays. Dr. Ferguson is here on Tuesdays and Thursdays. We're closed Wednesdays and over the weekends." She tried to walk away from him, but it didn't work.

Detective Ryder eyed the surroundings while he made small, obnoxious talk with the girl. Nothing seemed unusual about the office except that it wasn't very clean. The corners of the linoleum floor were filthy and cobwebs were hanging from the ceiling in front of the cracked plaster. But he expected that from a storefront health center. Behind the counter there was a small hallway with doors on either side. Probably treatment rooms, Bob thought. He shuddered to think how many people might be treated without proper sanitation of instruments.

He started to go behind the counter for a closer look, but the office girl stopped him, standing squarely in his way. I'm sorry sir, you'll have to come back when a doctor is in. Perhaps tomorrow.

"I could be dead tomorrow!" Bob was putting on quite a show for her. He did a quick turnaround and swooped Jackie up around the waist, lifting her off her feet. "Come on, let's get outta here."

Once outside he put her down, grabbed her around the neck and made her walk really close to him. Then, just before they got around the corner he brought her lips to his and kissed her passionately. Jackie was stunned for a moment, but didn't fight it. He looked over his shoulder before he motioned her to the car door and let her in.

"Man, I am so sorry about that kiss. Honestly. But she followed us out the door and I was afraid she'd be suspicious, so I thought I'd better kiss you to make it look like we're a couple." He started the car and took off, checking the rear view mirror as he left. "I don't think she came around the corner, though."

Right or wrong, the kiss felt good, warm and gentle, yet with emotion and strength. She missed Jonathan's touch and her heart ached at the thought that another man's embrace could actually get to her. She didn't want to give way to her feelings, so she suppressed them. Again it was silent.

This time the silence was short lived as the detective gave in to report his next move. "I'll have to go back to the clinic soon, but I need some time to check out the doctors."

They had driven far enough away from the center for him to feel safe, so he stopped the car before he continued the rest of the conversation. He pulled over on a side street, put the car in park and turned to look at Jackie. "Look, I'm really sorry about that kiss. It just seemed like the right thing to do at time. And if you tell anyone that you were with me today, I mean anyone, I could lose my job. They don't like it when we let civilians come along."

"Then why did you?" Jackie's question was valid and she was very interested in the answer.

"I guess I thought you deserved to see what was going on down here. After all, you were the one that found the lead."

"I hope it's a lead." Jackie sighed, turned her head towards the passenger window and rested her head against the back of the seat. Bob put the car in gear and pulled out. The rest of the ride was quiet. Jackie crawled in the back and changed again.

Home again to the sounds of the children, Jackie was an emotional wreck. Her head hurt. She didn't wait for Bob to get out of the car. Instead, she practically raced to the house shouting 'thank you' as she reached the front door. She was trying to escape the feeling of wanting to be touched by him again and running away seemed to be the best thing to do. When she got inside she looked through the curtains in the living room and watched him leave. She was weak and vulnerable and she knew it. She didn't want to feel those emotions.

"Hey." Jackie jumped as Celeste approached her and spoke.

"Hey back."

"How'd it go? Did you find anything out there?" Celeste was pulling on Jackie's arm trying to get her to sit on the sofa in the living room.

Jackie stared at the doll on the mantle. *Are you glaring at me? How do you always seem to know what I am thinking and feeling*, she thought.

"Jackie?" Celeste was trying to get information out of her. "You okay?"

"I'm fine. It's just so frustrating. I just can't believe that Jonathan would leave me like this, but there's not much proof that anything else is going on." Realizing how pathetic she sounded, she stood to her feet. "I've got to check on the kids. Are you staying for supper?"

"Me? No, I've got places to go, things to do. You know the drill. But I'll be back. Maybe tomorrow. Call me if you need anything." She pulled her keys out of her designer pants pocket and flipped them in the air. "Catch you later!"

As Jackie passed the desk in the kitchen she noticed the mail piling up. There among the bills was an envelope marked MRS. JONATHAN PENNINGTON- URGENT- OPEN IMMEDIATELY. There was no stamp, so it hadn't gone through the postal service. Her hands shook as she ripped at the tab of the envelope and pulled the contents out. In broken handwriting it read "Do only what I say and MAYBE you'll see your husband again."

Jackie gasped. *Maybe I'll see Jonathan again*? She continued to read the note.

"Come to the Coniac Cinema on Tuesday. Buy one ticket for "The Rage Within" and be in the theater at 1:50. NO LATER. Come alone. Don't do anything stupid like call the police!"

Trembling now, Jackie fell into the chair and buried her face in her hands. What next? If she told Celeste, the police or especially Bob about the note, Jonathan might be killed. *Why? What do you want from me? Why did it take so long for you to get in touch with me?* Panic set in. *How did this note get in the house*?

"Mommy? Mommy where are you?" It was Lizzy.

"In here honey. I'm in the kitchen." *Stay calm for the kids, Jackie*!

"Look what I made Mommy. Celeste helped me." She pulled a plaster cast of a tiny hand out from behind her back and shoved it under Jackie's nose. It was adorable, but it wasn't exactly what Jackie wanted to think about right then.

"It's wonderful Lizzy. Just wonderful. Where's your brother? And do you know where Mary is?" Jackie wanted to find out what Mary knew about the note.

Just then Mary opened the french doors from the back yard and entered the kitchen. "How'd you beat us, Lizzy?"

"I ran around to the front. I tricked you!" Lizzy was giggling.

Michael tapped Lizzy with his finger and said "Tag, you're it!" He ran up the back staircase as Lizzy chased after him. For the first time in a long time, he was laughing. It may have been only momentary, but it would have to do until Jonathan returned.

Mary caught Jackie sitting at the dinette table, staring outside. "Miss Jackie. Can I get you anything?"

Jackie wiped a tear. "No. Just sit with me, will you?" She was thinking of the note, but was afraid to talk about it with Mary. *What if the person who wrote it knew she talked to Mary? Would Mary's life be in danger?*

"Of course I'll sit with you." Mary was accustomed to easy conversation with Jackie. There was no pretense of relationship between the two of them- it was genuine.

Jackie stammered, "Mary, you know how much you mean to me, don't you? I mean, all this time you've been with us, I feel like we're family."

"That we are." Mary sat across from Jackie. *Why did this moment seem so awkward*, she thought. "What's on your mind?"

"It's just that I," Again she was struggling for words. "I rely so much on you. I kind of feel like you're my mother. I just don't know what I'd do without you. Sometimes I'm afraid I'll chase you away too. Or you'll die like all the others around me."

"What on earth are you talking about?" Mary knew a little bit about Jackie's past, but since no one spoke about any of it, she felt lost on the subject.

"Dr. Stanley," she hesitated thinking she needed to explain more. "You know, my therapist, keeps telling me that none of the deaths were my fault and that I must stop taking the blame, but it's so hard. Everyone seems to die around me. First it was Gina, then my father and then Jonathan's family. None of them would be gone if it hadn't been for me."

"Now listen here. I don't want to hear anymore of that from you. Your doctor is right. You weren't responsible for their deaths. When are you going to learn that death is as much a part of life as anything? No one is promised tomorrow. It's not your fault that they didn't survive. God took them when it was their time."

"They all died because they knew me."

"How in the world do you figure that?" Mary looked her square in the eyes, reached her arms across the table and pulled Jackie's hands into hers. "Sweetie, you can't blame yourself for a car accident."

"You don't know the whole story."

"Okay, then, tell me." Mary leaned back in her chair and braced for the story.

Jackie stared out the window for a few seconds, trying to decide if she wanted to relive the horrible scene. She sighed and then began. "Just after Jonathan and I started dating he brought me home to meet the family. They were all so friendly and I loved them from the start. They made me feel like, like I fit. That's always been problem for me, feeling like I fit anywhere. Anyway, his mother and father were wonderful to me." She hesitated, looked away as tears welled up in her eyes and then continued. "His sisters used to take me up to their room and show me pictures of their high school dances and their new clothes. They even let me borrow some of them. They were always laughing with me, helping me with my makeup or hair for a special date with Jonathan. They were the sisters I never had."

Mary didn't say anything as Jackie opened up to her.

"The closer I got to Jonathan, the more I wanted to be with his family. One day I suggested that we all go to the mountains to hike. I could tell his mother wasn't that interested in the idea, but everyone else thought it was great. We planned it for the following Saturday. Anyway, Jonathan said we'd meet them at Culver's Rock around 9:00 in the morning and get a good start on the day together.

Well, on Saturday, his mom packed us a picnic lunch and his dad put a cooler in the back of their new SUV. They even called us around 8:00, just before we left to say they were on their way.

The twins had just gotten their driver's licenses a few months earlier, but Jess wasn't as comfortable as Jen at the wheel. I convinced her all she needed was a little more driving time. So, when his mom called to make last minute arrangements, Jess grabbed the phone from her and announced to me that she was going to do the driving, just like I told her she should. Then she said 'if we get in an accident, it will be your fault."

Jackie continued the story choking on her words. " She wasn't used to the new SUV. The police said she probably didn't see the lights blinking on the railroad track because she was distracted. I guess they thought I'd be mad if they were late, so they picked up some donuts for breakfast. She didn't stop until she was on the tracks. I don't know why unless she panicked. They didn't have a chance. The train pushed them down the rails four hundred yards before it stopped. The twins and his dad died instantly. His mother hung on for almost a week.

"None of that was your fault, Jackie. None of it." Mary was insistent, but it didn't matter to Jackie.

"She was driving because of me. They were on their way to go hiking because I asked them to go. It wasn't their time, it was mine. I'm the one who convinced them to do it, and it cost them their lives. I struggle with that every single day. And now, Jonathan is missing. Don't you see, eventually everyone is hurt because of me. I don't want anything to happen to you or to the kids. I'm scared. I'm just so scared."

Mary didn't know how to comfort Jackie. She only knew how to put her arms around her and let her cry.

After a long embrace, Jackie decided to show the note she found earlier to Mary, praying it wouldn't endanger her life to know about it. She felt so desperate.

Mary studied the note and turned the paper over looking for a clue as to where it came from and who might have sent it, but there was nothing that could identify anyone involved with it- at least in Mary's eyes. Astonished, she stared at Jackie before she spoke. "You aren't thinking of going, are you?"

"I don't know what else to do. If I go to the police, Jonathan might die."

"Well, you should at least tell Detective Ryder. I'm sure he could help you." Mary stood to her feet in preparation for the reaction she anticipated.

"No police! I can't involve Bob in this at all or I might not see Jonathan again ever."

Mary began limping towards the sink to run the water. Washing dishes would help her keep from exploding. All she could think was hold your tongue, old woman! She wanted to say so much more, but she kept her mouth shut as she poured the soap into the hot water. *Old news to them*, she thought!

Jackie walked over to Mary and gently gave her one last hug from behind before she climbed the back staircase to look for her children. Hiring Mary was the best thing Jonathan had ever done for her. But Mary couldn't help her now and she knew it. Jackie had to do what was asked of her in the note. Tomorrow she would go alone to the theater so she could find out how to get Jonathan back.

Chapter 22

Tuesday morning - another day without Jonathan. How long had it been? Eight days? It felt longer than that. Jackie checked the papers for anything about his disappearance. *Old news to them.* Though she thought about letting the police know what was happening, she quickly changed her mind. *They'd just mess things up and the note said to come alone. Nothing could happen in a theater anyway. Too public.*

Mary arrived early. Jackie had asked her to come to watch the kids again so she could run some errands and they were already sitting in the living room. Michael was on the floor playing with his game boy and Mary was reading to Lizzy as she sat on the sofa.

10:30 AM. Jackie ran up the steps to her bedroom to grab her cell phone. Celeste walked through the front door, unannounced and saw Mary and the children together in the living room. Mary stopped reading, gave a slight downward look towards Lizzy who was nodding off to sleep, and a pleading eye to Celeste. 'Don't wake her!' Celeste remained quiet. Michael waved "hello" to Celeste and then pointed to the ceiling. His sign language was easily interpreted as Celeste turned to run up the steps. Jackie re-appeared just in time to see Celeste's hand on the railing and one foot on the first step.

"Going somewhere?" Celeste seemed anxious.

"Just need to run some errands." Jackie knew better than to tell Celeste about the note or the scheduled meeting at the theater. She would only badger her or beg to go. Besides, she had been warned - NO ONE WAS TO COME WITH HER.

"I'll come with you!"

"Not this time. Thanks. I really need to be alone for awhile. I need some space. You understand, don't you?

"Sure I've got plenty to do anyway."

Jackie was relieved. There was no hint of rebuttal or complaint. *Thank you God!* "I've got my cell phone if you need me Mary. Bye kid." It was a good thing no one gave her a hard time. Her palms were sweaty and her hands trembling. Her head ached, her stomach was in knots and nausea was causing her throat to close. She wished there was a way to avoid the meeting, but it was very clear what was expected of her.

There it is, the Coniac Cinema. It was easy to find a place to park since the lot was nearly empty. "One ticket for "The Rage Within" please." As she opened her purse, she fumbled and dropped her keys to the floor.

"Five-fifty please. The movie starts at 2:20, but you can go in and find your seat early if you want." The movie clerk watched Jackie as she pulled out a twenty-dollar bill. Her hand shook violently as she handed it to the woman behind the glass. "Are you okay, Miss?"

"I'm fine. Just a little jumpy I guess."

"Well this movie will probably make you jump more. Hope you're ready for it!" The clerk passed the ticket and change through the opening and watched Jackie stuff the dollar bills in her purse.

"Thanks." *If she only knew!* Jackie walked through the doors and gave her ticket to the young man standing at the threshold of the theater. It was very familiar to her, the buttered popcorn smell, and the video games off to the side. She'd been to this theater many times with Jonathan. He liked movies more than she did. His favorites were the ones that made his skin crawl, more like the "Rage Within" than "When Harry Met Sally."

She entered the theater and noticed she was the first one there. *Well, they did say it was pretty early.* Nervously she took a seat near the top of the stadium steps near the elevator. She wanted to be able to see everyone who came in from the lower seating area so she wouldn't be caught off guard. She chose her seat- third one in from the aisle. *Creature of habit.* It seemed darker than usual in the theater. *Probably just me worrying.* She knew the minute other people came she wouldn't feel so vulnerable.

She heard a noise from behind, like a swoosh, and then something was around her neck, choking and pulling her back in against the seat. Jackie grabbed for the cord around her neck to yank it from her throat but it wouldn't budge. Her legs were pushing against the seat in front of her to loosen the tension around her neck but the cord was getting tighter and tighter and Jackie couldn't feel her arms or legs anymore- just tingling. Her head was swimming and her heart racing. And then she felt nothing.

Just as her body went limp, three teenagers entered the theater laughing and joking, spilling popcorn and chiding each other. They didn't notice anyone hovering over a lifeless form at the top of the theater right away, but as the assailant moved to the exit they noticed Jackie lying back against the seat motionless.

"Hey, lady, lady, you okay?" The first boy was shaking her, the second standing in the aisle with his mouth hanging open and the third was watching the opening trailers on the screen.

"Hey Joe, Joe, go get the somebody will you!" The first boy was still trying to wake up the woman, but there was no response.

"Is she dead?" The boy in the aisle was reaching down to check for a pulse just like they did on TV, but couldn't find it on her wrist.

"How should I know? Do I look like a doctor? Just get me some help." He was shouting and loosening the rope around her neck at the same time.

Though it seemed like forever, the manager, ambulance and the police all came. They found Jackie did have a pulse and rushed her to the hospital. They took the boys to an office, closed the doors and questioned them over and over again.

"No, we didn't seen anyone else in the theater. She was like that when we got there. Yes, we touched the rope. How do you think it got loose? No they didn't know the victim. We just came to see a movie." On and on answering their questions. Eventually the police let the boys go.

Jackie was fortunate. A few more minutes and she would have been dead. Instead all she had was a nasty bruise on her throat though she could barely speak. The emergency room doctors were checking every inch of her body for evidence of any other bruising. Her arms were black and blue from flailing and fighting, but there was no skin under her fingernails. They weren't that lucky! No DNA. But at least the police were taking things seriously now.

So many questions. She couldn't speak so she either mouthed the answers or wrote on a piece of paper. She answered all their questions as best she could and completely truthful. After all, whoever wanted her to go to the theater alone obviously had no intentions of telling her where Jonathan was. For all she knew he was dead.

Although the doctor thought it best that she stay overnight just to be sure nothing else came up, she insisted on going home. She was afraid for her children and wanted to be with them. There was no convincing her to stay for her own good, so the police drove her home a few hours later.

Celeste raced to the door when she heard the car coming up the driveway. Mary held the kids back as Jackie was ushered inside, but Jackie broke free from the helping arms of a policeman, got down on her knees and hugged Michael and Lizzy as she sobbed.

"My God, Jackie. We were so worried. We thought you were dead." Celeste was hovering over the family as they huddled on the floor. Mary stood off to the side and wiped the tears from her eyes. *How much more* could the family take? First Jonathan went missing, then the flashlight intruder, the people following her and now this?   How much more?

Celeste broke the silence, "Let's get you up to bed Jackie. You need to lie down." Looking directly at the policeman she continued, "Thank you officers. I'll take it from here. Let's go, Jackie. Upstairs now!" She lifted her up off the floor and with an arm under Jackie's shoulders, forced her from her children and up to the bedroom. Michael started to follow, but Celeste ordered him back. "You stay with Mary, Michael. Your mother needs her rest."

Yanking the covers down, Celeste prodded Jackie into her bed without even changing her clothes. There was no resistance though Jackie really wanted to have her children next to her. She had no strength to fight Celeste, so she just gave in. Celeste headed to the bathroom for water, then reached for the medicine on the nightstand and took two of the pills from the bottle. Though Jackie questioned the amount of pills Celeste offered, Jackie obeyed anyway and they were swallowed in only a moment. The ivory satin sheets were inviting as Celeste tucked her into bed and left her alone so she could sleep.

A tear gently slid down the side of Jackie's nose, but she didn't have the strength to reach for a tissue to wipe it away. Besides, it was about the only feeling left in her body. She felt as if her she was watching herself lying there as she floated above, arms and legs twitching below. Her mind was racing. *Too much medication? Who cares? Mary and Celeste are taking care of the kids. Let the medicine knock me out, please*!

Thoughts of Jonathan darted around like sharp lightening bolts. His disappearance was so sudden and unexpected. There were no warning signs... no arguments; no money problems. *Why isn't he here? Where is he? Is he all right? Oh God, please don't let him be hurt. I need him. I love him. I miss him so much. How long has he been gone? Did he leave her?* No, she was sure of that. Things had been so much better between them. *His touch was softer, more sincere than ever before. He was still too busy with work, but he was more attentive to her needs as well as the children's. Wasn't it just last week he read them a story before he tucked them in their beds and kissed them goodnight*? No it had been longer than that, hadn't it? But how long? She couldn't think clearly. And who wanted her dead?

Jackie's bedroom was like a prison to her now. There was no comfort in the four poster mahogany bed where Jonathan used to hold her close. Instead there was pain. Jackie laid her head on her pillow and continued to think of Jonathan's touch. Tears were sliding down her cheeks again and she grabbed Jonathan's pillow, wrapped her arms around it and curled up on her side like an infant in a mother's womb. She buried her face in the softness of the feathers and could smell his scent. She drew in a deep breath- holding on to the fragrance hoping somehow it would bring him back to her. She began sobbing uncontrollably and the agonizing sound filled the entire room. Even with her head in the pillow, it didn't begin to muffle the sound of her cries.

To get a hold of herself Jackie began taking deep breaths- *inhale 1, 2, 3, 4, 5- exhale 1, 2,3,4,5.* This was the method her psychiatrist taught her to use when her anxiety level became intolerable. If she could breath slowly, then her body would adapt to the timing and she could relax.

Maybe some good would come out of her illness after all. Her mother had always said to try to learn from every life experience, but she hadn't been able to find the good during her depression. *But now- yes sir, now she could practice her relaxation exercises while under great duress. Isn't that a relief?* Now all she had to do was just breath slower and her sobs would stop and her grief would pass. Right. But ever so slowly she continued methodically to breathe. In and out. In through the nose, out through the mouth. Moment by moment. The medication was finally working. She was falling asleep. It was troubled sleep, but at least it was a diversion from the pain of Jonathan's disappearance, an intruder and now a would-be killer. She lay curled on her side, holding Jonathan's pillow and drifted off.

The house was quiet. Mary spent the night with the children and Celeste went home to freshen up.

Chapter 23

The relentless pounding on the front door was disturbing. Someone was obviously agitated and anxious. Mary limped to the door, peeked out the curtain and then unbolted and unlocked the door. "Detective Ryder, I'm so glad you came. Mrs. Pennington is upstairs, still sleeping."

Barely whispering because of her damaged throat, Jackie stood at the top of the stairs, "I'm up."

Detective Ryder bolted up the stairs, "I heard what happened yesterday. What were you thinking going there by yourself?"

She tried to answer, but the Detective put his hands across her lips to hush her. "Don't talk. You need to rest. I just came to make sure you were okay and by the looks of you, you're not."

Jackie immediately covered the bruise on her throat in embarrassment and leaned against the railing.

"Let's get you back to your bed."

"The kids" Jackie attempted to speak.

Detective Ryder interrupted her, "Mary is here and she's taking care of them." He directed her back to the bedroom as he continued talking. "When I called last night Celeste answered the phone and said you couldn't be disturbed and that I shouldn't come over. I hope you don't mind, but I had to see for myself how you are doing."

"I'm…"

"Don't talk. You'll strain your vocal chords. Just listen, okay?" Detective Ryder was moving her to the bed. "I've been digging into this NewStart Clinic thing. After what I've found out and what happened to you yesterday, I'd say we've got big trouble."

Jackie's eyes were partially glazed, and very troubled as she looked at Bob.

"Jonathan's law partner is in way over his head. He funded NewStart Clinic hoping for a big return, but after the initial start up money, the investment went sour. To cover his losses, he and his doctor friends started messing with the drugs- if you get my meaning- and pretty soon he was raking in the dough. I think Jonathan caught on because Peter Anderson was suddenly living high. Jonathan worked with the accountant on the books for the office and he knew things weren't going well enough for him to be spending so much money. I think Anderson knew that Jonathan was getting some evidence on him and thought Jonathan would eventually go to the police. I can't prove it yet, but I'm working on it."

"It wouldn't surprise me if he was the one that followed you from the office that day. He knows you've had some rough times and I bet he thought he could scare you into leaving town when he came around the house that night and left his note. Then I think he decided you knew more than you should and he came after you too. It makes sense to me." Detective Ryder could see he was overwhelming Jackie. but he continued, "I'm really sorry Jackie. It doesn't look very good considering all that's happened."

"You think he's dead, don't you?" Jackie couldn't have spoken those words in more than a whisper even if she hadn't just been brutally attacked.

"I'm not saying that, but if we don't find him soon, I don't know if we ever will." Detective Ryder walked toward the bedroom door. "I'm following up on a few more leads today and ..."

Jackie stood up to go with him. Detective Ryder turned back towards her. "Oh no, you don't. You stay right here. I said I'm following up- not you. You're not going anywhere. In fact, I'm going to see if I can get Celeste back over here to keep you out of trouble. You have no business leaving your bedroom. I'm sure if I tell her to make sure you don't go anywhere she'll take care of you!"

Jackie didn't argue. She slipped back onto the bed and curled up, defeated and alone.

"Jackie, I'll find him. I promise." Detective Ryder shoved his palm into his forehead as he stepped into the hallway closing the bedroom door behind him. *Stupid idiot. What were you thinking? I'll find him, I promise. You know better than to say that to anyone.* He was still kicking himself for the comments when he asked Mary to call Celeste to see if she could come over. He left the same way he had come in, through the front door in a whirlwind of harried thoughts.

Detective Ryder knew his theory was right. All he had to do was prove it. He sped out the drive and headed straight for the Center.

He waited around the corner of the building until he was sure the assistant was gone. He checked his watch. 12:15. He hoped she wasn't planning to stick around much longer. While he watched from his car, he thought about what his plan should be. There had to be a back door and he could easily pick the lock.

Wait. Is that her? Yes! He waited until she caught the bus before he got out of his car. Peering over his shoulder to check out the surroundings, trying not to look suspicious, he walked across the street with his head buried in his hooded shirt. When he got to the Center, he wiped the front glass with the sleeve of his hoody and tried to see if anyone else was inside. The place looked empty. Though he was sure the front door was locked, he jiggled the handle to be certain. It was.

He was startled by a sneeze behind him and suddenly felt very vulnerable. He turned around, wiped his nose with his arm to hide his face, kept his eyes low, and then looked around the opposite direction from the kid passing him on the sidewalk. He decided it would be better for him to approach the building from the alley in the back. He kept his back rounded and his gate slovenly as he walked through the alley.

Just as he suspected, the back of the building was more secluded and definitely easier to access without being detected. A dumpster partially blocked the entrance with garbage overflowing. Paper medical gowns flapped in the breeze as they had been thrown into the dumpster on top of everything. It was so full that the lid didn't close properly so there was a good chance that more of the garbage would be all over the lot when the wind picked up speed.

Though he knew he wasn't following procedure, Detective Ryder jimmied the lock and was inside without any problem. The clinic was squeezed between two other storefront buildings in disrepair. Interior offices were dark and windowless. It was a good thing his flashlight worked. Unlike the television series where the crime scene investigators used their flashlights instead of the overhead lights, Detective Ryder rarely used his and hadn't checked the batteries for some time. Detective work often fell short of the excitement promised to the recruits as they entered the force. Most of the time it was tedious leg work. But it was never supposed to be breaking and entering. *Oh well, some things you just have to do*, he thought.

Quietly he explored the rooms. There were three doors in the hallway. He opened the first one and stepped inside. He saw the usual things… a blood pressure kit hanging on the wall, a poster of AIDS prevention information and a ripped examination table covered with white paper. Nothing seemed out of the ordinary.

He went back into the hallway and opened the next door. It was a tiny bathroom. *Was that a roach crawling across the basin*? He shuddered as he closed the door.

He hit the jackpot when he opened the final doorway in the hall. It held all the office files and financial papers as well as a small desk cluttered with folders and paperwork. He started filtering through the piles, looking for anything that could prove there was something illegal going on.

He was reading a budget sheet when he heard the front door buzzer sound. He quickly shifted the papers and slipped behind boxes stacked to the ceiling. Dr. Ferguson entered with a disheveled man in his mid-twenties. His face was full of pockmarks and his dirty, black hair was as coarse as a ratty mane. His bloodshot eyes were filled with fire. There was an indescribable stench permeating the room. Detective Ryder nearly gagged as it filled his nostrils.

"I'm telling you, I can't pay you today. My partner and I are working with a cash flow deficit right now. I'll have it to you by Monday, I assure you." Dr. Ferguson was direct and adamant as he rambled on. "I don't understand why you're so angry. This is the first payment that's been late. We don't even have the stuff yet."

"Have the stuff? You don't have the stuff?" He was poking a knife at the doctor's face. "You don't get the STUFF 'til I have my money. You got that? I ain't no freakin' bank. You pay, or you don't get. It's as simple as that."

Dr. Ferguson stuck out his chest and shot his answer back. "Get that thing out of my face. Who do you think you are? If it wasn't for us, you'd be dead by now. So just cut the crap. I'll have your money by Monday morning. You just make sure you have what we need by then."

Detective Ryder could feel the tension building as Doctor Ferguson's voice elevated.

There was a scuffle as the dealer pushed the doctor into the desk. "Look man, don't screw with me. I need the cash now - not Monday. I'll give you 'till tomorrow to get it together. And just to let you know I mean business, here's a little something to remind you of our agreement." He put the knife to the doctor's cheek and slowly cut a two-inch line into the side of his face. He had been careful not to go too deep - just deep enough to draw blood. His filthy hands were pressed against Ferguson's chest before he pushed him off balance and the doctor fell to the ground. "I mean it, Doc. Don't mess with me." He left in a huff out the front door.

The doctor kept control of his emotions until the buzzer stopped ringing and the door slammed. As soon as he thought he was alone, he drew his hand to his face, felt his wound and checked his hand for blood. He stood up, collected his thoughts and dialed a number.

"Peter, its A.J.. We've got to meet. NOW! Manny was just here. He's out of control." There was a pause. "Meet me at Roxie's. Ten minutes!"

Chapter 24

Celeste whistled as she played games with the children and ordered Mary around asking for her to make vegetable soup for Jackie and steak and baked potatoes for the kids and her. As Mary filled the request, she stumbled over Celeste's sweater that had fallen off the ladder back chair in the dinette. *Can't even hang up her own things*! She used to like Celeste, but recently she was getting on her nerves a lot. *She was probably just spending too much time at the house*, Mary thought. She was getting pretty tired.

"Supper was delicious, Mary. You planning to leave soon so you can get something for yourself at home?" Celeste stood from the table, took another sip from her glass and then set it back on the table. "Come on kids. Let's get back to our game."

Mary was quietly mimicking Celeste as she started cleaning up the supper dishes. "You planning to leave soon so you can get something for yourself at home?" Mary thought to herself, *Mrs. Pennington always asked me to join them when I'm here past supper hour. And she always took her dishes to the sink- even made the kids help clean up. But Miss Fancy Pants won't lift a finger! I swear*! Mary began the cleanup as she limped across the kitchen with her arms full of dishes.

When she was finished Mary went into the living room and found Celeste asleep on the couch and the kids watching television. The room was a mess. Games were strewn all over the floor, blankets and pillows covering the rug and three different glasses - all Celeste's, were on Jackie's good table.

Mary started to pick up the glasses and then decided she'd had enough for the day. "I'll check on Mrs. Pennington and then I'm going home. You did say you'd be here tonight, didn't you?" She didn't care if she was waking Celeste up. She was supposed to be watching the children anyway and you can't do that when you're sleeping.

"It's okay, you can go. I'll check on Jackie soon. See you tomorrow." Celeste mumbled her goodbye from the couch.

Fifteen minutes later Celeste made her way upstairs to check on Jackie, handed her two more pills and some water and then coaxed her back to bed while Jackie begged Celeste to let the kids come upstairs for a few minutes.

"Later, when you're feeling better. Right now you need your rest." Insisted Celeste. "I'll be here tonight so you don't need worry. The pills I gave you should help you sleep."

Downstairs Lizzy was yanking on Michael's hair and he was punching his little sister to get her to let go. "Stop it you little jerk. Let go of my hair!" Michael was yelling at her as she ducked his punches.

"Mommy, Michael's hitting me!" Lizzy knew how to get Michael into trouble and lately she seemed to attack him more often.

Celeste walked into the room as Michael was raising his hand over his head to strike another blow. "Whoa, what are you doing?" Celeste had his arm in her hand before he could hit his sister again. "Don't you know better than to hit your little sister? I think you'd better just go right over to that corner, young man, and bury your head in it."

"Do what?"

"You heard me. Face the corner and don't move."

"But."

"Don't but me. I don't want to ever see you hit your sister again. Do you understand?" Celeste was growling the words as she spit them out. Michael decided he should obey her without another word, so he promptly stomped into the corner and stuck his nose in it.

Lizzy was crying as Celeste bent over to see if there were any bruises. "Beth, honey, are you hurt?"

"C.C., Mikey hit me." Lizzy was peering out an open, tearless eye to see how much of reaction she could get from Celeste. She got exactly what she was looking for.

Celeste was caressing her hair and scooping her into her arms. "You poor little thing. You okay?"

Under his breath, Michael complained to the wall, "Yea, I get my hair pulled out and Lizzy gets all the attention."

Five minutes later Celeste told Michael he could come away from the wall, scolding him for touching his sister once again. On her third finger shake in Michael's face, the telephone rang.

When Celeste picked up the phone an unidentified male spoke. "Mrs. Pennington?

"She's not available right now. May I ask who's calling?" Celeste sounded very professional as she spoke.

"This is Peter Anderson."

"And you're calling regarding?" She was very formal.

"I'm Jonathan's partner, Peter Anderson, and I just wanted to know how Mrs. Pennington is doing. I heard she had a bad experience recently." Mr. Anderson approached the conversation carefully. "I'm very concerned and was just calling to see how things are going."

"Things are going fine, Mr. Anderson but Jackie is resting upstairs and I don't want to disturb her."

Hesitating only a moment he continued, "Well, could you tell her we're all thinking of her at the office? Oh yes, and please tell her we're very anxious to have Jonathan back with us soon."

"Thank you. I will do that. Thank you for calling." Celeste was just as anxious to end the conversation with Mr. Anderson. His phone call had rattled her considerably, but she couldn't pinpoint why.

But he didn't hang up and instead continued, "By the way. Have the police come up with anything yet?"

"Yes, I think they have, but I don't know exactly what."

"Well, hmm, that's good, huh, very good. Perhaps you could have Mrs. Pennington call me when she is feeling better and fill me, I mean, us, in." Mr. Anderson's voice was shaky and he sounded flustered.

"I'll tell her. Thanks again for calling." Celeste hung up the phone before he could ask another question and quickly turned her attention to the TV.

Michael and Lizzy were playing a game on the floor next to her. With a sudden move, Celeste stood to her feet and announced, "I have to go out for a while, but I'll be back before you go to bed. Michael, your mother is sleeping upstairs if you need her for anything. I won't be very long, I promise. Maybe you should practice your piano lessons. I bet you haven't done that lately, have you?"

She didn't wait for an answer as she slipped her toes into the sandals beside the couch and headed for the front door. Michael just sat on the floor, his sister across from him, both of them looking stunned as she left. Michael got off the floor and walked to the staircase. He stood at the bottom and listened for any noises coming from his mother's room. Since he heard nothing at all he assumed his mother was sleeping and decided it was okay to practice as long as he didn't pound the piano.

Celeste was right. He hadn't touched the keyboard since his father disappeared. He began with finger warm ups. CDEFGABC, CBAGFEDC, over and over and over. Lizzy put her hands over her ears and then noticed her doll, Samantha lying beside her. She picked up the doll and covered the cloth ears so the doll wouldn't have to listen to the noise of the piano. Then she let out a giggle and snuggled with her baby doll.

Jackie awakened and looked at the clock beside her bed. She squinted and blinked her eyes, focusing on the numbers. *8:45 PM. That's pretty late for the kids to be up. Oh, that's right, Celeste is watching them. She'll probably forget to put them to bed. Maybe I should get up and see how they are.* Jackie put her feet over the edge of the bed and dangled them for a moment before she stood up. Suddenly swaying, she plopped her head back down on the pillow. *Guess I shouldn't get up just yet.* Nausea overtook her from the dizziness, but it was important that she knew how the kids were. She listened to Michael's piano playing and then between the notes heard Lizzy laughing. *They are okay. Good.*

Over and over Michael played the same song. Lessons were great, for those who enjoyed repetition. For anyone who had to listen to the same song again and again, it was tedious. Jackie continued to listen faithfully, grateful that Michael was so particular. *Whoops, sour note*! Michael started again, but suddenly his music stopped, practically mid note. Jackie listened for him to start again. Nothing. *That's not like Michael. He always finishes a song, even if it hasn't gone well.* She listened a few moments longer and then her heart began to pound. *Something isn't right. Michael wouldn't stop like that. He never stops like that.*

Struggling to get up and stumbling to her bedroom door, sweat had broken out on Jackie's brow. *Michael, Lizzy*! She moved to the stairs and listened over the railing desperately hoping to hear the piano again. Still there was nothing. "Michael? Lizzy? Celeste?" Jackie was waiting for their response. When no one answered, she started down the stairs. As she descended, her foot caught on her nightgown and she tumbled to the bottom of the stairs, hitting her head against the tiled entry floor.

Stunned and in pain, she couldn't move. Her cheek lay against the cold floor, something warm oozing underneath it. *Blood.* She could wiggle her fingers and toes, but she didn't have the strength to lift her head. Locks of black hair fell against her eyes as blood from her forehead slipped down to her nose. She tried to wipe it away, but she couldn't get her arm to move.

As she lay sprawled on the floor, she heard footsteps approaching. Drifting in and out of consciousness she tried to fight the feeling as much as possible. Suddenly she felt a hand touch her head and move her hair from her face. *Help me. Please, help me.* She could barely speak the words. She writhed in pain as she reached for the person touching her, but couldn't. Silently someone walked past her. *Don't leave me. Please, don't leave me. Where are my children?* Then she, too, was silent. She lay at the base of the stairs.

Chapter 25

"Celeste? Are you in there? Open up. It's me, Detective Ryder. Open up, will you? I need to talk to Jackie." It was a little after sunrise as Detective Ryder was knocking on the door but Celeste didn't answer. Impatient as he was, he tried to see into the center hall through the small window in the front door. Impossible to see much, he decided to look into the other windows around the house. Finally he found one window with the curtain pulled back just enough to see inside. There, in the center hall by the stairs, Jackie lay in a pool of blood. "Jackie, Jackie. Oh my God, Jackie!"

Without hesitation, the detective ripped off his shirt, wrapped his elbow in it and shoved his arm through the glass. He broke away the jagged pieces and crawled through the frame. As he raced toward Jackie, he tripped over a game on the living room floor.

"Jackie? Jackie, are you okay?" He was frantic as he touched her bloodied neck looking for a pulse. She was breathing on her own and her pulse was steady, but shallow. "Jackie. Hold on. I'm calling for an ambulance."

"The children. Where are the children?" She whispered.

Detective Ryder was on his cell phone dialing 911 as he scanned the room looking for Michael and Lizzy. There was no sign of either of them or Celeste.

It would be hours before Jackie could tell anyone what really happened. At the hospital she was x-rayed, stitched and admitted, protesting as best she could that she wanted to go home and search for her family. She couldn't even lift her head, she was so weak from the sedative and pain medicine. She sank into a much-needed sleep as Detective Ryder remained by her side.

Now that the children were missing the police picked up the case with more enthusiasm. Finally they believed her. Of course they did. After all,

Jonathan was still missing. She had been followed, nearly strangled to death and her children and Celeste gone. They took notice and hovered over Jackie as she sat up in her hospital bed trying to focus. Again with the questions. What happened? When did you last see your children? Who were they with? Do you have any idea who would have taken them? *Weren't these the same questions they ask when Jonathan disappeared? It doesn't do any good to ask these questions over and over again. Look for them. Don't just stand here talking to me. Every hour you spend talking to me means there's less chance of finding them.* Her eyes pleaded with Detective Ryder to make them stop. She burst into tears.

"That's enough." Detective Ryder stood to his feet poised for a fight with anyone who asked one more question. "Let's get back to the house and see what we can find."

"Jackie, Oh my God, Jackie. I'm so sorry. I didn't mean for this to happen." Celeste ran to Jackie's bedside and collapsed on the bed beside her, begging to be forgiven. Wasn't she supposed to be missing? For a moment they just stared at her.

"Where are Michael and Lizzy?' Jackie was crying, reaching her hands towards the blonde hair lying on the bed beside her.

"I don't know. I don't know. I only left for a little while. You were asleep and Michael said they'd be okay if I ran home to get my…" she tried to go on, but she broke down again.

"You left them alone? You left them alone? Oh God, no. Not my babies. Not my babies." Jackie was sobbing uncontrollably.

"I'm sorry. I'm so sorry. Please forgive me. Please."

One of the policemen gripped Celeste under the arm and brought her to her feet, " Get up please. We need to talk. Would you come with us?"

The policeman walked Celeste out the door and down the hall to a private waiting room and began to interrogate her. She kept repeating that she didn't know what happened. She didn't plan on being gone very long, but a friend phoned the apartment while she was getting a few things and time just got away. The next thing she knew, she was speeding down the street two hours later. She didn't mean to be gone so long. How could she be so stupid?

While the other policemen questioned Celeste, Detective Ryder stayed behind with Jackie. He reached over to her and touched her on the hand. It was awkward for him as he sat beside her on the bed trying to figure out how to comfort her. Before he could stop himself he was embracing her, letting her sobs break on his shoulder. "We'll find them, we'll find them. I promise. We'll find them." He rocked her back and forth and held her as he spoke.

The doctor came in a few minutes later. "Well, Mrs. Pennington amazingly you don't have any broken bones. Your head took quite a few stitches and your shoulder was dislocated, but I think you'll be okay."

"I want to go home." Jackie didn't acknowledge the doctor anymore than that. She only had one thing on her mind. Finding her children and Jonathan.

"If I remember correctly, when you get it in your head to go, nothing much will stop you. So, Detective Ryder, she's all yours. You will be sore. The shoulder will mend, but you must keep it still. At least promise me that. The sling you're wearing will only help you if you keep it on. You've suffered a concussion as well, but as long as you rest at home, you'll be okay. Someone should wake you every two hours for at least 24 hours"

It didn't really matter what the doctor was saying. Jackie was sitting on the edge of the bed motioning for her clothes before he finished his sentences. She asked the nurse for help and the gentlemen excused themselves so she could change. She didn't care that she was putting back on a bloodied nightgown. She was going home.

❧

At home, the Detective Ryder helped her up the steps and into the house. Mary was kneeling over the blood stained tile scrubbing it with a brush and soapy water. "Miss Jackie," she said as she stood to her feet. "How are you feeling? Let me help you." She took Jackie's good arm and led her into the spotless living room. "I've been cleaning up the mess here, but the blood is a little stubborn. Nobody called. I came as soon as I heard and I've waited by the phone for news. I can't believe it. The children and Celeste too." They were sitting on the couch consoling each other as Celeste walked into the house.

Mary looked up shocked, expecting to see Michael and Lizzy come up behind her. But they never did. Jackie could see Mary wanted an explanation and told her what had happened. Now Mary was glaring at Celeste. *She was supposed to watch the children. She would never have left them with that woman if she thought she'd let them out of her sight.* She felt like throwing the doll at her. Lizzy's doll, Samantha. Suddenly Mary was crying, holding the doll and sobbing. She and Jackie sat embracing each other as Celeste looked on from a distance. She left them alone and walked into the kitchen. It was almost time for lunch, as if anyone was hungry.

The house had been checked inside and out. There was no evidence of a break in or a struggle and except for the broken living room window, which the detective had smashed, the house was secure. To everyone's relief, the detectives brought in a surveillance van with all their equipment and set up in the driveway instead of the house. It was less chaotic and disruptive with it outside, but Jackie still had enough. She pressed her hand against her forehead.

"Come on, Jackie. Up to bed. Just for a while." Assisted by the strong arms of Detective Ryder, she carefully maneuvered the steps to her bedroom.

The door shut behind him and once again, she was confined and in tears. When would this nightmare end?

The hustle from all the officers kept the house alive as they pulled the investigation together. They put out an All Points Bulletin, the Amber Alert, and search parties were being formed. No one knew if Michael and Lizzy set out to look for Celeste together or if they were abducted. The big question was how someone could get in the house. All of the doors had been locked and bolted and without a key there wouldn't be a way in or out without breaking down the door. Who had keys? Mary did. But she loved the children and would never think of doing anything to them. What would be her motive? Celeste had a key, but lost it years ago. There was no one else besides Jonathan and...

The detectives were thinking aloud. "Mr. Pennington could have done this. We don't know where he is or why he is missing. Maybe the Pennington's relationship was completely unstable and he established a new residence and took them last night after he had a place for them to stay." Speculation was part of his job. "If he had been afraid of a custody battle, he could have just pulled them out and run off."

Detective Ryder didn't agree, but had a hard time convincing the others that his theory of Jonathan's partner being involved was credible. He could tell that the other officers were territorial. After all, this case wasn't even in his jurisdiction so what was he doing there in the first place?

A verbal battle was heating up as Mary walked in the dining room where the detectives were all arguing. She picked up her cane, raised it over her head and brought it down on the cushion of a chair. Everyone stopped talking as she walked through the room and into the kitchen.

"I think that's our cue to leave," said one of the detectives. "Let's go guys. We've got work to do at the precinct."

With Jackie resting upstairs, the detective walked into the kitchen to report to Mary that they were leaving. Celeste moved from room to room listening to the police and watching Mary go about daily chores as if nothing had happened to the children. She remained silent and calm - which was totally out of character.

Detective Ryder had become the spokesman for the house and ushered the officers outside. "I'll pick up the phone if anyone calls. You can listen from the van. I'm sure Mrs. Pennington will be down before long. She refused to take any medication at all."

A few moments later the house was quiet again. Mary was in the kitchen. Celeste sat in the living room sipping a cup of tea and Detective Ryder roamed the rooms, pacing. *What a mess!*

The hours dragged on. Mary stopped working and sat at the kitchen table staring out at the woods behind the house. Celeste walked in and tried to make small talk, but Mary just glared at her. *Stupid woman. She left the children alone and now they're gone*! Celeste could feel the tension and walked out the back door while Detective Ryder positioned himself in the front rooms pacing between the dining room to the living room and back again. It was hard to wait for any communication from the abductor. The ticking clock was the only noise in the room.

Upstairs Jackie awoke from yet another nightmare rose cautiously from the bed and pulled on a pair of blue jeans. She struggled with the sling around her aching shoulder. Zipping her pants was almost impossible and excruciatingly painful. She winced. It seemed too difficult to get a T-shirt over her head, so she got a button-down blouse, slid her arm out of the sling long enough to put it through the sleeve and then repositioned the binder.

She glanced at her bedside table. There were three prescription bottles sitting there, two from her doctor after falling down the stairs, and one bottle of sleeping pills from Celeste. The pain medication was definitely inviting, but she needed to think clearly. *No more pills for me at all*, she thought. *Whatever I've been taking cost me my children. If I had been more awake, Celeste wouldn't have been watching them instead of me, I wouldn't have fallen down the stairs and my children wouldn't have been taken from me.*

Jackie went into the master bathroom and splashed cold water on her swollen face. She didn't take time to examine her bloodshot eyes or the bruises covering her body. Make-up was neatly positioned on a glass tray near the sink, untouched. It didn't matter anymore. Nothing mattered now.

She toweled off, combed through her hair and left the room. Before she descended the stairs she looked into Michael's room, hoping to see him playing with his game boy on his bed. Of course, he wasn't there. She peered into Lizzy's room, pushing open the door. There on her bed she found Samantha, Lizzy's doll. *Mary must have put it there.* Jackie couldn't resist going over to the bed and stroking the doll's dress. She sat down on the bed, holding onto the doll as if it was Lizzy. "Noooooo….." She couldn't help herself. She could hear that she was screaming, but she couldn't stop.

Detective Ryder raced up the stairs and reached the bedroom before Mary could climb the back staircase. "Jackie? What is it? Jackie?"

Mary's limp was more pronounced as she, too, bounded into the room. The detective had already slid his arm around Jackie, holding her as she wept uncontrollably. Jackie's sling stopped Mary from embracing her, but it didn't prevent her from sitting as close to her as she could. Detective Ryder guided her from the bed to escort her back to her room, but Jackie pulled away from him and headed downstairs holding Lizzy's doll in her arms.

Halfway down the stairs the front door opened as Celeste came back into the house. "Jackie, you okay, honey?" She waited just inside the door for Jackie, Detective Ryder and Mary to come down and then she took Jackie's good arm and directed her to the couch. They sat together, Jackie's head buried in Celeste's shoulder. Detective Ryder and Mary exchanged disapproving glances. This would never have happened if Celeste hadn't left the children alone, and both of them held her accountable.

No one felt like eating supper, but Mary made sandwiches anyway just in case anyone got hungry. Mostly they sat in silence, taking turns staring at the news on the television and watching the silent phone. Helicopters were still circling the estate and volunteers were expanding their search after combing the grounds looking for clues. Lizzy and Michael had vanished without a trace and there was no evidence of who had taken them - or why they had been taken.

Once an hour a detective came inside to update the family about the search, but it was always the same thing. No one has seen them; the search, though expanded, hasn't turned up anything. "I know it's not what you wanted to hear, Mrs. Pennington, but we aren't giving up. Volunteers are working really hard to find them."

Celeste chimed in, "Do you think it would help if she made a statement to the press. You know, a plea for whoever took them to bring them back? I've seen that on TV before."

"We could certainly arrange for that, Mrs. Pennington, if it's what you want." The detective sat on the edge of the sofa waiting for Jackie to speak.

"Do you think I should, Bob?" She turned to Detective Ryder with pleading eyes - *Please, tell me what you think. I don't want to make any decisions anymore. I'll do whatever you say.*

"Set it up as soon as possible, will you?" Detective Ryder directed his comment to the other officer.

"I'll see what I can do, but I think it will probably be morning before we can get someone out here. It's almost 10:00." The detective was apologetic as he continued.

"I'm sorry, Mrs. Pennington, really I am."

"Thank you," was all she could muster in return.

"Maybe you should try to get some sleep. You're going to need it." Again Celeste was making suggestions for Jackie's well being.

"I'm not leaving this room. I don't want to go back upstairs."

As emphatic as she was, Celeste knew better than to argue with Jackie. Instead, she brought down pillows and blankets for everyone, including Mary who refused to go home for the night. Mary gave Jackie some hot chocolate and all three watched as she slowly sipped it. Detective Ryder was the first to gently encourage her to lay down on the sofa. He tucked a blanket in around her like a cocoon. It was 12:48 AM.

Chapter 26

How did the hours pass? Suddenly it was morning. Jackie could hear Celeste humming in the kitchen, making coffee as if nothing was wrong.

Mary hobbled into the living room with a tray, encouraging Jackie to take a bite. "You've got to eat something, honey. You need the strength. The press is already setting up outside."

Detective Ryder straightened up the room, folding blankets and topping them with the pillows. "I'll just run these up to the closet, if that's okay."

"Thanks." Jackie replied. She rose from the couch and headed to the bathroom to freshen up. She brushed through her hair, applied a little lipstick and wiped underneath her eyes to try to get rid of the dark circles. *What difference did it really make how she looked, anyway? All she wanted was to get her family back.* She left the bathroom and went upstairs to change her clothes. When she came back down, Detective Ryder was standing at the front door flanked by Celeste and Mary.

"Are you ready?" The detective grabbed hold of her elbow to support her as she walked out of the house to the steps where the reporters were standing with their microphones and cameras.

The statement came from the police chief who had volunteered to be a spokesman for the family. His speech was well written and poignant. He pleaded for the safe return of Jonathan and his children as well as offering a reward for any information regarding their whereabouts. As soon as his rehearsed comments were finished, he turned to Jackie and offered his hand for assistance to help her to the podium.

She spoke so softly that one of the reporters adjusted the microphone and asked her to repeat her plea. She started again. "I don't know who is doing this, and I don't know why, but I am pleading with you. Please return my family to me. Tell me what you want. I'll find a way to get it for you. Please, don't hurt my children. Michael is only nine and Lizzy is just…" she stumbled. "She's just a baby." Jackie broke down. Detective Ryder moved to her side and ushered her back into the house while Celeste and Mary followed.

The police chief returned to the platform. "On behalf of the family, I'd like to thank all those who are helping search for the children and Jonathan. Mrs. Pennington is grateful for the cards and letters and especially your prayers. Thank you."

The reporters began simultaneously asking questions that were left unanswered. "That's all we have at this time." The Chief of Police wasn't willing to give any information regarding the investigation. "I'm sorry, we can't get into any details. Thank you for coming."

The press conference was over almost as quickly as it began. The crews gathered their cameras, lights and cords and left abruptly, scurrying to yet another breaking story. Children went missing everyday, but there was an abandoned warehouse on fire and that made spectacular footage. To add to the excitement, a woman's charred body was discovered at the scene. A death was more interesting to their audience- unless, of course, it was the death of an innocent child.

It had been over twenty-four hours since Jackie had seen her children. She knew that every hour was critical if they were to be found alive. But there were no calls for ransom, no answers as to why they were gone, just like Jonathan who had now been missing for twelve days.

Celeste was the first to admit she had other things she needed to do. She apologized profusely and promised to return by suppertime. She hurried out the door.

Detective Ryder sat Jackie beside him on the couch and pulled both her hands to him. "Jackie, tell me about Jonathan. I need to know anything and everything you can think of. Don't leave anything out."

"Why?" Jackie pulled her hands away from his and inched her way to the side of the couch. "What are you thinking?"

"I'm not thinking. That's the problem. I felt so sure of myself at first. I thought it had to be Peter Anderson and something to do with his clinic, but now that the kids are missing too, I can't fit all the pieces together." He watched the expression on her face as her eyes closed and she heaved a heavy sigh. "I need to know more about your life, how you met, who your friends are… anything that will put the puzzle together." He leaned into her. "Don't hold back on me. Please!"

"Where do you want me to start?" Jackie seemed ill at ease, but willing.

"Tell me how you met and started dating. We'll go from there."

"We met at Virginia Commonwealth University. He was in law school and I was in the College of Education. I'd seen him around, but he was always with a couple of other people, usually girls. I slipped and fell outside of the library and he came to my rescue and got them to call an ambulance for me." Jackie was condensing the version she always told her children, telling him only that he was popular and she was like cellophane- invisible to the crowd.

Detective Ryder chided her. "If you were so invisible then how come he fell so hard for you? Damsel in distress syndrome?"

"Maybe." Jackie blushed. "It was probably one of the reasons I fell so hard for him. He had no idea who I was, but he made sure I was taken care of at the scene and then tried to get in the ambulance with me. They wouldn't let him in. I could hear him ask which hospital they were taking me to when they closed the doors. They yelled out the answer, but he didn't hear them. He just assumed they'd take me to the nearest hospital, but I wasn't at that one.

Detective Ryder was taking notes. Taking notes on a twelve-year-old story! What did that have to do with her family missing? Jackie trusted Bob and continued without missing a beat.

"Jonathan went to the wrong hospital and started asking every staff member in the emergency room where I was."

Detective Ryder interrupted her. "How did he know what your name was if no one in his crowd knew you?"

"He picked my books up from the ground where I fell and looked through them until he found identification in one of them."

With a smug look, the detective replied. "Clever guy!"

"Yes, very. Anyway, he told me later that they practically threw him out on his…" She decided she didn't want to describe what he almost landed on and continued. "Well, they politely asked him to leave because he was creating such a ruckus. He really thought I was there and that they were just being difficult. It wasn't until he began pacing back and forth in front of the emergency room that the security man asked him if he had considered that I might be at another hospital." She chuckled. "He said it was as if he was struck by lighting. Every hair on his neck was standing up. He hailed a cab and headed to the right one."

"And then?

"Then they wouldn't let him in to see me. He didn't lie when they asked him if he was a relative. He couldn't even say he was a good friend. After all, we had never met before!"

"I'd have lied!" Detective Ryder was smiling as he scribbled down the names of the hospitals. It probably didn't have anything to do with the disappearance of Jackie's family, but he didn't want to leave any holes in his investigation this time.

"Yes, well. He didn't. Instead he tried to wait until they released me, but he must have been getting a cup of coffee when Cindy came to pick me up."

"Cindy?" Detective Ryder hadn't heard that name before and perked up thinking maybe it was a new lead.

"Cindy was my only friend at college. Mom and Dad couldn't travel from Indiana, so she borrowed her landlord's car and drove me back to my room. I had no idea Jonathan was waiting all that time. The nurse told me someone was asking about me, but I just assumed the nurse was mistaken. Anyway, Jonathan started asking around about me and sat on the stoop outside the library- shivering in the cold- just to figure out who I was. He told me later that all his friends told him to forget about me, but he just couldn't."

"Smart guy, if you ask me." As soon as Detective Ryder said that, he regretted it. He didn't want her to think he was moving in on her. Not that he wouldn't love to get close to her, but this was neither the time nor his place right now. He admitted to himself that he had mixed emotions about finding Jonathan at first, but now her children were missing too and it put a different spin on the whole thing.

Although he really didn't believe it, he had entertained the idea that Jonathan had left Jackie- who knew why. But now that the kids were gone too, he didn't think that was a possibility at all. Something awful was happening and he needed to get to the bottom of it for her sake.

"Even though he knew my name, no one knew where I lived, so sitting around the steps of the library finally paid off- for him and for me. I had been so embarrassed about making a scene when I fell that I had deliberately stayed away from the place. But when I needed to look up something for my English paper, I had to go back there. He stood to his feet and ran up to me. I was so scared. He was shaking me and saying, "It's you! It's you!" I remember standing there, frozen in my tracks. I knew what he meant, but I had no idea he'd been looking for me. He put his arms around me and squeezed. My arms just hung at my sides, I was so dumbfounded."

Detective Ryder was listening, pretending it didn't matter to him that she was reliving a time he wished he could have experienced with her.

"I don't know exactly what happened after that. He just never let go. Well, you know what I mean. He walked me to classes, we studied together at the library, and he took me to the movies. I'd never let anyone get that close to me before, and whenever I said we were moving too fast, he'd just laugh and say 'Too fast according to whom?'"

"How about your mutual friends? Who were they?" The detective was trying to find someone who may have been jealous of their relationship.

"Didn't really have any. Jonathan barely had time for me while he was studying for the bar, and Cindy and I hardly saw each other. In fact, we didn't know who to have stand up for us at our wedding. We always thought it would just be his twin sisters, but they died in a car accident along with Jonathan's parents."

"I know. I asked Mary about Jonathan's family when I first started the investigation. Really tragic. Was that rough on him?"

"Rough on him? That's an understatement. He hardly got out of bed for weeks. I was the only one he'd let in his apartment. His cousin tried to see him, but he just couldn't stand the idea of talking to anyone. We sat on his couch and stared at the television instead of studying. He even missed some classes. It was a bad semester for both of us, but we got through it. At least, I thought we did."

"What's that suppose to mean?" The questioning eyes gave him away before his lips moved.

"Jonathan recovered. I didn't do as well as he did. He's an amazing man. He pulled himself together and finished fourth in his class, passed the bar and started practicing law with a big firm. He was an immediate success. I, on the other hand, had Michael and then fell apart."

"Fell apart?"

"I had a breakdown. Jonathan came home night after night and found me yelling, or crying, or sitting on the couch staring into space. He had to find someone to watch Michael because he was so worried about me. He's the most understanding guy in the world. He'd walk in the bedroom where I had buried my head under the covers, lift them and gently kiss me on the forehead. I'd just look up at him and start to bawl. What a baby I was!"

"What happened? Was it really because his family was gone?"

"That wasn't the only thing that had happened in my life and I had a hard time accepting the fact that it wasn't my fault that so many people were dead." She could tell that Bob was shocked by her comments and began to explain. "My best friend, Gina, drowned when we were playing by the river without permission. She was only seven. His parents and sisters died because I told

Jess she should drive more often to get over her fear of it. She was distracted and went over the tracks when a train was coming."

"And that was your fault?" He couldn't believe she could really feel that way.

"Then my father had a massive heart attack and I wasn't there for him. I didn't come until the weekend and he died before I got to see him. Pretty pathetic, aren't I?"

"What do you mean by that?"

"I mean, all these years of therapy and I still feel responsible for everything that went on. I fight it everyday. Right now I want to scream and tell you and Celeste and Mary to run for your lives before you are cursed like everyone else in my life. It's really all I can do to keep still inside." The tears were back again. *Why can't I be stronger?*

"Wow!" He really didn't have a clue what to say. 'Wow' was the only thing that came out of his mouth.

"Yea, tell me about it. I didn't want you to see this side of me. I thought maybe I could prove to someone that I wouldn't fall apart. Here I am, no closer to the truth about where my kids or Jonathan are and I'm just sitting on my couch lamenting over my past."

"Did you forget I asked you to give me details about your life so that I could get a clearer picture?" The detective put his pad and paper down and moved closer to Jackie. With one hand on her chin, he lifted her face and forced her to look into his eyes. "It hasn't been easy for you, Jackie. I know that. I've checked you out. I know about your mental collapse and your hospital stay. I know you've seen a psychologist in the past, and I know that you keep in contact on an as needed basis. There's nothing to be ashamed of. You've won more battles than I've even been in! You are strong. And good. And I don't believe I'm cursed because I know you."

She moved her head away from his hand trying to avoid eye contact.

"When we find your family, you'll see just how important you are to them. I'm sorry you've had such a tough time, but we'll get whoever did this. I know we will."

All she could do was nod her head. She hoped he was right.

Chapter 27

It was Kathy's body the firemen discovered at the warehouse. A.J. and Peter had fought over the best location to dump her. Peter had wanted to wrap her in a plastic bag and discard her in a remote location. Dr. Ferguson had argued that it would appear to be a homicide that way and since they had injected her, he thought they could make it look as if she died from an overdose. He had the forethought to put more needle marks in her arms and even between her toes to prove she had been using for a long time.

So, Peter went along with his friend's plan- including the fire and dumped Kathy's body in the warehouse before they torched it. They thought it would be more difficult to identify a charred body since it would remove any trace of evidence left behind.

There was only one problem. The body was rescued from the fire before the ankle bracelet Kathy wore could be destroyed. Dr. Ferguson was usually a very detail oriented man, but finding an I.D. bracelet on a dead body was a huge mistake.

The police soon established that the 'Kathy' engraved on the gold chain was indeed the same person whose car was impounded.

Linking her to the law office of Anderson and Pennington was just a step away. Peter was flushed with rage and worry. His life was being destroyed. His loyal employee and partner had seen to that. Now what was he to do? He knew his old pal, Dr. Ferguson wouldn't be implicated. His tracks were covered.

Peter didn't want to keep Kathy alive as long as they had but Dr. Ferguson insisted. He didn't think she would even be missed since she didn't have any family so discarding her body in the dump would be simple. No one would care or notice. But Dr. Ferguson kept her drugged in the empty, upstairs apartment above Peter's garage. His friend, the good doctor, helped him tie her to the bed and left syringes filled with narcotics so that if she came around she could quickly be put under again.

A.J. taught him how to inject her and warned him to continue the injections every six hours- no matter what. Peter followed his instructions religiously, returning from the office at odd times to make sure she was still unconscious. He listened to the news faithfully and realized that no one even knew that Kathy was missing. He thought to himself, see, she really is a nobody and nobody will even know she is gone.

The police didn't investigate Kathy's disappearance because no one had talked to them about a missing person. Nothing indicated foul play at the scene, and there was no reason to doubt the innocence of an abandoned vehicle in the alley. The tire, after all, was completely deflated and the car could not have been driven in that condition. The abandoned car would remain in the lot until the owner contacted the department to retrieve it, and if no one claimed it, it really didn't matter.

Too bad. Perhaps if they had retraced the last few hours of Kathy's life immediately after they had found the car, they could have saved her. It took Peter that long to determine what to do with her once he realized that she was out to destroy him. She thought he hadn't seen the copies she'd made, but he had learned how to deceive people early in life and he covered his tracks well. He had briefly glimpsed the contents as they were strewn across the floor. The word 'confidential' was plastered on every sheet. She had obviously found Jonathan's evidence and was taking it to the police.

That was why he decided to walk around the block, away from the building when he did. He knew she would feel safer if he wasn't hanging out at the office, but he needed to be able to follow her once she left. His pocketknife came in handy when he used it to puncture her tire. She didn't even notice how low it was until she was a block from the firm.

He had waited patiently out of view until he saw her drive off in her car with a flat tire. He was laughing as he made a dash for his own car and followed her down the street and into the alley. It was easier than he ever dreamed possible. Catching up to her took only minutes. And getting the rope was sheer genius. Peter took pride in his ability to think and make quick decisions. The idea to abduct Kathy was good- he knew he had to stop her- but now what was he supposed to do with her?

When he pulled up behind her in his BMW, she checked her rearview mirror and saw him get out of the car. All Kathy could think was how glad she was that she had decided not to take the copied paperwork with her. If Peter Anderson had seen those files with her outside of the office, he would have fired her right then and there. It was company policy that all files remained in the building unless there was written permission from the attorney stating the reason it should be released for out-of-building recording. And she didn't have permission from anyone.

As an afterthought, Kathy had returned to the office and shoved the copies in a file drawer in the storage room, next to the exit. The archive section was a wonderful hiding place for papers no one else should see. Jonathan's only mistake was trusting Kathy with his secret. Now Kathy knew where he put his highly sensitive materials.

When Peter approached the car, Kathy was opening her purse and fumbling for her cell phone. She barely had it flipped open when Peter jerked open the door and yanked her out of her seat and onto the ground in the alley. *Why had she been so stupid?* Kathy thought. Pulling off into a dead end alley made her too vulnerable and sure enough, her greatest fear had become a reality.

Peter kept his voiced hushed as he bent over her. "You've been trying to destroy me for a long time now, haven't you?" He had a tight hold on her upper arm and a knee in her ribs. Having caught her off-guard, he pulled her up and pushed her into his car, strapping her hands behind her back with a rope he bought from the store around the corner from his building just an hour earlier.

But he hadn't planned it out well enough. Now he was stuck with an employee tied up in the back of his BMW. Where could he go? Should he take her home to the wife saying, "Hi Honey, I'm home?" or "Guess who's coming to dinner?"

NewStart Clinic. I'll take her there, he thought. Peter felt certain that he could get her to talk at the clinic and then he would find out where he stood with Jonathan and the police. He had to know how much the cops knew so that he could make up a viable story for them if they were going to come after him.

The clinic wasn't far from the office. When they arrived, Peter pulled around back and maneuvered Kathy inside, carefully looking over his shoulder all the while. The back lot was extremely secluded and therefore, quiet. No one was around to see her struggle or hear her scream.

His impulsive move didn't seem so intelligent anymore. What was he doing with her? All he wanted to do was know what kind of things she could use against him. He didn't really want to hurt her. But now, he didn't seem to have a choice. She could wind up at the police station as soon as he let her go. She'd make it sound like she was kidnapped instead of just detained and they'd have him in jail before he knew what hit him. Feeling more desperate with every new thought of how absurd this move was for him, he forced her into one of the examination rooms and tied her on the table with the rest of the rope.

"You brought this on yourself, Kathy. I tried to be nice to you and all you did was slap me in the face. I'd really like to know what you have against me. Where are those papers you copied?" Peter was pacing back and forth next to the metal table.

"What papers?" Kathy was stalling. She knew what he was referring to.

"What papers? The papers you were illegally copying in my office, at my firm. The ones that had confidential stamped all over them! I know what you were planning to do with them. Now where are they?" His voice was no longer hushed as he shouted into her face, realizing that he should have checked her car for them.

"I don't know what you're talking about. The only papers I copied were the files I told you that needed to be discussed at Monday's meeting. I left them there, in Jonathan's office."

Peter stormed out of the room and slammed the door. Kathy began struggling with the ropes, hoping they would loosen and she could escape while Peter was so frazzled, but he had tied her up too well. She was helpless and frightened.

It took a while for Peter to establish his next move. A sudden stroke of genius! He'd call Dr. Ferguson. He was the one that got him into this mess in the first place and he would have to help him get out of it!

"A.J, this is Peter. You've got to come to the clinic right away." Peter's voice was commanding.

"I was just there a little while ago. Can't this wait? I've got company."

"No, it can't. Get over here now!"

While Peter waited for A.J. to get there, he discretely looked out every window, checking to see if anyone was lurking around outside. The streets were unusually quiet for a late Saturday afternoon in the neighborhood.

Fifteen minutes later, A.J. slid his key in the back door lock and was inside hunting for Peter. "Don't open that door," Peter cried out as he walked down the hall from the clinic's waiting room.

"Yes, sir!" A.J. replied sarcastically.

Peter moved faster and ushered A.J. into the office beside the examining room where he held Kathy prisoner. "We've got a problem."

"We've got a problem? I don't recall having any problems." Another sarcastic statement.

"Okay, I've got a problem, which will soon involve you. Is that better?" Peter could be just as nasty as anyone else and sarcasm rolled off his tongue with ease.

"What are you talking about?"

"One of my secretaries knows everything. I had to bring her here to keep her from going to the police."

"You what?"

"You heard me. She was going to go to the police and tell them everything. What else could I do?"

"You brought her here? What'd you plan to do with her?" A.J. was furious at Peter.

"That's the problem. I don't know what to do now. She denies knowing anything and if I turn her loose, she'll run to the police saying I kidnapped her." There was panic in Peter's voice.

"You did kidnap her you idiot! You've made a real mess here and now you want me to clean it up. That's priceless!" A.J. was so aggravated at Peter that he punched the wall between his office and the examining room. Kathy's startled scream was piercing. A.J. heard the noise. "Wow, you weren't kidding, were you?"

"I don't kid about things like this. I'm telling you, we've got to do something."

"And what is it you propose we do? Kill her?" A.J. was now calmer, breathing deeply to restore control to his body.

"Don't be so caustic. I asked you to come here to help me. I know I made a mistake, but I thought that maybe you could help me figure out what to do. I don't want to go to jail and if she gets away from us, we will!"

"What's this "we" bit? I don't recall grabbing her out of the office." A.J.'s protesting of innocence made Peter sick.

"Look, if it wasn't for you, I wouldn't be in this trouble in the first place. You are as much a part of this as if you picked her up yourself. And, just for the record, I grabbed her out of her car, not the office. And nobody saw me. I made sure of that!"

"Alright, shut up, will you? I need time to think. Go quiet your friend down in there while I decide how to do this."

A.J. mulled ideas over in his head. Letting her go just didn't seem to be an option. But killing her seemed so extreme. In the end, he couldn't come up with a plan that would spare her life.

Peter checked on Kathy while he waited for Dr. Ferguson's brilliant solution while Kathy pleaded with her captor. "Let me go, Mr. Anderson. I promise I won't say a word. We'll just forget this ever happened. I'll resign with a letter to the firm and mail it. I don't even have to step foot in the office again. You can even have all my personal things sent to my house. Just let me go." Kathy looked pathetic as she begged for her life.

"I seem to remember a time when I approached you with a request and you turned me down flat. In fact, you threatened a lawsuit if I so much as touched you again. And now you want me to believe that if I let you go you will just quietly leave and never mention this incident to a soul? I doubt that very much." As Peter talked, he was looking at all the supplies in the room.

"What do you want from me? I don't know anything. You've got it all wrong." She was pleading for his trust.

"Doesn't matter anymore, now, does it?" Peter's comments were interrupted by A.J.'s call for him. "I'll be back soon. You just rest now."

Dr. Ferguson stopped him outside in the hall. "Look, I don't like this one bit, but I've been thinking. Our only choice is to get rid of her. You're right, if we don't, she'll go to the police and we'll both be locked up."

"Have you got a gun?" Peter's eyes widened as he questioned him.

"I think I've got something better. In this business, there are ways of making a homicide look like a suicide or, better yet, an overdose. I see that kind of thing all the time. All we need to do is sedate her, get her away from the clinic and then inject her and like magic, no more Kathy, no more problems!" A.J. was proud of his idea and confident that they could get away with it.

For Peter, the only thing that mattered was that she wouldn't compromise his precious lifestyle. Reluctantly he agreed and watched as A.J. walked into the examining room, introduced himself to his victim and began calmly talking about the treatment she would need.

"Well, hello, Kathy, is it? Nice to meet you. I'll be your doctor today." He bent over her and looked into her eyes. "Nothing to be afraid of now. I'll take good care of you."

Kathy squirmed and started to scream, but the good doctor muffled her cries with his hand. "Now, now, you don't want to frighten the neighbors, do you? This won't hurt a bit. In fact, you'll be asleep in no time. And won't that feel good? Just relax now." He motioned to Peter to come to her side. "Whisper sweet nothings to her while I get the needle ready will you? I can't stand it when people scream in my ear."

He went to the clinic's stash of medicine and pulled out a bottle. A small dose would settle her down and make her more cooperative. The rest would be given later, when they needed it.

As the doctor approached Kathy, she bit Peter's hand. He screamed out in pain and then pushed hard down on her chest and mouth to keep her from moving. "To think I ever cared about you! Do it, A.J., do it!"

Only Kathy's eyes could express her fear now. They widened in horror as she followed the needle to her arm and watched him plunge it in the vein. Heavily sedated, with a man on either side of her, Peter and A.J. then dragged Kathy out of the clinic with her legs dangling behind her.

They didn't even need to lock the doors of the BMW. Kathy wasn't going to cause anymore trouble.

After arguing about whether to kill her or let her go, both Dr. Ferguson and Peter determined that it was too dangerous to free her, but they needed time to devise their plan. Keeping her alive for a week wasn't really the problem. Finding the right place to ditch the body was.

Peter knew he shouldn't listen to his friend the doctor, but he didn't know what else to do.

*
Kathy lay in the rumpled bed, half dazed and dehydrated and her heart raced as she anticipated the next time Peter would return to give her another injection and immobilize her again. Each time he came back, Kathy feared it would be her last. She knew he was planning to kill her, but she just didn't know when.

As she lay in the bed, arms roped to the posts, she dozed fitfully. It had to be the shot he gave her that made her feel so groggy. Every four hours, like clockwork, he was at her side, filling her veins with just enough medicine to keep her quiet. Whenever she came out of the stupor, it would be time for another plunge, and there he was!

In her drugged state, Kathy would only be slightly aware of her surroundings and try to fight off the affects of the injection. It was during those half-conscious moments that she would sift through her past, looking for the reason she lay bound and gagged awaiting death.

How did she get where she was? Was God punishing her? She couldn't even wipe the tear running down her cheek as she thought about how her life had turned out. Her mother always said she end up in trouble. And now she was.

She was dreaming about Mildred, and as Kathy lay in the bed strapped to the posts, she begged God to spare her life and promised Him she would do better if only He would let her live. Mildred hadn't taught her to negotiate with God, but somehow it seemed like the only hope Kathy had left. Peter would return soon and he could easily kill her. How did she get messed up with him anyway? She fell back into a fitful sleep and began dreaming again.

She was dreaming about Mildred and how much they had grown to love each other. *After a year of living together, Mildred had settled into her status as a retired secretary with ease as Kathy took over full responsibility at the church and then came home to take care of the house. It seemed as if Mildred had less and less energy, but she never complained. When Kathy would tell Mildred she should see a doctor, Mildred would just sweetly look at her and say she was fine- just fine.*

Denial was a big part of their lives. Mildred would say she was fine, and Kathy wouldn't argue because she wanted to believe it was true. But when Kathy came home from the office one day, there was no denying that Mildred was very, very ill.

Mildred was lying on the floor in the living room, unable to move her right side or speak at all and it was nearly two minutes before Kathy called 911 because she was so distressed seeing her like that. The ambulance arrived seven minutes later. She knew the exact time because she kept checking her watch worrying about when they would come.

The doctor said it was a stroke. Kathy remained by Mildred's side in a constant vigil, sometimes crying, sometimes praying, as Mildred looked into Kathy's eyes with despair- not for herself, but for the anguish Kathy was experiencing. She tried to form the words "I'm not afraid to die" but Kathy misunderstood and thought she said, "I'm afraid to die." With that, Kathy would gently comb back Mildred's hair with her fingertips, wash her face with a warm cloth and hold her hand in hopes of comforting her best friend.

Mildred died from a massive heart attack two days later. Kathy planned the service and burial in the old church cemetery just as Mildred had requested in her will. Unbeknownst to Kathy, Mildred left her most of her estate- over fifty thousand dollars. Since Mildred had lived so frugally, Kathy had no idea she had so much money. In dutiful Christian fashion, Mildred made sure that her church received ten percent of the estate and had prepaid her own funeral arrangements. There was nothing left for Kathy to do but mourn the loss of the only person who so honestly and willingly loved her. Brokenhearted, she kept Mildred's things just the way she left them in her bedroom and for months Kathy continued to sleep on the pullout couch. Over the next few years, Kathy took computer course work, which improved her secretarial skills, and eventually she landed a job at Peter Anderson's law firm.

Now, as she lay in her drugged stupor, Kathy was inwardly kicking herself for copying those stupid papers. That was what made Peter suspicious of her in the first place and that's why he was willing to kill her. If Peter had been a better employer, she wouldn't have felt the need to look for work elsewhere, but she felt she had no choice. He was a bitter, unethical man. That's why she had copied the papers and started to take them out of the office. She was going to another attorney for advice on protecting clients at the Anderson firm because she knew Peter was cheating them. In her fitful dreams, she could see the anger in his face as he bent over the files that had fallen on the floor. Kathy's skin was crawling as she thought about Peter and how disgusting he was.

Just as she squirmed again in an attempt to loosen the ties around her, Peter let the door slam behind him as he entered the room where Kathy was tied to the bed. She pulled away from him as she approached her.

"Poor Kathy. I forgot to give you your injection, didn't I? And look, you're coming around, aren't you?" Peter's cynical and diabolical intent was clear as Kathy opened her eyes and saw his face looming above her. He bent over her and gently kissed her on the cheek. "Now that would be called sexual harassment at the office, wouldn't it? Well, you won't have to worry about that anymore! You know, I really didn't want to do this but you forced me to, Kathy."

She blinked back the tears and pulled away from him, but it was no use. He had won. The needle came from his right hand and was inserted into her vein. He had become a pro. One gentle push, and so long Kathy.

He called Dr. Ferguson to help him get her to the warehouse.

Chapter 28

It wasn't that they didn't want to stay. Honestly, they would, but there were no ransom calls and the police department was forced to tear down their unit and have the detectives conduct the investigation from the office instead. The most likely theory was that Jonathan had removed them from the house to avoid a lengthy custody battle.

Jackie cried as she looked out the living room window while they drove away. *They'll never find them now. Don't go. Please, don't go.* But they left without hearing her pleading because she didn't speak. She just stared out the window as her tears fell down her cheeks.

Detective Ryder had used up his vacation time and was forced to return to Beach City. "I'm really sorry, Jackie. I don't want to leave you alone, but if I don't show up for my shift, back home, they'll fire me. I'll be back as often as I can. I'll call you every day, if that's okay with you. I promise I won't give up looking, but I've got to do it from my office. I'll call the department here everyday and bug 'em until we find the kids. I won't let them stop looking, honestly".

He could hardly release her from their embrace and glanced back at her every other step as he approached his car. He wanted to say he'd stay, who cares about a job, but he didn't dare. As he waved goodbye, Jackie sat on the front porch step and nodded her head before she dropped it. She fidgeted with her hair before she buried her eyes in her hands.

As soon as Detective Ryder was out of sight down the long, wooded driveway, Mary stepped onto the front porch from the entryway. Limping to Jackie's side, she dropped down beside her and sweetly, gently wrapped her arm around her. They sat together until the sun began to go behind the trees.

The phone rang. Jackie jumped, but Mary put her hand on her shoulder as if to say "you stay" and she spoke. "I'll answer it."

Mary listened for a few minutes then replied "okay". There was little resistance offered to the caller.

She stepped back out on the porch, plopped down and stared at the ground.

"Who was that?"

"It was Harold. He wants me to come home tonight."

Mary's husband insisted that she come home before her health suffered anymore. He didn't understand how important it was for Mary to stay with Jackie. After all, he would say, the Penningtons aren't her family, he is. She broke down as she hugged Jackie, "I'm sorry, I'm so sorry. I'll be back as soon as I can tomorrow morning. It's just…"

"I know, Mary. I understand." Jackie said flatly. A half-hour later Mary's husband drove up. After a long embraced, she released her hug and watched as Mary waved goodbye from the car.

That only left Celeste, who had been coming and going most of the time anyway. Jackie walked up to the wingback chair Celeste was wrapped in, "It's okay, Celeste, you can go home. I'll be okay."

"I don't think you should be alone. I can stay." Celeste's protest seemed genuine, but Jackie wanted her to go.

"Maybe I'll feel differently in the middle of the night, but right now, I just want to be alone." Celeste embraced Jackie, but Jackie didn't respond.

"Listen, all you have to do is call me on my cell or at home. You know I'll come right back."

"I know. Thanks."

It took Celeste all of five minutes to get out the door leaving Jackie alone. Completely alone.

Jackie didn't eat the food Mary left for her. She couldn't stomach anything. She paced the house, listened to the news, and waited for the call that would get her children back. She picked up her cordless phone and climbed the steps to the master bathroom for a quick shower. There, on the bedside table were the pills that could help her escape her physical and emotional pain. After fighting with herself, she chose the bottle that would put her to sleep, temporarily. The pills that Celeste had gotten for her worked well and since there was no one to be awake for, Jackie decided it was okay to take two.

After her shower, Jackie returned to the sofa. She didn't want to sleep in her bed anymore. She preferred the couch. She checked the house to make sure the doors and windows were all locked before she lay down. She fell asleep easily once the pills took effect.

She heard it. She was sure. It was the sound of someone walking around the house. But she felt so groggy, so out of it. *I shouldn't have taken the pills.* Jackie listened again. It sounded as if it was coming from the kitchen. She tiptoed through the living room and into the dining room. As she went by the front door she noticed it was still bolted. *How could someone get in?* The basement door creaked as if it was closing and Jackie froze waiting for the sound of more footsteps.   Nothing.

What should I do? If she followed someone downstairs, she would be helpless if they attacked her. If she waited for them to come upstairs again, they could get her then too. But if she left the house, then she might miss the only opportunity she had to find out who took her children. She remained quiet and waited.

An hour passed with Jackie sitting alone, waiting for the intruder to come back up. No *one would stay in the basement. Jackie, you are such a fool. There wasn't anyone in the house.* Once again, she blamed the pills she had taken. She tried to sleep, but couldn't so she flipped on the television and watched a movie.

Outside Detective Ryder was sitting on Jackie's doorstep waiting for some sign of life in the house unaware that Jackie was watching T.V. He hadn't wanted to wake her, but he needed to be with her. He finished his shift at 11:00 PM and had driven back to make sure Jackie was okay. He put his hand on the button to press the bell as Jackie opened the door.

"Jackie, I..." Stumbling over his words he continued. "I just needed to see how you are. Uh, how are you?"

"Can't sleep too much, you know?"

"I know. Me neither."

"I took a couple sleeping pills last night hoping I could sleep better. Instead I had horrible dreams and even thought someone was in the house."

You could hear the panic in his voice as he responded. "In the house? You thought someone was here?"

"I even tiptoed around and crouched here in the corner of the dining room for an hour. How stupid is that?"

"What happened? What made you think someone was here?"

"I heard footsteps. That's what woke me. Then I heard something in the kitchen and I crept into the dining room to listen without being seen. I was sure I heard the creaking of the basement door. I listened for an hour and then felt pretty stupid. Every door was bolted. No one could have come in the house. I'm sure of it.

"Where's Celeste? I thought she was staying with you." Detective Ryder was obviously perturbed.

"I sent her home. I just couldn't look at her anymore. I don't know who I blame more, her or me. If I hadn't taken the pills, I would have been watching my own children. If I hadn't let her stay and take care of them, they wouldn't be missing now. It's just such a mess."

The detective moved the blanket on the couch to sit down.

"Samantha!" Jackie was frantically looking under the cover and couch.

"What?"

"Lizzy's doll. I've been sleeping with it since they disappeared. Now it's missing too. "

"Well, it's got to be here somewhere."

"It's not." Jackie was lifting blankets and pillows, throwing things around. "Look! It's not here."

"Listen, did you hear that?" Now it was Bob who was hearing things.

"What?"

"Shhh. Listen. I heard something in the basement." He drew his gun and headed for the basement staircase in the kitchen. "Stay here." He demanded.

Jackie didn't obey him. Instead, she followed close behind as he drew his gun. When he reached the door he held his left hand up to keep her at bay and slowly opened the basement door while standing to the side. Then with a fast move he held up his gun and scanned the stairwell. He flipped on the light and took one controlled step at a time. Jackie remained at the top of the stairs, cell phone in hand, ready to call the police at his command.

After inspecting the entire downstairs, Detective Ryder called up "Jackie, come down here."

"What is it?" Her dislocated shoulder ached so much she held it close to her side as she descended the stairs.

"What is this?" He was holding up a wig and a black hooded sweatshirt.

"I don't know. Where did you find it?" Jackie examined it closely as he led her to the fruit cellar. "In here. The shirt was right by the door, but the wig was clear across the room on the floor."

"It's not mine. I don't know whose it is." Jackie examined the shirt looking for some recognition of it. There was a coconut splattered on the floor. "Look at this. I bet that happened when the policeman came down here the day the prowler was outside."

"Didn't he see the wig or the sweatshirt?"

"He said something about feeling hair on the coconut later, but nothing about a wig or shirt. Maybe it wasn't there before."

"Well, how did it get here then?" The detective searched the room again, but found nothing else. Together they looked over the entire basement.

Jackie began moving the boxes across the room and gasped. "Bob, look at this." There behind some well-placed boxes was a small opening, only big enough to crawl through. She knelt down and started to crawl on her hands and knees.

"No you don't! I'm going first! Do you have a flashlight?"

"Somewhere around here." She found one a few minutes later and handed it to the Detective. "Be careful."

"Do you know where this goes?"

"Are you kidding? I didn't even know it was here!"

They began crawling on their hands and knees in the dark. Jackie suffered with every painful move trying to avoid using her right shoulder. "Looks to me as if someone else has been using this tunnel. I haven't run into a spider web yet."

"Spiders!" Jackie cringed as she spoke.

They crawled silently for fifteen minutes. "Is this thing ever going to end?"

"Shhh. I see light." Detective Ryder cautioned Jackie not to speak for fear someone would be waiting for them. He came up through brush and weeds and stood to his feet just in time to receive a blow to the back of the head with a shovel. Jackie saw him fall, screamed and turned around in the tunnel to retreat. Before she could begin the crawl back someone was grabbing at her ankles pulling her out of the tunnel.

"Let go. Let go" Jackie was screaming and kicking, but she was no match for her assailant, especially with one arm in a sling. Within minutes the fight was over and she was bound, gagged and blindfolded. The pain from her shoulder was intolerable and the blow to her head caused her to black out. She was dragged from the woods to a car waiting nearby. Her tiny body was flung into the trunk and the lid closed.

Detective Ryder blinked his eyes trying to focus. He was lying sprawled over the dirt and leaves surrounding him and he spit the debris from his mouth. His senses were just returning when he heard an engine start and looked up to see license numbers QJP700. He repeated the number three times, " QJP700, QJP700, QJP700". There was no way to catch up to the car. He could barely sit up. He grabbed his cell phone and dialed 911.

"We have a kidnapping in progress. License QJP700, repeat, license QJP700. Make of car is unknown, but it was a small sports car. Color unknown. Suspect has taken Jacqueline Pennington from her estate. I don't know the victim's condition other than a dislocated shoulder from a previous injury. The victim's husband has been missing for over two weeks and her children for three days."

The operator questioned him. " What? Oh, address not known but on record. The police have a missing persons file on Jonathan Pennington. They may need to look it up." He felt dizzy as he hung up the phone and lay on the ground to collect his thoughts and regain his strength.

Chapter 29

There was a click of a lock as the bedroom door opened. "Beth, look what I found! It's Samantha. I bet you were pretty worried about her, weren't you?" The doll was gently laid on the bed before the door closed. Michael watched as it was shut and locked again.

Lizzy ran to retrieve her doll and retreated to the bed made just for her. There she hugged her dolly and softly cried for her Mommy. Michael sat on the twin bed across the room from her. His game boy and a few of his favorite books were strewn over the top of his blanket, but he stared blankly at Lizzy. She had curled up into a ball huddled with Samantha, stroking the hair and saying "Everything will be okay, don't you worry, Samantha, everything will be okay."

The eight-by-ten room had one second-hand dresser, two twin beds and rustic bare wood floors. The windows were covered with boards nailed to the interior frame with brightly colored fabric draped over them to mask their dingy, dirty look. A television set was sitting on top of the dresser with rabbit ears twisted to find a station. A few play clothes for both Michael and Lizzy were tucked neatly in the drawers.

The tiny bathroom beside their room was overcrowded. A chipped bathtub with rust stains and a lime-coated faucet was squeezed between two interior walls. A cracked mirror hung above the soiled and spotted pedestal sink. The bolts on the toilet were filthy and loose, causing it to rock when even a small child sat on it. It frightened Lizzy every time she used it. There were putrid stains on the floor and inside the bowl and the ripped linoleum was full of dirt and grime from years of neglect.

In the room down the hall you could hear the rhythmic clanking and rubbing of chains. An extra bolt on the outside of the door was shifted open and the door unlocked. The conversation was barely audible to the children as they started talking.

"Why are you doing this? Please, just let us go. We'll get you help. I promise." Jonathan was pleading with his abductor, but there was no way he would be unchained. She had made that perfectly clear. The bathroom floor where he was forced to remain was equally as disgusting as his children's, but at least a rug had been provided for him to sleep on. The pipes were rusted together at the base of the sink. Though he had been trying to escape ever since he was taken, the chains were too strong to break and the pipes weren't giving way.

His captor refused to converse and walked out without a word.

Chapter 30

Detective Ryder was questioned repeatedly at the Pennington estate and showed his frustration about the delay in the investigation. "Look, you're wasting time. We've got to find Jackie before it's too late. Did you find out who owns the car?"

"It's registered to a Celeste Hanover. Ever heard of her?"

"That's Jackie's friend. She's been staying with her since Jonathan went missing. Did she report it stolen?" Detective Ryder was running images through his mind. *Was she there when the prowler came? Where was she when Jackie was attacked at the theater? Wasn't she there when the kids disappeared? No, she left. Or so she said. Could she really be behind this?*

It all made sense. When Jonathan disappeared nothing was missing from the ocean cottage. He never started his run because his shoes were still there. She could easily have met him there, asked him to go for a ride and then never let him return. She had access to the house, knew how the investigation was going, knew the kids' routines and could have followed Jackie anywhere she went. But why?

"We've got to find her. Did you try her apartment?" You could hear the panic in is voice.

"No one was there. The manager said he hasn't seen her for over two weeks, except for overnight once with a couple kids and their mom."

"That was Jackie. She stayed with Celeste one night after Jackie had a prowler at her house. Did the manager say anything else?"

"Just that Celeste was always bragging about her cute little Honda Z3 and the house she bought down by Duck Lake. Said she'd be out by the end of the month."

"Then that's where we should start. Did she say where on Duck Lake?"

"Nope."

"Let's go. We'll call the records department on the way. They should know something." Detective Ryder led the others to their cars.

Chapter 31

When she returned to the room, Celeste calmly delivered Jonathan his meal- a ham and cheese sandwich. She stroked his head and kissed his cheek and he squirmed to get away. She stiffened and spilled his juice on his pants. "Oh so sorry. I don't know how that happened. Let me wipe that up for you." She opened the palm of her hand and slid it towards the front of his pants. He took his chained hands and pushed her off of him.

Celeste lost her balance and fell against the sink. "This is exactly why I can't let you go. You haven't learned how to treat me yet. Didn't anyone ever tell you not to push the ones you love?"

"I've never loved you. Can't you get that through your head?" Jonathan's face was beat red and he was screaming at her. Though he was normally even tempered, she had gotten the best of him.

"Nasty, nasty. Can't imagine what you'd be like if your hands were free." She turned to leave and then looked back at him. "Oh, by the way. I brought the little wife back with me. Of course, she won't be your little wife for long. That will be my job. I was willing to let her alone, but she had to stick her uppity nose in my business, so I'll just make other arrangements for her now. I've got her out in the garage with the rest of the trash until I come up with a deadly accident for her. What'd you think? Should she drown? Or maybe she should she burn? I'm sure it will happen tonight, whatever I do!" she paused to watch him squirm. " Time will tell!" As she left, she blew him a kiss and gently closed the bathroom door.

She opened it only a second later, "Oh, Johnny Boy." Her acidic tone was making Jonathan shiver. " I've always wanted to call you that, 'Johnny Boy.'" She gestured open hands as if dancing, then pulled out a candy bar from her

Liz Clayborne jacket pocket and began eating it in front of him, savoring every bite and even pushing it to his nose. He pulled away in disgust.

"Oh honey, you are just so ungrateful. I'm amazed that I could love someone so mean spirited. But, I do recall the first day I was introduced to you. You remember it, don't you? You were such a hotty." She bent down close to him again, "Still are, for that matter, although you could use a shave."

"Jackie didn't know how good she had it. When she was wallowing in self-pity all those months in therapy, all I could think of was how beautiful you were and how ridiculously pitiful she was. You never left her side. I couldn't believe she didn't see how good her life really was. She was so annoying. It was all I could do to be nice to her. Dr. Stanley never let me see the files, but I knew she was a loony tune without ever reading his notes."

She continued as Jonathan sat quietly. "I quit a few weeks after she stopped seeing him when my inheritance came through. Mamma died and left me her house and a little bit of spending money from her life insurance. I'm not rich, but I'll be okay now that you and I are together."

Celeste loved egging him on. "She was so out of it, she didn't even know I was Dr. Stanley's assistant when I introduced myself later. I pretended I was one of her high school buddies and she believed me. God, was she dumb! I don't get it. How'd she ever graduate from college anyway?"

Celeste sat on the bathroom floor just far enough away from Jonathan so he couldn't kick her. "All I had to do was call the high school, pick a name from her high school yearbook they sent to me, and pretend I was her. I figured out what restaurant she liked to go to, waited around and when she showed up, I introduced myself to her as her long lost buddy, Celeste, from school."

She changed positions on the floor. "Did that medicine she overdosed on fry her brain? No matter what I said she agreed with me. Man, I had to work hard to become her best friend. She was always so paranoid about her friends dying that she kept to herself. What a battle! It was worth it though. Now I have you and Beth."

Jonathan was livid listening to her go on about Jackie. It was true. She was gullible and easily frightened, but he had been so protective of her that he thought she was stronger than she really was. He had no idea that Celeste wasn't really her high school friend.

"Well, I need to go now. I've got things to do." She walked out, then turned around again. "Oh yes, I was wondering. Did you ever take out a life insurance policy on Jackie? It would come in so handy - especially if it doubles with accidental death." She smiled and promptly shut the door again. He heard the lock click and threw his sandwich across the room into the tub. Frantically he started yanking and pulling on his chains to no avail.

Celeste walked down the hall and unlocked the children's door again. "Come on kids, let's go outside before it gets dark and play for awhile." Celeste was coaxing Michael and Lizzy out. "Beth, leave Samantha on the bed and come with me. She'll be there when you get back. I promise."

"Where's my Mommy?" Lizzy was still crying as Celeste took her by the hand and led her out the back door. The wooded lot was secluded on all four sides. Through the trees you could barely see the lake at the bottom of the hill. Celeste took hold of Lizzy's tiny wrist and forcefully tugged on Michael's shirt with her other hand. "Come on. I brought a ball from home for you. You need some exercise and fresh air."

For the next few minutes they threw the ball back and forth. Michael kept moving closer to Lizzy, and further from Celeste. Lizzy could barely catch the ball and kept running down the hill after it. Michael made sure he threw the ball harder at Celeste each time and when he felt certain he could reach Lizzy, he purposely overthrew the ball so that Celeste would have to chase it. When Celeste started down the hill to get it, Michael grabbed Lizzy by the hand and took off in the opposite direction and up the hill. Celeste was so engrossed in retrieving the ball she didn't hear them running away at first. It was only after they were yards from her that she began chasing after them.

"Michael, you'd better come back. It will be dark soon and you know how scared Beth will be if you don't bring her in. Michael, I'm not kidding." She was out of breath as she ran up the hill. She had to stop to catch it. "Michael, you come back here now!"

Go ahead and scream. I don't care. I want to go home and you can't stop me! Michael didn't dare speak, but he could think whatever he wanted. Lizzy begged him to slow down.

"We can't stop yet, Lizzy. She might get us. We have to keep moving," Michael was urging Lizzy to keep running. Lizzy tripped on a branch and started to cry when she saw the blood coming from the scratch on her leg.

"Shhh, please don't cry, Lizzy. Celeste will hear us." He picked her up and dragged her away as fast as he could.

Celeste wasn't able to climb the hill fast enough to keep up and finally stopped. She yelled at them. "Fine, stay out here. I don't care. There's no one out there who will help you anyway. You'll be back when you get hungry or tired. And maybe when it's dark, the animals will try to eat you. You'll be so frightened, you'll beg for me to come and get you. And when that happens, maybe I'll come and, and maybe I won't." Celeste turned and walked back towards the house. "Your call, Michael. Come back when you want."

Lizzy was just about to scream when Michael covered her mouth. "Don't say anything. She's just trying to scare us."

'"Well, I am scared!" Lizzy cried.

"I'll take care of you. We'll get to the road and someone will help us. You'll see."

"Which way is the road?" Lizzy waited for her brother to answer. "Michael, which way is the road?"

"Huh, I think it's up there." He pointed away from the house and up the hill. "We'll be there soon."

Celeste went back inside, unlocked the bathroom door where Jonathan was still chained, splashed her face with cold water and growled, "That son of yours is quite the man. He just took your little girl deep into the woods trying to get away. He thinks he's so smart, but he's heading in the opposite direction of the road. Too bad. They'll either be back cause they're so scared, or they'll get lost." She paused for effect and looked at Jonathan. "Either way is fine with me if he's going to act like that. Maybe something wild will get him." She snarled as she started to leave. " Oh yea, in case you were wondering, I've been thinking about what to do with Jackie. I've made a decision. Tonight is the night and I might as well handle it while the kids are gone. It'll be easier without them around anyway. So, I'll be gone for awhile. She and I are going to take a nice boat ride to the middle of the lake. I've found a few trinkets to attach to a nice ankle bracelet for her. But, don't worry, I have a few sleeping pills I can give her before we go. I wouldn't want her to suffer too much. You know?" She kicked up her heel, pointed her finger playfully and made a click with her tongue. "See you, sweetie!"

It was dark now. The children had been alone in the woods for nearly an hour, and Michael was sure they were going in circles searching for the road. He had been dragging his little sister up and down the hills so long that he had to rest himself. They sat together to catch their breath.

In the meantime, Celeste went out to the detached garage about 200 yards from the house and opened the swinging door. She chuckled as she saw Jackie sitting by the old tire and gasoline can. "Wow, honey, you're looking mighty fine." She was mocking her as she spoke. "Brought you out something to drink and a few pills to calm you down. Are you thirsty?" Celeste removed the tape covering her mouth long enough to force water down Jackie's throat.

Jackie glared at her, but couldn't do anything as the water went down. She choked and gagged.

"Good girl. You'll be a lot easier to deal with when you can't walk away from me. You're such a puny little thing anyway. What did Jonathan see in you?" She maneuvered a small, round, plastic snow sled into position near her. " This will help me get you down to the boat. You like boats don't you?" She didn't wait for an answer but loved watching Jackie's eyes as they expanded in fright.

"Oh, that's right, you're afraid of the water, aren't you? Something about one of your little girl friends drowning in a river? I'm right, aren't I? Yes I think I am." Celeste smiled big and nodded her head. "Perfect ending for you then, isn't it? Drowning." She thought to herself, *man, am I good or what*?

Jackie fought as best she could but the rope Celeste used to bind her was wrapped around her chest and waist so her arms wouldn't move. Her mouth had been taped shut again, but at least the blindfold had been removed. Her feet were bound with the same rope used to bind her chest. Celeste picked Jackie up and transferred her from the floor to the sled. "Convenient, huh? The people who lived here before left a few things behind. Works for me!"

Jackie shifted her body and fell to the side, almost off the sled. "Aw, come on Jackie. Don't make this harder than it has to be. Just relax. It'll be over before you know it."

It took nearly fifteen minutes to get her on the sled. She began trudging down the hill to the boat, but the sled would only go a few feet and then it would get stuck on branches. Celeste cursed. "This is ridiculous.   You're more trouble than you're worth. She shoved Jackie off the sled and started rolling her down the hill. The branches tore at her skin and her shoulder was jarred unmercifully. With her mouth still duct-taped, Jackie couldn't even cry out. She was like a rag doll with no arms. She felt just like her doll in the elevator when she was a little girl. She couldn't move, couldn't scream, and was barely conscious. She thought of her children and Jonathan. *Be safe. I loved you so much.*

Chapter 32

Detective Ryder and Officer Brennan rode in an unmarked car, exceeding the speed limit and running red lights as they drove to Duck Lake. Two other police cars used their cruisers to clear the streets as they went, sirens blaring all the way. Although the winding roads were more difficult to navigate in the dark than the city streets of Richmond, they skillfully maneuvered the mountainous terrain. Light rain was making it difficult to see much in front of them and a deer bounded across the road and forced the officer driving to swerve in order to miss it. Tires screeched as all three cars barely avoided hitting each other.

With no other oncoming traffic, the cars were on their way in seconds. Detective Ryder never spoke of the deer but instead radioed orders to the others, "Cut the lights. The house should be just over the hill."

The unkempt house was tucked into the woods with a winding gravel lane. The policemen parked their cars just south of the home, around the bend, just out of sight. Five men and one woman got out of the cars, quietly closing their doors. A surprise arrival would benefit their invasion.

"You two take the left side, I'll go in the back. Wait for my call! You guys search the woods. She's got those kids somewhere." Detective Ryder was very protective and used his hands to gesture 'shhh' as they motioned each other to new positions.

As they each found an entrance door, he radioed again. "NOW!"

"Police." They yelled and simultaneously kicked in the doors rushing the house. As trained, they scattered and began a defensive search - guarding their bodies with sudden, calculated moves and guns drawn. Shouts of "Clear" could be heard as each door was shoved open and areas identified as unoccupied.

The female officer spoke up, "'In here." She had opened the bathroom door where Jonathan was chained. "I've got something."

Officer Brennan was at her side in moments with Detective Ryder a few paces behind him. They checked their surroundings before stooping over the man with his wrists bleeding.

Jonathan spoke in frantic tones. "She's going to kill her. Celeste is going to kill Jackie. She said she was going to dump her body in the lake. Hurry, please."

"Stay here with him." Detective Ryder ordered. "I'll go see what I can find."

He raced out the back door and slid all the way down the hill trying to get to the lake. He could see Celeste putting Jackie into the boat.

"Celeste, stop!" Detective Ryder was only feet from the dock as Celeste took the rope off the poles, hopped in the boat and started the engine. He reached the dock, yanked off his shoes and jacket and dove into the lake, swimming after the boat.

Not far from the shore, Celeste panicked and dumped Jackie over the edge of the boat, her arms and legs still bound.

"No, don't!" Was all Detective Ryder could get out before Jackie's body hit the water. He swam to where she was dropped and dove deep to find her. On impact, Jackie regained consciousness and was squirming within the confines of her bindings. She was sinking to the bottom of the lake with each second that went by. She held her breath as the boat sped away.

Detective Ryder surfaced once again and dove deeper. This time he reached her body and fought to bring her to the surface. He flipped her on her back, grabbed her under the chin and pulled her to the shore. Officer Brennan was on the bank and waded to his side to help bring her on the grass. She wasn't breathing.

Quickly they began breathing for her. "Come on, Jackie, breathe, breathe!" Detective Ryder was pleading.

After a few more artificial breaths, Jackie began coughing. They rolled her to her side so she could bring up lake water as they loosened her bindings.

When she could speak, she cried. "The children. Where are the children?"

"We've got people combing the area. We're looking for them everywhere. Let's get you some help!" He had Detective Brennan radio for another ambulance and spoke again. "Jackie, you'll be safe now. Detective Brennan will take care of you. The ambulance is on its way." He covered her with his jacket and wiped her hair away from her eyes, gently brushing a tear from her cheek as he whispered to her. "Jonathan is alive, Jackie. He's in the house."

She couldn't speak, but her eyes said it all… thank you God!

He put on his shoes and ran back up the hill towards the house. "Celeste is in the boat. She took off that way." He shouted, hoping someone could hear him. An officer rounded the corner and again Detective Ryder was shouting orders. "Get to the shore and watch for her boat. Don't let her get away!" The light drizzle had turned to a steady pouring of rain.

Chapter 33

"Stay close, Lizzy. We'll be okay under the tree." Michael was comforting Lizzy as he had his arm around her trying to keep her warm. "We'll wait for the rain to stop and then we'll look for the road again."

"I'm scared. I want to go back to C.C."

"We can't do that! We've got to get away from her and find Mom. C.C. has Daddy. I know she does. And if she could keep him, she could keep us and we'll never see Mom again." Michael had recognized his father's voice at the house and was finally filling in the blanks. "We can't go back there. If we stay here, maybe someone will find us."

Lizzy was weeping softly into her brother's chest. "I don't want to stay here." Just as she finished her sentence, she heard a branch break and fall out of the tree. She screamed in fear.

"Shhh, Lizzy, be quiet." He covered her mouth again and then let it go. "We can't let her find us."

Huddled beneath the tree, they shivered from fear and shrank from every noise.

Lizzy gasped and turned her head toward the sound she heard.

"It's just another branch falling." Michael said as he tried to reassure his sister. "We're okay." Another snap and then another. Michael jumped up, grabbed Lizzy's hand and cried out, "Run, Lizzy, run."

Celeste drove past the dock and rammed the boat into shore. Running full speed up the hill, she had heard Michael's screams and found them. She swept them both up, one on each hip and they hung sideways in her arms. Both of them began to scream. "Let me go. Let me go"

"Thought you could get away, did you? Not so fast now, Michael, are you? I've had it with you. Always picking on Beth. It's time you found out what it's like to have someone bigger picking on you."

Michael couldn't figure out what she was talking about. "What do you mean, picking on Lizzy?"

"You know exactly what I mean, young man. You're always hitting her and calling her names. But not anymore, no sir. Beth and I will be just fine on our own. Even without your father. I'll make sure the police find you, all right. I'll leave you wrapped around a tree so the wild animals can get you. By the time they find you, Beth and I will be long gone. "

"C.C. no! Don't hurt Michael. Please… don't hurt Michael." Lizzy was begging Celeste to put them both down.

Celeste yanked Michael to an upright position while dropping Lizzy from her arms. She found a tree and flung Michael against it. Thick grapevine dragged the ground and gave Celeste a great idea. She wrapped it tightly around the tree with Michael between it. Then she looped it through itself to hold him to the trunk. When he was sufficiently bound, she pinched his cheeks and spoke. "See ya, Mikey."

Off they went further into the woods leaving Michael behind, tied to a tree and screaming. In the distance, Detective Ryder could hear something. "Quiet. Did you hear that?" They listened again and then ran towards the sound of Michael's screaming.

Michael's cries halted abruptly as a wildcat came out of the brush. As it stalked his prey, the cat circled Michael from the outer edge of tree branches and inspected the area before its planned attack. Slowly it paced, back and forth with its head up and moving from side to side, growling.

Michael stiffened up and screamed as loud as he could. As the cat leapt at Michael, Detective Ryder's shot felled it. "Michael, are you okay? Where's Lizzy?"

"Celeste took her. They went that way." Michael was pointing away from the house, deeper into the woods.

"Can you walk?" Detective Ryder was helping Michael up as Michael focused on the wildcat that nearly attacked him. "It's dead. It can't hurt you anymore. I need to find Lizzy. Can you make it?" He was moving him away from the cat and up the hill.

"Yea. I'm fine. Let's go."

Celeste pulled Lizzy further up the hill only flinching for a moment when the gun went off.

"I'm tired, C.C. I wanna go home. Please, let me go home." Lizzy was crying.

"We've got to hurry now, Beth. Let's go. I can't carry you either, but we've got to keep moving." Celeste was twisting her arm, dragging her across the brush.

Lizzy stopped walking and sat down. "I'm not going anywhere. I want my mother!"

Celeste pulled her up. "Get up." There was no response from Lizzy. "Get up now!" She yanked her up by her arm.

Lizzy screamed in pain as her arm dangled at her side. She cried uncontrollably. "You hurt me, C.C., you hurt me!"

"Oh, honey, I am so sorry." She bent over Lizzy to look at her arm, heard the brush crunch a few feet from her and turned to see Detective Ryder, gun drawn and in position.

"Step away from Lizzy, Celeste." Detective Ryder was prepared to shoot.

"Well, looky here, if it isn't beautiful Bob to the rescue! Well isn't that just ducky? Okay, let's just cut the theatrics. I'm not stupid, you know. I can tell when I'm beaten." Celeste was matter of fact. "I haven't got a gun and I'm not trained in karate, so…"

It was finished. She put her hands over her head as he commanded and he pulled them down to cuff her. "You have the right to remain silent.…"

As Celeste was being dragged away, she called out to Lizzy, "You know I love you Beth. I did it because I love you. Nothing can stop that! Don't forget it!"

Chapter 34

Peter had made too many mistakes. He sat in his office, staring at the clock. Time was running out for him, and he knew it. He was kicking himself for being such an idiot. Kathy didn't have any papers on her. She apparently wasn't planning to go to the police when he abducted her. He was sure he could be linked to her disappearance if he lost his watch when he dragged her from her car- which had been hauled away by the police before he could search for it. Stupid watch. He knew it fell off his wrist easily, but he didn't notice it was gone until after they killed her. And it wasn't a cheap watch either. He was sure his office staff could identify it by the initials on the underside-P.A.

Peter Anderson. The good guy gone bad, the lawyer with no grounds for appeal, the idiot that ruined his life by listening to other people. Peter was bashing his hand against his head.

Well, none of it mattered anymore. It would soon be over for him. He was not going to jail. That was for sure.

Epilogue

Jackie was groggy when she woke up in yet another hospital bed. Jonathan was sitting in a chair he had pulled to her side and was gripping her free hand as the I.V. drip in her left arm slowly moved through the tube. She had suffered multiple bruises and cuts from being rolled down the hill and with each move she made, she moaned. Her body ached from being pulled across the ground, and her shoulder muscle had torn during the ordeal. But she was alive.

Jonathan leaned forward, moved Jackie's hand to his lips and kissed it. As he stood to stroke her hair, Mary limped into the hospital room holding the hands of both children. Although Lizzy's arm had been separated at the elbow when Celeste was dragging her, the doctor was able to reposition it and no cast or sling was necessary. The children ran to their mother's side but were cautioned not to hug her because she was so fragile. Soon they were on the bed gently kissing her cheek.

As if on cue, Detective Ryder timidly entered behind Mary and walked over to Jonathan. He reached out his hand and shook it. "I hope I'm not intruding."

As Jonathan stood, he couldn't hold back his emotion and embraced him. "Not at all. Thank you so much for all you've done."

The detective felt awkward accepting such a gesture, and pulled out of it as soon as he felt he could. "Just doing my job. And obviously not well enough!" He went to Jackie's side. "I'm sorry I didn't see it coming before. I was so sure that Peter Anderson was involved."

"You know he's dead, don't you?" Jonathan interjected.

"Dead? What happened?"

"He put a gun to his head and put a bullet in his skull. Died instantly."

"Wow. What was that about?" The detective was definitely surprised by the revelation.

"I knew he'd been messing around with that NewStart Clinic, but I didn't know how bad it really was. It seems he thought that my secretary, Kathy, was going to turn him in, so he killed her. Then when he knew he could be connected to her death, I think he panicked. The police think he killed himself after they found her body."

Jonathan held Jackie's hand and tightened the grip for a second.

Detective Ryder was speechless for a moment, then noticed Michael's wide eyes and changed the subject. "Did you know that your home has a history? From the look on Jackie and Jonathan's faces, he could tell they had no idea what he meant. He continued. "It seems the Underground Railroad used it for slaves who were running from their masters during the 1860s. The tunnel helped them get into the woods without being spotted. After the Civil War, no one bothered to board it up or fill it in."

He watched their reaction as he continued. "Celeste must have stumbled across the tunnel on one of her little adventures with the kids in the woods. That's how she got in your house. All those times you thought you heard something, but could never pinpoint it-that was Celeste. She'd come in through the tunnel and nose around looking through your things. After a while she started to fantasize that she was Jonathan's wife.

Jonathan interjected, "That's one of the reasons we went to the ocean. I needed to get away from the firm and I thought we should get away from Celeste for awhile too. She always seemed to be hanging around. I still can't figure out how she knew where we were at the beach."

Jackie closed her eyes. "That was my fault. I called her to gloat over the fact that I was sipping lemonade by the dunes of the beach. She asked me where, so I told her."

Jonathan shook his head. "She came to the door when I was about to go for a run. Said she wanted to talk to me about you. So, I took a ride with her. She offered me a drink of water and all of the sudden I was so ill, I couldn't lift my head."

"Drugs. Apparently she knows a lot about them. The pills she gave you weren't sleeping pills, Jackie. They were hallucinogens." Detective Ryder was filling in all the gaps. "She got the pills off the street and exchanged them for the ones in the bottle. Pretty slick, huh? I'm not sure when she decided to play house with your family, but she certainly had the lake house ready. She bought it a few months back. The wig and shirt in your cellar were disguises she used so she wouldn't be recognized if she was seen.

Jonathan stood to his feet. "I can't thank you enough for your help. I don't know what else to say except," he paused, trying to remain composed. "I owe you so much."

"You're welcome." Detective Ryder smiled as he prepared to leave. "May I?" He looked for approval as he bent over Jackie to give her a kiss on the forehead. "You are a very brave woman, Mrs. Pennington. I hope you can get some rest now." He touched her hand, turned to leave and then spoke to Jonathan again. "Your son was very brave too and very smart. I was amazed to hear how he and Lizzy escaped from Celeste. He was really using his head."

He went over to Michael and lifted his hand to mess up Michael's hair.

Michael's hand met his in the air. "Don't touch the locks, man." Michael said with a smile.

Grasping the outstretched palm, Detective Ryder replied, "Proud to know you kid. You'd make a great detective some day - or an escape artist!" Then he turned to Lizzy, still tucked in beside her mother, playing with her doll. He leaned close to her ear and spoke. Lizzy giggled and whispered in her doll's ear as the Detective winked before leaving the room.

Michael was eager to know what the detective had said. "What did he say, Lizzy? What did he say?"

Lizzy refused to answer no matter how much badgering she received. Jonathan and Jackie just smiled at each other and said nothing They were a family again.

About the Author

Having previously published a short story, *Sometimes We Cry*, Linda J. Clark is now debuting her novel, *Shadow Stalking*. She works at GlenOak High School in Canton, Ohio and devotes much of her free time to writing novels, short stories and plays, as well as directing and choreographing musicals. She lives in Massillon, Ohio with her husband, Dennis.

Printed in the United States
48242LVS00005B/22-156